OCEAN CITY M.D.

Tom Croft

ISBN 0-9661994-0-5

Palmer & Stewart Publishing
853 Broadway, Suite 1516
New York, New York 10003

Library of Congress Catalog Card Number: 98-96247

ISBN: 0-9661994-0-5

June 1998

10   9   8   7   6   5   4   3   2   1

Manufactured in the United States of America.

I would like to thank the following individuals. Without your help this book would never have been written.

Chip Croft
Jean Croft
John Edmonds
Lee Leonhardt
Kim Loveland
Teresa McBride
Andrea Posin

SPECIAL THANKS
to
Tom Eicher
and Image Graphics
This book would not have been printed with out his help and expertise.

v

OCEAN CITY
M.D.

Tom Croft

Chapter 1
Tuesday, July 14

Looking up, Billy Lee could barely make out the shape of the sun rising above the horizon of the ocean. The cool morning air was just beginning to warm up, burning away the light misty fog that lay throughout the town. A soft breeze drifted in off the ocean and over the beach, carrying with it the scent of saltwater and suntan lotion.

Reaching in his shirt pocket with two fingers, he pulled a Marlboro from the open pack. Placing the cigarette between his lips, he reached into the pocket of his cut-off jeans, pulling out his old Zippo Fisherman's Special. Flipping it open with his thumb, he lit his first and most valued cigarette of the day.

The sixteen foot Boston Whaler drifted quickly down the inlet, pushed by the incoming tides. Billy watched as the sun would suddenly appear between the buildings, then just as quickly disappear, playing tag with him as his boat drifted along. The constant chugging of his 75HP Mercury outboard ruined the quiet serenity of the morning, occasionally belching a cloud of white smoke with a loud pop.

Normally, at this time of the year, he would be up on the Thoroughfare by Ocean Pines where most of the flounder and the fishermen who chased them had migrated. But when he got in his boat this morning, he had a feeling that maybe, just maybe, there might still be one or two big fifteen pounders laying on the bottom of the inlet waiting for him.

The tide had pushed his boat down to the Route 50 bridge that connects the mainland to Ocean City. Reaching back, he cranked up the motor, the spinning propeller sending the bow riding high in the air. The little boat struggled against the incoming tide as it made its way up to the opening of the inlet. For the fifth time this morning, Billy let the boat idle, and lowered his bucktail lure back into the water. An experienced fisherman, he sat patiently awaiting his first strike, as his boat was pushed back by the tide along the rock jetty.

Drifting by the pier, he glanced at the empty pilings where the large fishing boats had been tied up a few hours earlier. He day dreamed about being out on one of those boats fighting a big blue marlin. Making a mental note, he decided to save some money and one day treat himself to an outing on one. It was the same mental note he had been making for the past thirty years but had never managed to save that first dollar.

His boat drifted down to the bridge again and he motored back up to the tip of the jetty. Taking the old engine out of gear, he watched as one of the big fishing boats slipped out of the last remnants of the mist, sliding quietly into the bay.

Damn, that's odd? he thought as he watched the boat gently glide by. The only reason a boat would come back at this time of day was if it was damaged or in trouble.

The man at the helm of the boat was dressed in a loud Hawaiian print shirt. He was casually drinking a cup of coffee and smoking a cigarette as if nothing was wrong. The boat pulled up to the dock about 50 yards away. Two men jumped over the side, tying the boat off. Not wanting to drift into her stern, Billy decided to pull back up to the mouth of the inlet. As he drifted back down past Wicomico Street, he turned around to look at the fishing boat. A large truck was pulling up to where she was docked. He couldn't quite make out what kind of truck it was, but could see that someone had written "Do Not Wish Me!" on the dirty bay door. Being a writer, he couldn't help being intrigued by the writing. Had it been written by some moron who couldn't spell "Wash" or was there some more hidden meaning in the word "Wish."

As Billy was about to pass the stern, someone stepped off the boat, opening the bay door of the truck. Two seconds later, ten Asians, seven males and three females, hurried off the boat, climbing into the back of the truck. They were dressed in rags and looked filthy. Their faces and clothes encrusted in dirt, looking as if they had not bathed in weeks. As the last one climbed in the truck, the man who had opened the door closed it. When the door was locked, he pounded twice on the side of the truck and it pulled away. Making a right turn onto Dorchester Street, the truck disappeared around the corner. All this took place in less time than it had taken Billy's boat to drift from the stern to the bow of the fishing boat.

Billy sat there thinking, trying to figure out why the Asians had been on the boat as he neared the bridge once again. Out of the corner of his eye, he noticed something on the pier. Shading his eyes against the morning sun with his hand, he saw a dark blue police cruiser. Standing next to it was John

Eastwick, a policeman with the Ocean City Police Department.

Billy had known Eastwick all his life, always considering him to have the intelligence and personality of a slug. It mystified Billy why his ex-wife, Jill, had left him ten years ago for a slow-whited bully like John Eastwick. Billy tried to avoid him in the small, closely knit community. But, like a bad cold, he would run into Eastwick at least once or twice a year in this small town that six months out of the year, housed less than five thousand people.

Eastwick was parked just a few feet from where the truck had been. He must have watched the whole bizarre scene unfold. There was no way he could have missed it. Turning his head again, Billy saw Eastwick staring down at him ominously through a pair of mirrored sunglasses. He could almost feel the eyes behind the glasses boring a hole into him. Not willing to give into Eastwick in any shape or form, Billy cranked up the engine just enough to keep him even with the tide. Sitting there, almost frozen in the stream, he returned Eastwick's stony glare. After thirty seconds, he felt he had proved his point, revved the engine higher and sped back up to the tip of the jetty.

As Billy let the engine idle and began drifting back, he turned to look behind him. Eastwick's car was gone. Looking back down the estuary, he saw the truck driving across the Route 50 bridge. It was leaving Ocean City, followed closely by a dark blue Ocean City police car.

It was approaching 7:30, time to go home, clean up and get to work. Pulling in his line, Billy turned his small boat around and motored up the bay in the direction of his mobile home. Passing the fishing boat for the last time, he glanced at the transom to read her name. She was called *"Bow Wow."*

Chapter 2

Motoring up the bay to his trailer, Billy kept replaying what had happened on the fishing boat. He was sure of what he had seen, he just couldn't bring himself to admit it. The two mile trip to where he docked his boat on Robin Drive off 26th Street took about twenty minutes. As he was pulling up to the dock, his old Mercury outboard began sputtering and then died. Picking up an oar he paddled the last few feet to the dock. Tying off his boat, he walked across the sandy vacant lot to Sunset Drive where his mobile home was parked.

Billy had spent the last twenty-two years living in the rusting old hulk of a trailer. Three more years of making payments and he would own it. Considered an eye sore by the community, it was the only place in town he could afford to live. The small paycheck he earned working for the *Ocean City Times* as a reporter was barely enough to make ends meet. During their eight year marriage, Jill had always been pushing him to go out and find a better paying position. After she left him, he lost all interest in getting ahead in this world. Now, at the age of forty-five, life had passed him by. He knew there were no "better jobs" out there for a man of his age. It was a sad fact of life that he had learned to accept. He would spend the rest of his working days as a third rate reporter for a local, tourist oriented newspaper.

Unlocking the front door to the trailer, he heard the air conditioner kick in, attempting unsuccessfully, to cool the metal box down to a livable temperature. Sweat was beginning to bead on his forehead as he opened the refrigerator door to see what was inside for breakfast. Looking around, he saw various uneaten dishes of fish, a bottle of lemon juice and a bottle of orange juice with just a little bit left in the bottom. Pulling out the orange juice he lifted it to his lips, drinking what was left. Tossing the bottle into the overflowing trash can, it rolled off onto the floor. He watched it bounce twice, breathing a sigh of relief when it didn't shatter into thousands of pieces. Reaching back into the refrigerator, he took out the lemon juice. Walking over to the sink, he washed his hands with it and a little soap to get rid of the fishy smell. There was a single coffee mug sitting upside down in the strainer by the sink along with a knife, spoon, fork, glass and a single plate. These were his only surviving eating utensils. He had been telling himself for months to go out and buy a few more, but never seemed to get around to it. Picking up the coffee mug, he turned it over and sat it on the small countertop with one hand as he reached up to the open cabinet with the other, pulling out a large jar of Folgers instant coffee. Opening the jar he poured in just enough to cover the bottom of his cup, then screwed the top back on, replacing the canister on the shelf. Flipping the hot water handle on the sink, he held his finger under the running water until it got very warm and then filled his coffee cup. Picking up his one clean spoon, he stirred it a couple of times. Pulling off his favorite old fishing shirt and cutoff jeans, he put on a clean pair of jeans along with a white dress shirt, then picked up his favorite and only necktie, pulling it over his head. Tying neckties took too much time, so he never untied the knot, he would just loosen the tie enough to lift it off and then back on his head next time. Tightening the knot around his neck, he looked in the mirror as he ran a comb through his graying and thinning brown hair. As he walked out of the trailer, he picked up his coffee mug and headed for the car.

Life at the beach is rough on cars. The constant blowing of salt in the air and rain causes cars to deteriorate rapidly. That and the fact he couldn't afford to buy new cars caused him to always buy old Jeep's. He had owned Jeep's that were at least ten years old for the past twenty-five years. The convertible tops were always taken off after he purchased them and he would drive the Jeep topless the year round, rain or shine, freezing cold or sweltering heat. Over the years it had come to be his trademark and made him somewhat of a character in the small community.

July was the beginning of the high point for the tourist season. All the shops and restaurants wanted stories on their establishments to run in the Ocean City Times, just as the tourists were invading the city. Billy had made arrangements to stop at five restaurants and a discount store on his way into the office this morning. He would drive down Philadelphia Avenue toward his office, stopping at one of the businesses every few blocks to interview the owners or managers about what was new and newsworthy in their establishments. It would take all morning and was a total waste of time. He knew just what to write about each place, having written the same thing about each one for the past twenty years. Nothing would be new or different, but he had to do it anyway, to make the owners and managers happy. Tomorrow Eli, the owner and publisher of the paper, would follow up behind him, calling on each place he had been, selling them a large four color ad in the newspaper that would run with their story. This was how the paper made its money, soaking the shops and restaurants for big ads that would run with their stories. It was a gimmick and on the edge of being a con job, but the arrangement had worked well for longer than Billy had been with the paper, and no one was going to change it as long as it produced profits.

His last interview was at a restaurant on Dorchester Street. Bored to near death, he feigned interest, as he talked with the new owner who explained in minutia how fantastic his secret steamed crab recipe was. Shaking with excitement, he told Billy about the long lines that were there each night as customers waited in anticipation to get into his restaurant. He was the fourth man to own this same restaurant in the past fifteen years, Billy had interviewed each one every year and they always said the same thing verbatim. The last stop was just a block from the newspaper offices at the corner of Somerset and Baltimore Avenue, so he decided to leave the Jeep where it was and walk the block to the paper. As he bounded up the old steps to the offices on the second floor, he could smell crabs being cooked for the lunch crowd in the first floor restaurant. Another secret seasoning he mused to himself. They all claimed they used secret seasonings on their crabs, but everyone from the locals to the vacationers knew it was Old Bay Seasoning. Always was and always would be. It was another tradition that no one, including the tourists, wanted to change.

"Hi Bev! How's it hanging today?" Billy said with a smile as he picked up a handful of messages and headed to his computer.

"Same as always Billy. Same as always.... Oh, Billy, Eli's looking for you," she yelled as he walked away.

"Do me a favor, tell him to kiss my ass, will ya?" Billy yelled back as he disappeared around a corner, just missing running into Eli.

"Kiss who's ass?" Eli asked as he walked by, reading proofs from today's paper.

"You know that's one of those things I've always had trouble with, is it who's ass or whom's ass?" Billy asked facetiously.

"You know very well it's who's. What are we talking about?" Eli sounded confused.

"Bev told me you were looking for me, I told her to tell you to kiss my ass," Billy said with a smile as he carefully navigated the tight space between his computer and the wall.

"Billy, you need to work on that little attitude adjustment we discussed the other day," Eli said with a concerned look on his face.

"Eli! Why do we keep having this same conversation? I don't like you. I never have and I probably never will!"

"Billy. You remember our discussion from the other day. I want you to clean up your act and act a little more professionally around here. All right. Now, did you get those interviews I sent you out for this morning?"

"Yes, I got those interviews you sent me out for this morning. And I'll get the interviews you want me to go out on this afternoon," Billy said in a monotone as Eli walked away reading his proofs. "Oh, hey, Eli, come back here for a minute, would you?"

"Yes, what is it now?" Eli asked, now bored with their conversation.

"Something really weird happened this morning, I was ..."

"That's just great, Billy," Eli interrupted. "Let's talk about it later. Make an appointment and we'll discuss it next week," he muttered as he walked away still reading the proofs.

"Hey, Eli! Thanks for taking such a fucking interest in the news. Maybe you should try a little fucking attitude adjustment, you schmuck!" Billy yelled at Eli as he walked away.

Before typing up the stories from the day's interviews, he got up and walked over to the vending machines for a cold Coke and pack of crackers for lunch. As he walked back to his desk, he stopped for a few minutes to look out the front windows of the building to the inlet where he had been fishing that morning. It took only an hour for him to write up the five stories about the places he had covered in the morning, and the ones he had covered on his way home last night. Glancing up at the clock on the wall he saw it was two o'clock, time to start his return trip back up Philadelphia Avenue, interviewing a new group of restaurant and store owners.

"Hey Janet!" he yelled over to the good looking young woman who had the nightmarish job of composing and balancing the ads and stories together so they made sense.

"Yea, Billy, what is it?"

"Stories for Wednesday are in the computer, the file's marked KMA797."

"Any earth shattering news I should know about before I read your gut wrenching prose?" Janet asked sarcastically.

"Hell yes. I wrote exposes on four restaurants, each with a new and secret seasoning for steaming their crabs. All of Ocean City's been talking about it, haven't you heard?"

"Damn, don't know how I missed that one. I'll be sure to save a special spot on page one for those stories. Let me take a guess, all four restaurants smelled the same inside, Old Bay Seasoning. Right?"

"You got it, Schweetheart. Well, I'm off to interview another group of enterprising restaurateurs. I can't wait to find out just what secret seasoning they're using on their steamed crabs," Billy was saying as he walked out the door.

The temperature was in the upper nineties with high humidity making the combination seem like a hot wall as Billy walked out of the office. The heat engulfed him, and he stopped for a few seconds to let his body adjust to the stifling temperature. Standing there, attempting to breathe, he looked across the street and saw Jonathan Banks walking up Somerset toward the inlet. Jonathan Banks was one of the true characters of Ocean City. He was referred to lovingly by all who knew him as the 'Mayor' of Ocean City. No one knew his exact age. He was an old black man who wandered the city doing repair work and odd jobs for boat owners and hotels in the lower Ocean City area. He knew everything about everyone in the town, what was happening and what would happen. He was a fixture in Ocean City long before Billy had arrived and probably would be long after he was gone. The two men had spent many a happy and drunken night together closing down bars. Billy had been fighting with Eli for years to do a feature story on Jonathan, but Eli had always been against it. To Eli, the fact that Jonathan was practically a bum was bad enough, but he was also black, and in this area the years had changed but not the thinking or the attitude.

"Tourists don't want to leave the cities and come to a place like this to read about some bum walking the streets of Ocean City," Eli would say. "And not only that, he's black and in case you haven't noticed, there's still a hell of a lot of racism on the Eastern Shore, and it's not just African Americans, they don't care too much for Jews either."

"Hey, Joe-nathan," Billy yelled across the street. Jonathan turned and waved his hand wide over his head as Billy made the treacherous crossing, across the street. As always, it was jammed with tourists, cruising the city looking for parking spaces they were never going to find.

"Billy Lee, hey man, what's happenin? Ain't seen you for several weeks," Jonathan said with a wide smile on his face, happy to see his old friend.

"Tis the time of the season," Billy said sarcastically. "Yea man, it's been a while. They've got me runnin' like crazy."

"We all got to do what we got to do, Billy boy!"

"Yea, unfortunately. Listen, you ever run across a big fishing boat called *"Bow Wow?"*

"Sure have, fixed the little engine on his dink last week. Had a bent drive shaft not enough to stop it from runnin' but just enough to make it chug. Took me an hour and a half to fix it. He'd had it over at old Captain Bob's repair place for two weeks and they couldn't fix it."

"Who owns the boat, what you know about him?"

"Man name of St. John, real nice guy. Owns that plant over near the airport where they make dog food. Why's he calls the boat *'Bow Wow.'* Laughed like hell first time I heard that one. Owns a dog food company and calls his boat *'Bow Wow,'* Jonathan doubled over laughing.

"Dog food plant?" Billy said in surprise. "I didn't know we had a damn dog food plant around here. How long's it been here?"

"Shit, Billy, you got to get off this old sand bar more often, there's a whole 'nother life outside this old city. Plants been there for little over two years now, near the airport, just off of Stephen Decatur Highway on Keel Drive. Big old place, 'bout forty people working there. Called Dr. St. John's Pet Foods. Sits right in the middle of a cornfield. You know Gail Jonas, least you did when you was porkin her a few years ago, she's got a real good office job there."

"Oh shit, yea, I think I heard about that place. They have a company plane. Heard one of the pilots that fly's the billboards up and down the beach complaining about how they almost hit each other a couple of weeks ago."

"Yea, I remember that, that's them. Only that wasn't Dr. St. John. One of his partners I think. Seen him around too, real creepy guy. He's some doctor from one of them old Russian countries. Hey, what say we hit a few bars tonight, down a whole bunch of beers?"

"Can't. Got to fix the old Merc, she died on me this morning when I was pullin' into the dock. Think it was that damn fuel line again. Don't know what it is, I've cleaned that fuel line a hundred times, but it keeps fouling up on me."

"Damn, Billy! Why don't you get rid of that old thing, you been rebuilding and fixing that thing for ten years now. It's had it. Told you last time I helped you fix it, you was wastein' your time and money on that old thing."

"Can't let that old engine beat me. Hell, I been fighin' that thing so long it's gotten personal. It's me or it. 'Sides, I've replaced just about every part in it, she's as good as new."

"Billy boy. It's a piece o' shit. Got a line on a good used one, cheap price too."

"No way, Joe-nathan," he said with a sly smile.

"Have's it your way. But when it dies and it will soon, come see old Jonathan. You know I'll fix you up good," he smiled.

"Yes, I do. Yes, I do. Listen man, got to go. Maybe we can get together tomorrow night for some drinks," he was saying as he started walking away.

"Sounds good, Billy boy. Until that time. Until that time," Jonathan said as he smiled and turned to leave.

Billy lucked out and was able to get his interviews over a few hours sooner than he had hoped. Stopping by the Burger King near 62nd Street, he picked up a cheeseburger and fries for dinner along with a cold case of Old Milwaukee beer from a convenience store. Eating his burger as he drove back down the Coastal Highway to his mobile home, he was wondering if he could get his motor fixed and get out on the bay to do a little fishing tonight. Stopping by the trailer, he put the beer in the refrigerator, except for one six pack, then grabbed his tool kit and portable radio. The trailer was smelling like garbage, so he decided to take out the trash. He put it in the beat up old metal trash can in front of his trailer. As he was dropping the bag in the container, the orange juice bottle from this morning fell out onto the ground, but unlike this morning, luck was not with him, and it broke into a thousand pieces.

"Poetic justice, I suppose," he said to himself, bending down and picking up most of the large pieces.

Looking around he saw no one was watching and walked away leaving the rest of the broken glass on the ground. Strolling across the vacant lot to where his boat was docked, he could see a few kids on the landing, dipping nets into the water to catch crabs. One of the kids on a dock up the road pulled in two huge females and all the kids ran up there in hopes of catching more. Climbing into the old Boston Whaler, Billy popped open a beer and turned on his radio to the oldies station. Carefully, almost lovingly, he pried the top off of the old Mercury and started tinkering with the fuel lines as Martha and the Vandellas began belting out *Heat Wave*. An hour and two beers later he had cleaned the fuel lines and the carburetor. As he placed the housing back on the engine, he heard the six o'clock news begin. Not paying attention to the news, he cranked up the engine, it started for a second, turned over twice, then sputtered to a stop belching a gray cloud of smoke. Suddenly, he found himself listening to the radio.

"The ship was loaded with over 500 illegal aliens. All Chinese, who had each paid as much as ten thousand dollars to be smuggled into the United States. Coast Guard officials said they had been tracking the boat up the East Coast before intercepting it late this afternoon off the coast of New Jersey as it was nearing New York City. Officials said they did not want a repeat of what happened three weeks ago, when another boat came into New York harbor and ran aground allowing most of the illegal aliens to get onshore before the authorities arrived. Coast Guard officials who boarded the boat said that the people on board were living in some of the most unbearable conditions they had ever encountered. They stated that the people on board were so dirty and their conditions so squalid, that they were afraid of possible disease contamination. More news after these words from one of our sponsors."

"Hey, Come on down to old Captain Phil's Crab House. Old Captain Phil has come up with a special crab seasoning that will make your mouth water and scream for more."

Sitting there in the late afternoon sun, Billy smiled to himself. He was right, at first he thought he was crazy but now he knew he was right, they were smuggling in illegal Chinese aliens this morning. But why in the hell would they smuggle them into Ocean City? There was no problem finding people to work at menial labor in this part of the State, that was all there ever had been on the Eastern shore and the only work most of the work force had ever known. Ten Chinese aliens? Why would you send a big boat like that out for just ten people? Future workers for the dog food plant? Nah!

Cranking up the engine again, it sputtered several times and almost died, then kicked in and started purring as if she were brand new. As the boat sat there idling, Billy looked out at the bay, contemplating whether he should cast off in search of a flounder or head for the *Windjammer Bar*. Turning the engine off, he climbed out of the boat, picked up his tools and walked back to his trailer. After washing his hands and putting on a clean sweatshirt, he got into his Jeep and drove up the Coastal Highway to the *Windjammer*. As he was getting out of his Jeep in the parking lot, he could see the black clouds moving in quickly from the west, setting up for what looked like a good thunderstorm. He was glad he had made the decision to go to the bar, one thing he did not like was getting caught out on the water in a thunderstorm. As he reached the front door of the bar he could hear the first loud claps of thunder rolling like cannons over the waters of the bay.

The inside of the crowded bar, like all good bars, smelled from a combination of stale beer and cigarette smoke. Loud rock music was blasting from large speakers that were hung on the walls. Groups of people were mingling around, looking for a love connection for the night. Billy always felt out of place in the bars now, they were mostly filled with twenty and thirty year old singles cruising for a pick up. At his age, 45, he felt more like a chaperone than a player. Surveying the crowded bar, he hoped to find Gail Jonas. This had been one of their favorite hangouts when they were dating. After ten minutes he was about to leave when he saw her, behind the bar, serving drinks. Making his way through the crowded room he managed to find a seat at the bar next to a couple of young men in their early twenties. As he sat there, waiting for the bartender, he couldn't help but overhear the two young men talking about trying to pick up a couple of women.

"Hey man, check out the cute chick over there. I bet I could pick that babe up," said one of the men as he laughed in a loud oafish manner.

"I don't know dude, you are a beast dude, but dude she's got a good body, but I bet you've got to take her out to get any," said the other who then also started laughing like an idiot.

"Yea, you know, she is cute and all, you know, but you know, she could be like, you know, be dating that dude she's with you know."

"You know, you're right, you know dude, she is like, you know, sort of hanging close to that guy, you know. I'll bet, you know, she is his date, you know."

Damn, Billy thought to himself. Did I sound that stupid when I was that age or are we raising an elite group of illiterate boobs to take over the next generation?

"BILLY LEE! Hey, babe. God damn, it's great to see you," said Gail with a big smile as she walked down the bar to where he was sitting. "Where have you been? It's been at least a year since I seen ya."

"Yea, I know," Billy said with a warm smile. "Wow you are really looking great. What'ja do, new hair style?"

"Yep, that and I lost fifteen pounds, been pumping iron and working out," Gail said as she stepped back, held out her arms and turned, showing him her body. "What can I get you honey?"

"Anything on draft that's not light. God, you really look fantastic. And what the hell's that on you finger, you get engaged?" he exclaimed.

"You better believe it is, that's why I got my bod in shape, you remember Ron Langhorn, that's my man," she said as she pulled a pitcher from under the bar and filled it from the tap in front of him. When she finished, she pushed the pitcher, along with an empty mug, across the oak bar to Billy and winked, "On the house hon, you know they charge too much for beer here," she was saying in a quiet voice as she leaned across the bar.

"Thanks, appreciate it, you know how me and money don't go together," he said shrugging his shoulders.

"That means you're still working for Eli then. How's he doing, you guys still getting along as good as you used to?"

"Oh Hell yea, best buds, like always," Billy said as they both broke down laughing.

"Excuse me mam, you know, could we, you know, like get a couple more bottles of, you know, like Budweiser, you know," said one of the young men next to Billy.

"Yes sir," said Gail reaching in the refrigerated cabinet and pulling out two bottles of Budweiser. "That'll be five dollars."

"Thanks, you know, like great," said the young man as he reached in his pocket, pulled out a five dollar bill and dropped it on the bar. "You know, like you can keep the change, you know," he said as he turned around with his friend to keep watching the action in the bar.

Billy looked at Gail who put her lips together as if to whistle as she raised her eyebrows, then blinked as she shook her head in a short quick motion implying the man was a real idiot.

"When did you start working here?" Billy asked.

"Oh, bout six months ago, after I got engaged. Tryin' to put some money away for married life."

"Yea, know what you mean. Hey, I heard some time ago you were working for some company near the airport."

"Need six drafts, Gail," a waitress called across the bar from behind Billy.

"Yea, been there over a year now. They make dog food, can you fuckin' believe it?" she said as she started filling beer mugs and sliding them to the waitress on the other side of him. "It's a really great job though, I'm the office manager. Never thought I'd say this but I love the work. It's really great. The guy who runs the place is really nice. There are a couple other guys who own it with him, but I never see much of them. They're always over in the research section doing some shit."

"Yea, I heard about him. His name's, ahhhhhh, St. John, right?"

"Yep, that's him, Dr. Will St. John, one of the greatest guys I ever worked for."

"Who are the other owners?"

"Like I said they're always in the research section. It's a special section you can only get into if you have one of those credit card type things and punch in a password code. So, let's see, there's Dr. Ling, he's a Chink, and Dr. Jackanock, he's a Commie from Yugoslavia or whatever it's called now. No one likes him, he's creepy as hell. We all call him Dr. Jackolantern, behind his back," she laughed.

"Wow, all Doctors. They MD's, Ph.D's or DVM's?"

"Don't know about those initials, don't care about those initials. I just want Dr. St. John's signature on the bottom of my pay check at the end of the week. Hey, you know what? You ought to do one of your little stories about the place. I'll bet they would like that. They never seem to advertise. I think it would do them good. Why don't you call Dr. St. John? I'll bet he'd love it. Yea, sure just a minute, Hon," she was saying as she moved down the bar, filling two pitchers of draft that she gave to one of the waitresses. Grabbing another pitcher she filled it, came back up the bar and put it in front of Billy.

"Sorry, Babe, but I got to get back to work. Listen, it was really nice to see you again. Keep in touch. I want you to come to the weddin'. It's going to be in November after the tourists leave, of course. Take care and I'll be back to top off that pitcher from time to time if ya want," she said with a smile that warmed his heart.

"Thanks, Gail, of all the loves in my life you were always the kindest and sweetest," he said with sincerity.

"Oh Billy, you are so full of it, but I love you anyway," she said with a big smile as she winked and walked down to the other end of the bar.

He could just barely hear the rumbles of thunder over the loud classic rock music. As he looked out one of the windows in the corner of the bar, sheets of rain obscured his vision of the parking lot as the storm raged on.

"God, am I ever glad I didn't go fishing tonight," he said softly to himself, the first pitcher beginning to make him feel a little high.

Noticing that the two seats next to him were now empty, he looked around the room to see if the two boobs had managed to pick up some girls. At the other end of the bar he could see the two young men walking out the front door into the pouring rain with two pretty blondes.

"God, life sucks. The losers are conquering the universe. We're doomed, we're all doomed!" he said to himself.

As he finished his second pitcher, Gail came back and refilled it again. He had just poured another mug of beer when he felt someone brush by him and sit in the vacant stool next to him.

"WELL, WELL, WELL, if it isn't my old buddy, Billy Lee."

Turning his head to the right, he saw that it was John Eastwick. "Hi, John," Billy said quietly, turning to stare straight ahead, not looking at the man beside him.

"Yes, Sireee, it's been a long time, Billy. Odd, I thought I saw you this morning and now, here you are again tonight. This little sand bar just keeps gettin' smaller and smaller, don't it sport?" Eastwick said emphasizing the word "sport."

"Yea," Billy shrugged, not wanting to talk to the man or even acknowledge his presence. He had known Eastwick all his life and had disliked the man before his wife left to move in with Eastwick. He was six years younger than Billy and always had a reputation as a guy with a bad temper, who liked beating up people for little or no reason. He was a tough guy who liked violence, a bully you could count on to terrorize and pick on people smaller than he was. There had also been numerous rumors around the police department of cover ups from Eastwick's too heavy use with a night stick during arrests.

"You know, Billy, somethin' I always wanted to ask you but never got the chance," Eastwick said swiveling on his bar stool to face him.

"Oh, yea," Billy replied trying to sound bored.

"Yea! We seem to get together like this so infrequently. I never got at chance to ask, but do you mind me fucking Jill. After all she was your wife at one time," he said playing at sounding sincere.

Billy could not see his face but imagined Eastwick was smiling as he made the statement.

"Free world, she's free. Don't matter to me what she does," Billy replied, still looking straight ahead.

"You don't know how happy that makes me feel. I always thought that maybe you had a grudge against me and Jill, you bein' her old husband and all. Like this morning when she was giving me this great blow job before I went to work. Man she was moanin' like Hell when I came in her mouth. You remember how great she was at given BJ's don't you Billy. Oh shit, that's right. I remember now, she told me she never once sucked you off while you were married. Too bad, she really knows how to give a man a real good blow job. Well, I guess I better get goin'. Got to get back on duty and all that. Now Billy, you ain't been drinkin' too much there, have you boy? I wouldn't want to have to arrest you for drunkin' drivin' tonight."

Billy felt Eastwick slap him hard on his shoulder, much harder than was necessary, as he got up to leave. He didn't like admitting it to himself, but Eastwick had achieved everything he had intended to do. He had put a cold knife right through Billy's heart and scared the hell out of him at the same time. Sitting at the bar, staring straight ahead for several minutes, he tried not to think about anything. Finally, he looked around and was glad to see that Eastwick was gone.

He was too depressed to stay out anymore and decided to just go home to try to sleep it off. As he walked out of the bar, the rain was still coming down heavily but the lightning and thunder had moved on down the beach toward Virginia. He was already drenched by the time he climbed into his Jeep. The seats, soaked by the rain, made a squishing noise as he sat down. Starting the car, he pulled out of the parking lot and headed home. Two blocks away from the bar, the rain started to let up and was now just a light mist. Looking into his rear view mirror he saw that there was an Ocean City Police car just behind him. Staring hard, to see through the steamy windshield of the police cruiser, he could just barely make out that it was John Eastwick who was driving. The streets were crowded with tourists in their cars, traffic backed up for blocks and going no where because of the thunder storm. Billy inched his car along the highway, nervously glancing in the rear view mirror every few minutes, to see if Eastwick was still behind him. When he was a few hundred feet from the turn to his trailer, he saw the blue lights start spinning in his rear view mirror and heard Eastwick beep the siren twice. Making a right turn onto Sunset Drive, Eastwick pulled around on his left side, made a U-turn and went racing back down the Coastal Highway in the opposite direction. As Billy pulled into the parking space by his trailer, he got out of the Jeep and fell to his knees on the wet grass throwing up from fear.

"God, I hate that man," he said as he leaned over to wretch again.

Chapter 3
Wednesday, July 15

The pounding of rock music on the clock radio synchronized with the pounding of the hangover in Billy's head. Laying in the early morning darkness he tried to decide if he should get up and go fishing. His hangover won the battle. He decided to get up, take some aspirin and go back to bed for a few more hours of sleep before going to work. Laying in the darkness, his mind started to drift back over what had happened last night. He was angry with himself for letting Eastwick get to him and furious with Eastwick for pushing him around. An hour later as the sun was beginning to break into daylight over the ocean, he decided to get out of bed and get a Coke to help settle his stomach. The air conditioner came on as he sat down at his small kitchen table. The little bit of cool air it put out helped to relieve the pain in his head as it gently blew across his face. The cold Coke made him feel somewhat better, and as he took the last drink he reached for a cigarette.

Looking through the small dirty window at the end of his mobile home, he watched the fishermen drifting silently on the bay trolling for flounder and bass. Acting on an impulse, Billy picked up the phone book and began thumbing through the business pages. When he came to Dr. St. John's Pet Foods, he hesitated for a second, then picked up a pen and wrote the number and address on a pad on the table. Knowing it was too early to call, he decided to take a shower and shave. Two hours later he was back sitting at the kitchen table, dressed and ready to go to work. While taking his shower he had decided to just forget the whole thing about the Asian people, but as he was shaving a few minutes later he had changed his mind again. As he sat looking at the phone number on the table he kept trying to figure what it was about this whole thing that was eating at him.

"Good morning. Dr. St. John's Pet Foods, can I help you?" the receptionist said in a cheery voice.

Billy sat there, frozen not sure of what he was doing.

"Helloooooooooo, is anyone there?" she asked.

"Ah, yea. Excuse me. Dr. St. John please."

"Yes, and who should I say is calling?"

"Ah... Mr. Lee with the *Ocean City Times*," he stammered.

"Yes sir, Mr. Lee. One moment please," responded the cheery voice.

"Hello," said Dr. St. John in a strong, vibrant voice.

"Good morning. My name's William Lee. I'm a reporter with the *Ocean City Times*. Our newspaper primarily focuses on human interest stories in the Ocean City area and I would like to set up an appointment to drop by, and interview you about your company for the paper," Billy said as he cringed, thinking how he must have sounded like an inept moron to Dr. St. John.

"Wonderful, we could use the publicity. When would you like to come by? You're welcome any time," said Dr. St. John in a robust tone.

"Well, ahhhhh. What would be convenient for you?" Surprised, Billy hadn't expected Dr. St. John to be so eager.

"I may have to be out of town later in the week. Right now would be fantastic. Any chance you could come by this morning?"

"Well, Ahhh. Yea, sure. I can be there in, I guess twenty minutes. I mean if that's too soon I, we, can set something up for another time."

"Nonsense, come right on over. See you in twenty minutes. You know how to get here?" asked Dr. St. John.

"Ahh, yea. Be there in twenty minutes," Billy's voice trailed off.

"OK, see you then."

After hanging up the phone Billy put his face in his hands as he leaned on the table.

"What the <u>HELL</u> am I doing? That guy doesn't sound like he's hiding anything. Christ! If I interview him for the paper, Eli will never run the story and give me holy hell for wasting my time writing it. He can't sell this guy a big color ad and he won't want a piece about a dog food company. I'm fucked. I'm royally fucked," Billy sighed as he got up from the table and left.

Driving down Philadelphia Avenue toward the Route 50 bridge, he kept looking at the places he was supposed to have visited this morning. He knew he was going to be in big trouble for not going on these morning interviews, timing was important. It was all prearranged, he would interview the people then Eli would follow up the next day to sell them an ad. Break the chain of progress and you slow down the whole operation. He knew Eli was really going to chew his ass off for missing those interviews.

Crossing the Route 50 bridge he could see there were only a few people leaving Ocean City but a long line of cars flowing into the city from points west. About a mile outside of the city he made a left on to Stephen Decatur Highway and followed it down to Keel Drive. As he made a left on Keel he thought he could see the company as Jonathan Banks had described it.

The building was sitting in the middle of a large corn field, the tall corn surrounding the complex engulfed the building, enclosing it in a green protective enclosure. Billy had expected it to be an old sinister looking building, with a bunch of good ol' boys standing around a loading dock doing nothing. But, as he pulled into the parking lot, he was surprised and shocked by the building. It was constructed of brick and steel in a very expensive hi-tech design. There was a little green strip of grass about fifteen feet wide that ran from the highway down to the front of the building. Two asphalt driveways ran parallel along the strip, one marked for delivery vehicles led around to the rear of the building and the other marked "Employees and Guests" led to a parking lot on the other side of the building. Surrounding the building and parking lots was a chain link fence, separating it from the corn that was trying to force its way back into the parking lot. On top of the fence, going around the perimeter was coiled strands of razor sharp concertina wire.

Pulling into the parking lot Billy had a sinking feeling in his stomach that he was chasing a dead end. This place looked too prosperous to be caught up in the importation of a few illegal aliens, but he was stuck. He had come too far to walk away. One quick interview and leave, let Eli chew him out, then just forget the whole thing, like he should have done from the beginning.

The dry, cool air made his head feel better as he entered the marble tiled foyer of the building. A pretty blond receptionist was sitting at a desk next to two very large and soft looking leather chairs. There was a glass and chrome coffee table sitting next to a rack full of magazines. This registered as a plus with Billy, an old salesman's trick. You could guess how well you would be treated by the way the reception area looked. If it was soft and comfortable you knew the people you were about to meet would, most likely, treat you with respect. If the reception area was little more than a wooden chair and an old industry magazine, you were in big trouble, they didn't want to talk to or see anyone.

The receptionist had a big smile on her face as Billy walked up to her. Looking into her eyes, he was sure he was falling in love.

"William Lee to see Dr. St. John," he said returning her smile with a big one of his own.

"He will be with you in just a minute, Mr. Lee. Can I get you a cup of coffee or a soft drink?"

"God, I'd kill for some coffee. Could you please get me a cup with just a little sugar in it?" Billy said putting his hands together as if in prayer.

"Sure thing, Mr. Lee, I'll be right back," she said with a smile as she got up and walked out.

After she left, Billy walked casually up to her desk and glanced at what was laying on top of it. There seemed to be nothing unusual, memo pad, phone message book and a phone system with eight lines. The young woman came back in and handed him a china cup filled with coffee.

"What, no Styrofoam?" he joked.

"Dr. St. John hates it. He'll only let us drink out of ceramic or china cups."

"Nice guy," Billy said as he took a drink of coffee that brought a wide smile to his face. "God, that is really great coffee."

"What can I say," said the receptionist. "Dr. St. John has always said he doesn't want his employees or guests drinking some foul gruel. We love it too. We drink gallons of it."

"Don't blame you. I would too. Can I get a few hundred cups to go?" Billy asked as the receptionist started to giggle.

"Mr. Lee. I presume," said Dr. St. John from behind Billy.

Startled, Billy turned around. He was shocked, he had been expecting some old, balding guy with glasses who looked like he lived in a lab 24 hours a day, but Dr. St. John was younger than Billy, probably not quite 40. The doctor had a full head of elegantly cut rich dark hair with just the slightest bit of gray at the temples and a dark smooth tan. Instead of a lab coat he was dressed in an expensive looking pair of jeans that were cut to fit perfectly, the kind of jeans that have that "lived in" and faded look that cost several hundred dollars a pair. He was wearing a red print Hawaiian shirt, that on anyone else would have looked ridiculous, but on Dr. St. John it, somehow, seemed to fit. Billy was not sure, but because of the Hawaiian shirt, he thought that he may have been the one who was piloting the boat that brought the illegal aliens in yesterday.

"Yes, Dr. St. John?" Billy asked searching his shirt pocket for a business card. Finally finding one, he nervously handed it to Dr. St. John.

"Well," said Dr. St. John looking at the business card. "To begin with, the term Doctor is just a bit too pretentious for me. Please call me Will."

Billy reached out and they shook hands. Will's hand shake was firm but not in an attempt to show power.

"William R. Lee," said Dr. St. John as he looked at the card again. Turning, he walked slowly through the door into the offices as Billy followed closely behind. "What's the "R" stand for?"

"Robert," Billy said trying to keep up with Dr. St. John.

"William Robert?" Dr. St. John said with a big smile as he looked back at Billy. "William Robert, c'mon you've got to be kidding?"

"Yes, sir, you've got it!" Billy said emphatically as he nodded his head.

Dr. St. John stopped and turned suddenly, Billy almost running into him.

"Billy Bob?" he questioned with a smile.

"Yep, 'fraid so," Billy replied looking embarrassed.
"Billy Bob? Son of a gun, I've never met a Billy Bob before," Dr. St. John said, his smile warm, "especially with a last name like Lee."

"Well, it's not exactly my favorite name either. My father was from around here. He met my mother when he was in the Army in Mississippi. She picked the name out. I guess it would have been perfect if they'd stayed in Mississippi, but after I was born they moved back here. I had one hell of a time living it down when I was small. Took a long time to get away from that handle."

"I'll bet," Dr. St. John said with a warm smile as he put his arm on Billy's back. "Well, Billy Bob, let's get on with the guided tour. If you have any questions, just ask."

"Yes, Sir," replied Billy with a smile.

"This is the general office area. Computers, billing, payroll, accounting, etc. the real and very boring stuff you have to deal with everyday," Dr. St. John said stretching his arms out wide as he headed for the doors marked "factory." Before following Dr. St. John through the doors he saw Gail off to the left talking on the phone, and they waved to each other. When he walked through the doors, Dr. St. John was standing there wearing a hard hat and holding out one for him.

"There's no danger. Our insurance company requires that everyone who comes in here wears one or they'll jack up the premiums on us out of sight. The bloodsuckers!" Dr. St. John said with a smile.

The plant was noisy, as Billy looked around he could see cans of dog food being packed and sliding down wire paths then on to conveyor belts, all movement working its way toward the end of the building where the cans were being packed into boxes.

"It's really a very simple operation. You grind up the meats over there in that machine, usually spare parts and poor cuts from horses and cows. We mix in a lot soy to make it go a lot further, some vitamins and minerals and a large helping from that ugly looking mixture in the clear Plexiglas tank over there. That's the secret ingredients that makes ours better than anyone else. It's great for your dog, some stuff we've developed that will let your animal live longer and healthier. We're awaiting final word on the patents and should have them by the end of the month. It's really quite unique, took our research department a long time to develop, and it's just beginning to be recognized. In a year or two we'll be national, all the rage, ripe to be bought out by one of the big boys for enough money to retire and buy a BIG island in the Bahamas."

Looking around, Billy smiled. "So, you've done all this just to put it together and then sell it. Why not go along for the ride and reap the profits?"

"Well yea, you could do that, but Billy, it's boring as hell, endless meetings with pinheads and bean counters who'll spend hours just trying to decide which color of ink to use on a brochure or how many pens and paper clips to buy. I have been involved in a number of enterprises and the real fun is in setting them up and getting them running smoothly. It's a little akin to playing with an erector set, but with very BIG pieces. It's a real challenge to put your visions together, see them come together, growing from nothing, but once it's up and running, the fun stops and it just becomes work and, after all, work is boring. You're a writer, look in the dictionary under fun, I'll bet you a million bucks you won't find the word "work" listed anywhere. So, just take the cash and run to the bank. It's been fun up to now, but I have visions of boredom and monotony beginning to appear as we continue to grow. Now, over there is our packing machines, state-of-the-art, those little son-of-a-guns can pack 100,000 cans a day. We are, as you can see, nowhere near that capacity yet, but, we can expand and grow as demand builds. Once packed, the cans come down those conveyors over there and into cartons which are put on trucks or held until other trucks can take them away. You'll, also, notice this place is clean, sanitary clean, equal to any restaurant or other food processing plant that produces food for human consumption. Since we're processing food for animals we do not have to conform to all the laws and regulations we would have to if we were canning for human consumption, but we do anyway. We want it to conform to the same rules and laws if people were going to eat the dog food. We produce a first class, quality product, we are proud of it and want it to look that way. Right now we have sales people working up the coast to Maine and we're really hitting big in New York City right now. Any questions? This is really kind of cut and dried stuff, hope I'm not boring you?"

"No, not at all. In fact, I find this all very fascinating. Are you the sole owner, Sir, or do you have other investors?"

"I own 50% of the stock. Dr. Ling my old friend and partner owns 25% and Dr. Jacknaock owns 25%. That's all," said Dr. St. John as he gestured with his hands.

"Are they here?"

"Yes, they're over there, through that very secure looking locked door with all kinds of alarms, bells and whistles on it. That's our research section, all hush hush and hands off. No one is allowed in and I'm sorry Billy, that means you too. I would love to be able to show it to you along with some of the things we are planning for the future, but in the interest of corporate security. I hope you understand," Dr. St. John said apologetically.

"Really slick operation! If you don't mind me asking how'd you finance it?"

"Well, let's see. Banks are scum sucking slime, I'd rather die than ever be indebted to one. So I did it myself with my own money. I know they teach you in the text books not to risk all of your own cash, but what the hell, life is a gamble anyway," Dr. St. John was said as he leaned over and whispered in Billy's ear. "I probably shouldn't tell you this Billy, but I had rich parents, really, really rich parents."

"Must be nice," Billy replied.

"Billy, I'm not going to lie to you. Yea! It's great man. Everyone should be born rich," Dr. St. John said as he folded his arms, leaning back against one of the conveyors.

Billy was laughing with Dr. St. John as they walked back into the office area.

"Well, Billy, I'm sorry but that's about it. There isn't a lot here. Any questions?"

"Nope! You're right it's a very simple operation. Wish I'd thought of it!" he said.

"Sooooo," said Dr. St. John. "Think you can write a good story on us."

"I'll tell you, Will, I'll give it my best shot. Listen it was really nice of you to see me on such short notice and give me a guided tour. I really appreciate it."

"Billy Bob, it was my pleasure. Take care and if you have any follow up questions, please call or stop by if you're in the area," said Dr. St. John as he held out his hand.

"No problem, Will, thanks again!"

Walking to his car, Billy couldn't help thinking he really liked Will St. John, he was just a great guy. He decided to wait until he had written the story and then take it back to Dr. St. John to read. If, more likely when, Eli decided not to run the story, he could return to Dr. St. John and explain it all to him, blaming Eli, then with a little luck, he could talk about fishing in hopes of an invitation to go deep sea fishing.

Sitting in his Jeep scheming, Billy reached into his brief case pulling out the list of people he was supposed to see that day. Luckily, the meeting with Dr. St. John had only taken forty-five minutes so there was still a chance he could save his neck and see the people before noon. Putting the Jeep in reverse he turned to look behind him as he backed up. He stopped suddenly as he saw an Ocean City Police car pull into the parking lot, his eyes following it intently as it drove down and pulled up in front of the building into a space marked "security." John Eastwick got out of the car and casually walked into the building. Billy backed the car out and pulled up to the entrance of the employee parking lot, looking at the other road that said "Deliveries" and pulled over onto it. The road wound down and around to the back of the building where there was a loading dock. Parked next to it was a silver truck with "Wish me" written on the back. Looking at the truck, Billy remembered the dirty faces of the Asian. Had he just been played for a fool?

It was necessary for Billy to do the interviews with the other businesses before returning to the office. Eli would be waiting for him. All of the interviews had been quick and short, there was no time to schmooze the people or listen to endless boring talks about their future plans for growth. Back at the office well before noon, Billy walked right to his desk without saying a word to anyone. Picking up the phone he called information for the number of the *Washington Post* and dialed it.

"Good morning, *Washington Post*," said a very bored and tired voice.

"Metro desk, Oliver Garret, please," Billy said quickly.

"Just one moment,"

"Garret," the voice barked at him.

"Oliver, this is Billy Lee, How ya doin?" he asked, wishing he had taken time to think about what he was going to say before calling.

"Who?" the voice barked back.

"Billy Lee, from Ocean City, the *Ocean City Times*. Remember?"

"Oh yea, Lee, Ahh, how you doing? Been a long time," said Oliver with less edge to his voice but sounding a bit cautious.

"Oliver, I need a favor," Billy knew the answer he was about to receive, but had to ask the question just that way.

"Christ, come on, give me a break. Everyone I've ever known who knows I work for the *Post* calls me up for favors. Lee, you were a nice guy and I enjoyed working on the paper with you that summer. Look Lee there's nothing I can do for you!"

"Whoa, wait, hold on Oliver. I'm not looking for a job. I need some information for a story I'm working on," Billy cut in.

"Look Lee, I'm very busy. This isn't Ocean City. This is the Post. We have tight deadlines. I'm in the middle of a story. I can't just...."

"God damnit, Oliver. You remember when you got busted by the cops in Ocean City for pot. Who came in and bailed your ass out? Who was friends with the cops who busted you, and who got them to drop the whole thing and destroy the records that you were ever arrested? Who, God damn it, WHO? ME, THAT'S WHO. Do you think you'd have that great job right now if you'd been convicted of a felony for possession of pot? That's what it was back then. Hell no, you'd have also probably spent some time in jail. Hey, thanks man. Thanks for helping me out when I need help." Billy yelled into the phone.

"Oh, all right, damn it. But Lee, we're even after this, OK?" whined Oliver into the phone.

"I need you to do just one thing for me, check out a name. I want a detailed check on it and send all the information you get to me, OK?"

"Yea, yea, OK. Come on, I have to get back to work," Oliver said in an unhappy and submissive voice.

"The guy's name is Dr. Will or William St. John. I think he's from Maryland but I'm not sure."

"Well, gee, golly Billy. Thanks for narrowing the area down so much. I'm sure our research department will really be glad about that," said Oliver sarcastically.

"How quickly can you get back to me?"

"Late this afternoon or tomorrow morning. I'll FedEx what ever I get to your attention at the paper. Listen, that name rings a bell, I can't remember just what, but I've heard it before. What are you working on Billy?" Oliver asked in a more friendly tone trying to get some information.

"Oliver, I'm not sure yet. It's something really odd. If I told you what I had so far you'd laugh. Listen, if I get anything out of this, you interested in sharing a byline if it's worthy?" Billy asked holding his breath waiting for the answer.

"Yea, sure Billy. I'm always interested in a good story. But you have to do all the research and I get most of the credit for it, research and story. I know it stinks but that's the way we always do it. I also get total rewrite. If that's agreeable to you, contact me when you get something substantial. You know Billy, I probably shouldn't say this, but you were, at least when I was there, a damn good writer. Yea, I'm interested. Call me here or at home if you have any questions or need anything. My home number's (703) 555-7555. Good luck Billy, I'll get back to you later," said Oliver in a voice that was warm and sounded friendly.

"OK, Oliver. It's a deal. Listen, thanks, I'm sorry I had to twist your arm that way about the grass stuff," he said trying to sound as sincere as possible.

"No problem, Billy, take care and keep in touch," Oliver was saying as he hung up the phone.

Billy felt pumped up now. If he could get this story to pan out and get a byline in the Post he could have a chance of finally, after all these years, going somewhere, anywhere, away from Eli. For the first time in more years than he could remember, he was beginning to feel powerful again.

"Billy?" Bev was saying as she walked up to his desk.

"Bev! How's it going today?" Billy asked with enthusiasm.

"Billy. You didn't pick up your messages when you came in," Bev said in a soft voice as if something were wrong. She reached out handing him the messages in her right hand while still holding back one in her left.

"Thanks Bev," Billy said as he looked back at his desk lost in thought.

"Billy," she said reluctantly.

"What Bev!" he was becoming irritated with her now. He needed time to think.

"Billy, there was another message too."

"So, what was it?" he asked testily.

"It's from Jill, she wants you to call her."

The life seemed to drain from Billy's face. He reached out and took the note, it just had her name with a phone number under it.

"Did you get a chance to talk to her, Bev?" Billy asked reluctantly.

"Yea, we talked for about twenty minutes,"

"OK, Lay it on me," he was trying to sound cool but his insides were grinding. Jill, his ex-wife had never called him in the ten years since she had left.

"She's doing fine. Least that's what she said. Let's face it. We were both kind of nervous. Anyway, she opened a small store. Upscale gift shop in upper Ocean City, one of those trendy new strip shops around 144th Street near Fenwick Island. She wants you to do a story on it. I asked her about how she and John were getting on. She blew the question off. That was all," Bev said.

"What time did she call?" Billy asked looking at the note once again.

"'bout nine,"

"OK, thanks," he said relieved that Jill had called before he had talked to Will St. John this morning.

Sitting at his desk, lost in thought, he kept wondering why Jill had called. Was it just about the store or could it possibly mean something else. He softly cursed at himself for thinking it could be something else? She had just opened a new store and needed the coverage in the paper. That was all it was, but still, after all these years he wanted to see her and talk to her again. Until now there had never been a reasonable excuse for calling her, he was thinking as he grabbed the phone and dialed the number.

"*Jill's Place*," he recognized her voice instantly and his heart began beating rapidly. Sweat broke out on his forehead and a knot twisted in the pit of his stomach.

"Jill?" Billy wished he had something clever to say or could have sounded more in control, he was barely able to breathe normally as he held the phone in his hand.

"Billy! My God after all these years. I can't believe it, but I still recognize your voice," she sounded cheerful, no sound of any distaste or anger in her voice.

"Well, you know," Billy stammered. "So, Jill's Place, after all these years you finally managed to open a store, congratulations." Damn it, Billy said to himself. What's with talking on phones lately. Every time I do it I sound like some idiot!

"Yep, finally did it. Been saving for years. I knew it would happen and it did. I could use some exposure. I know that it's imposing on you, but is there any chance you could, please do a story on my shop?" Billy loved how she said the word 'please.' It stirred emotions hidden long ago.

"Of course, you know I'd be happy to, when can we get together?"

"Whenever you want," his heart was racing wildly at the prospect.

"Would tonight be pushing it? I've got an employee who comes in at five this afternoon, I'll be off after she shows up. I have to go to New York on a buying trip late tomorrow. I'll only be gone a day, but, ahhh," Billy was amused and smiled. She was stammering like a fool too, as nervous as he was. It felt good being on equal ground.

"Sure, I'll be there around 4:30 or 5:00. What's the address?"

"I'm right on the Coastal Highway at 144th Street. It's a new group of stores, you can't miss it. It's called *Jill's Place*. Oops, I guess you know that already, sorry. See you then."

"OK, see you then," Billy hung up the phone.

A wave of euphoria swept over him, suddenly followed by cold fear. He had wanted to see her for years, just to talk to her again. He had never tried to kid himself by saying he didn't love her anymore. In fact, he had always known he was still in love with her, even after all these years, he still had that feeling.

Watching the clock all afternoon, he typed up the stories he had briefly talked with the people about earlier this morning. Eli had no interviews planned for this afternoon. He had left early, deciding to play golf at Ocean Pines. At three o'clock Billy shut off his computer and ran out of the office. The late afternoon traffic filled with vacationers was miserable and seemed worse than usual. It was as if everyone was trying, intentionally, to keep him from seeing Jill. His Jeep slid to a stop in front of his trailer. Jumping out, he ran inside to take a shower, shave and change his clothes.

At exactly 4:30 he was sitting on the shoulder of the road at Coastal Highway and 140th Street, a panic attack gripping his body. He wanted to see her, but fear was preventing him from driving that last block to her store. A police car pulled up behind him and Billy jumped in fear thinking it was John Eastwick as he looked in the rear view mirror. Turning cautiously he saw it was Mike Moran, a Maryland State Trooper he had known for years.

"Hey, Billy, you Ok?" Mike called from the speaker mounted on top of his car.

Billy lifted his hand to wave that he was all right to the trooper who pulled back into traffic and waved as he passed by.

"OK, Sport. It's now or never!" he said to himself as he pulled back into traffic and up to 144th Street.

The little strip shopping center looked familiar, he remembered interviewing a couple of store owners there last year. He saw the sign *Jill's Place* on one of the stores and was sure it had been the same location he had interviewed someone else last year. Pulling the car into the parking lot, he could see Jill standing by a cash register at the front of the store. Her hair still as blond as it had been years ago, and her body still as svelte as it had always been. Standing there wearing a pair of white shorts, she had a rich deep tan, her legs looking just as beautiful and shapely as the day he had first met her. The place looked expensive from the outside, lots of pricey porcelain and glass figurines on display in the window.

Walking in the front door, he saw her turn, looking at him with a big smile that made his heart melt. She walked up to him, giving him a big hug. He could smell the fragrance of *White Shoulders* perfume. It immediately brought back pleasant memories from years past.

"I'm sorry, but I have to say it. You look just as beautiful as you always did," Billy said smiling, hoping she couldn't tell that his knees were knocking. His heart was beating at twice its normal rate.

"Well, I see you still have a penchant for charm and I thank you for that. But, let's face it I'm not that young anymore and this old bod does have a few miles on it," she said with a warm smile.

"Yea, well those miles look like they were gentle ones. You really do look great."

"I thank you again, kind sir. So, where do we begin?"

"I guess we begin with, has life been treating you well?"

"Like all lives. It's had its ups and downs. But enough of that, I'm sure you don't want to hear my tales of woe. After all, you are here on business," her smile wasn't quite as wide and warm as it had been and he picked up on it right away.

"Sure, we can get to that. I think I've told you a gazillion times what and how I write these stories. Hell, I'll bet you could write the whole story yourself. But, if there are tales of woe, who better than an old friend to talk with?" he was still smiling and hoped she could read the concern for her in his voice.

"Same old Billy, always the nice guy. Listen, really, I didn't bring you here to talk about me. I appreciate your concern, but I really need to talk about my business. I need the publicity, I've got to get some bodies through here and it's got to be quick," her smile was gone now and he could really see how troubled she was.

"Business problems?" he asked sounding concerned.

"No, not yet. I've been able to generate enough business to pay the bills and cover my debts, but I need to do a lot better and soon, or I won't be able to make it through the winter when the traffic really drops off," her smile came back. "And, yea I could write the story myself but I would rather have a real pro do it, someone I can trust to do it up right."

"Great, we'll find someone that fits that description and really make it a great story."

"Billy,' she said laughing. "Come on, get serious, you know you were the best writer I have ever read or seen. Speaking of which, whatever happened to that great American novel you were always talking about writing?"

"I wrote it. Then I made a really big mistake," he was saying with a serious look on his face.

"What was that?" she asked curiously.

"I read it. It was boring as hell. It made Russian novels look exciting. So one April night, I made a bon fire out of it. It burned much better than it read," Billy gestured with his hands.

"Oh you, you're too hard on yourself. You shouldn't have burned it, damn you. I'm sure it was great. I wish I could have read it." Her concern for the book made him feel good. It was nice that someone else besides him cared.

"I don't think so," he said sheepishly shaking his head. "The guys from the fire department, who came to put out the brush fire it started, read several pages and they could hardly stand up from laughing so hard."

Jill doubled over in laughter, and it made Billy feel good that he could still make her laugh like he used too.

"Listen, I'll write the story on *Jill's Place,* and I promise I'll make it good. But, after it runs, the guy who owns the paper, Eli, will come by and try and push you into signing for a big expensive four color ad. Don't do it. It will be a waste of your money. The story will sell the place. The ad, if you take it, will be worthless."

"Yea, Yea, I know. I remember the way it works. Don't worry, I have no intentions of buying into that ad thing. So, what do you need to know, where do we start?" she asked clapping her hands and rubbing her palms together.

"Where do we start, are you kidding? I've written this story a thousand times, but this time I'm going write it so it sings, deal?"

"Deal!" she said loudly.

They were both smiling and she held out her hand for him to shake. When his hand touched hers he could feel his heart melt for about the fifth time since he had been there.

"Here's Lisa, she has the late shift tonight until eleven," Jill said turning to the young woman who was walking through the door. Billy also turned and looked at her. She was a beautiful girl of about twenty with short black hair and a rich golden tan, undoubtedly a summer worker. The beach employers loved them, mostly college and some high school students, they would work all summer for very little money, just to hang around the beach and get a great tan. It was one of the things that helped keep most of the shaky summer businesses alive from year to year.

"Hi, Lisa," Jill said with a smile. "There's not much for you to do tonight, just watch the register. I restocked all the shelves this afternoon."

"OK," said Lisa as she walked by Jill and into the rear of the store.

Once Lisa had gone by, Jill turned back and looked at Billy with a serious look on her face.

"Billy. I know I can't pay you for writing the story. Can I, would you, let me take you out to dinner tonight? Please. I really want to," she insisted.

"Thanks, but I... Really, thanks, but no ... I better not, I'm sure you have better things to do. Really, thanks," he was growing angry at himself for stammering like a dullard.

"Please. It's as much for me as it is for you. I've haven't been out in weeks, Hell, it's probably months. Please, oh please, Billy," she pleaded.

"OK, but, ahh. Well, what about John? I mean, we've never been on too friendly terms. It might get you and me in trouble," he said giving more emphasis to the word "me".

"I thought, maybe you had heard. John ditched me, big time, about eight months ago. Haven't seen him since he left and hope I don't ever see him again. The prick!" she said making her last statement sound very bitter.

"No, I'm sorry. I didn't know... Well, Ahhhh... OK, let's have dinner. But I pay!" Billy could feel his heart fluttering.

He tried to look concerned on the outside, but inside he was jumping up and down with joy like a little boy.

"Not a chance, this is my treat. Besides, if you take me out to dinner, you won't have any money to eat with for a month. You forget Billy Lee, we used to be married. I know how much money you don't have," she said sounding serious but with a smile on her face.

"Unfortunately, as always, you are right," he sighed. "Ok, you can pay, but nowhere expensive. I still have a little pride left."

"I promise. Hang on for a second, I'll go back and strong arm some reservations. Be right back."

As she turned and walked away, his eyes dropped to her hips.

"Damn," he said quietly to himself. "She is just as beautiful as the first time I met her."

A few minutes later she came out of the back room smiling.

"Got it, two reservations at Fagers Island for an hour from now. Let's go," she said excitedly as she walked by, taking his hand and leading him toward the front door.

"Wow, great... Oh Yea... Nice cheap little place like Fagers Island. Nothing more expensive you could find?" he asked sarcastically.

"I owe you one, Billy Lee. Actually, I owe you a bunch! If you don't accept, you won't get to enjoy my scintillating company and gut wrenching sob story over dinner," there was a smile on Jill's face, but Billy knew her well enough to see that there was sadness in the way she said it.

"Damn, you put it that way. How could I resist? Let's go, but I drive," he said as he pushed open the front door for her.

"WHOA! HOLD ON! NO WAY! NOT A CHANCE! I saw you pull up. You are still driving those damned old, topless Jeeps. NO, I'll drive. Billy, you have got to change your life just a touch, get a top on your Jeep!" she said with a laugh as she took his arm and walked him through the doorway.

Leading him to her car, he was surprised to see she was driving a Cadilac Eldorado. It was about two years old, but in excellent condition and a very expensive car. He opened the door for her and as she got in, smiled warmly at him, saying "Thank you!" That made, at least, the fifth time his heart had melted tonight. He made a mental note to himself, as he walked around to the passengers side, to start keeping a better count.

"Nice car, you had it long?" he said as she made a right turn onto the Coastal Highway heading back into lower Ocean City.

"Yes, it is, I love it. I got it from a friend of mine last year. Really got a great deal on it."

As they drove along he suddenly became panicky. He couldn't think of anything to talk about. After all these years of hoping for just one more chance to talk with her here he was drawing a blank. Looking over at her, he thought he could see some discomfort in her face too.

"We are going to have to talk about it sooner or later Billy, you know that," she said quietly, not taking her eyes off of the road.

"What?" Billy asked. He knew exactly what she was trying to say but hoped to avoid it for as long as possible. He wanted to enjoy his time with her and was afraid if they started talking too much it could ruin the moment.

"Billy, it happened we split. Sooner or later it's going to come up. We can do it now, put it behind us and move on, or we can wait and do it later. It's up to you," she said turning to look at him in a serious manner.

"Oh God, do I ever remember that look. OK! Let's do it now, let's get it over with," he tried not to put an edge on his voice but could not help it.

"It wasn't you, it was me," she said coldly.

He couldn't help himself and started to laugh loudly.

"What's so funny about that?" she asked.

"I'm sorry I couldn't help it. It reminded me of a segment on the old *Seinfeld* TV show. The guy who plays George, always had a way of getting out of a situation with a woman by saying 'it wasn't you, it was me.' I'm sorry I didn't mean to laugh but the way you said it, you sounded exactly like him," Billy said quickly trying to calm her down. "Look, it happened ten years ago, why don't we just let sleeping dogs lie and just let it go."

"I'm not going to lie to you Billy. I still have feelings for you. I've always had feelings for you. When I saw you get out of your Jeep tonight it really gave me a rush, just like it used to when we were dating," she blurted out.

"What the hell are you talking about? Feelings for me. Are you serious? You left me for John Eastwick. Yea, that showed a shit load of feelings for me," he quickly blurted out, shocked at how easily he had become angry.

"There you see," she said with a smile. "Now! Now! We can talk about it!

"Damn it, damn it, damn it to hell, there you go, just like you always used to do. You're pushing my buttons again!" his voice loud but not angry.

"I was always great at that, wasn't I?" she said with a laugh. "Jeez, we'll be at the restaurant in a few minutes. You were right let's put it off till after we eat."

"WHAT?" he exclaimed. "I told you I didn't want to talk about it. But noooooooooo, you started pushing buttons. I said let's forget it but noooooooooooo, you said we had to talk about it. Nowwwwwwwww that we're here you don't want to talk about it. Nooooooooo wayyyyyyyyy. We're going in and talk about it over dinner. HELL! I want everyone to hear us talk about it! BECAUSE YOU HAD TO BRING <u>IT</u> UP," as he finished he could see she was laughing so hard that she had tears in her eyes. She pulled into a parking space barely missing a very pricy BMW. After placing the car into park, she reached over and touched his cheek, rubbing her fingers along his chin.

The maitre d' seated them immediately when they walked into the restaurant. Billy was more than a little surprised when he saw Jill casually palm the man a tip that looked like several twenties folded together.

"So, what do you want to eat?" she asked quietly after the maitre d' left.

"I'll leave it up to you. You're buying," he said picking up the menu and glancing at it as the waiter arrived at the table.

"Two double scotch's with ice and two lobster dinners, you can pick the lobsters, large ones please. We also want baked potatoes with sour cream, salad with house dressing and the asparagus if you still have any fresh ones left." Billy was taken back at how quickly she barked out the orders.

"I take it Billy, you still like a double scotch before your dinner," she said as she smiled and looked into his eyes.

"Definitely! Hell, I've been known on many occasions to just have the scotch instead of dinner, sans ice," he said with a smile. "Do you know how much two lobster dinners are going to cost you?" his voice now serious.

"Yea, and you know what, I think you're worth it. Even if you don't," she stated returning the serious look he was giving her.

"It's crazy. I could eat for a month on what we're spending for dinner, wait, I take that back, I could eat for three months on that," he whispered across the table to her.

"No, it's not crazy Billy. You could eat for six months on what I'm paying for this dinner. Hell, all you ever wanted to do was fish for those damn flounders and then eat them. With all the fish you eat, or at least ate, you should live to be a hundred. I'm sure you still indulge to excess in your fishing, don't you?"

"But of course, my dear, you would expect less of me?" in an attempt to sound like Cary Grant.

"Very funny. Christ, I think the last time I was fishing was when we went. God, how long ago that must have been," she said wistfully.

"So, now that we are in a crowded place with people eavesdropping on our every word and move, why did you leave me?" he asked with a smile.

"Billy! You were the sweetest, nicest man I ever met or loved," she said reaching out and placing her hand on top of his.

"Damn, that's really hitting below the belt, Jill. Please, that hurts, don't be so rough on me," he said in a serious tone but with a smile.

"You were, I mean are. Billy! Damn it, you always do this to me. I get so twisted around I can't talk straight. I once told you about the men I used to date before I met you, do you remember that?"

"Wow," he said, his mind trying to search back as the waiter brought them their drinks. "Yea, I do. I used to tease you about it. You said you always dated bums and losers. I thought you were joking, you were too beautiful to date scum like that."

"There was something in me back then. I can't explain it but I liked to live close to the edge. I liked men who were rough and unpredictable. I would push them to the edge and then back off. It's a little, no, it's a lot like playing with fire. You just keep trying till you get burnt," she said holding her drink and staring off into space.

"Ever get burnt?" he asked trying to bring her back.

"Yes, once, very badly. All the way to my soul," she said quietly, her voice trailing off at the end.

"I did that to you?" he asked in surprise.

"No, like I said, you were the kindest, gentlest man I ever met. That's what I've always loved about you. I never once saw you try to prove you were rough or tough."

"I don't know about that, there are a couple of fish out there that got away from me that might just want to argue that point with you." he said with a smile, trying to lighten up the conversation a little.

"When I met you, I'd just come to Ocean City, rebounding from a real, real loser. It was time for someone nice in my life and I met, then fell in love with you. But after a few years I started feeling the need for that edge again. It wasn't going to come from you, and I thank God about that. So, that is when John Eastwick slithered into my life. I met him at one of the local grocery stores, I don't remember which one, but I do remember that it was early spring. I knew he was bad news and it really turned me on. Then, one day, I went to lunch with him. I know I shouldn't have, but I did. At lunch he spilled some food on his pants, so after we ate, he wanted to go back to his place to change. When we got there I told him I'd wait outside. He pushed me in the door and we had sex on his rug in the living room. It was more like rape, but at the time it seemed like sex and I tried Billy, I really tried, but I couldn't help myself. I fell hard for that S.O.B. Strange, his idea of sex was practically to beat me up, which he did on numerous occasions. I was living in Hell for years. Beatings and rapes, that was all that it was. I wanted to leave, but I guess I was the classic victim. I had no where to go, my parents had died by then, and I had absolutely no friends left in the whole world. Still don't! So it was either stay with him or live on a street corner. I stayed," her voice quivering slightly as it trailed off.

"Thanks for sharing that with me. Gee, there's nothing more fun, hearing how my wife had sex with another guy. LOOK, you could have called me," he said softly and sincerely.

"After what I did to you, no I couldn't. I was too embarrassed. Anyway, after a couple of years he got tired of me and started playing around with other women. God, I feel so sorry for them. So, he left me home alone most of the time. Occasionally he would come home for his version of sex, but it wasn't too often, over time he came home less frequently. Then, a little over eight months ago, I came home and all his clothes were gone. I jumped with joy. I had managed to hide most of the money my parents had left me. I bought a condo at the Golden Sands, nice beach front two bedroom deal on the eleventh floor. Moved in and have been living happily ever after." Billy could see tears in her eyes.

"Seen him since he left?"

"No, not a word. I have a big dead bolt on my door and there are security guards there. I warned them about him, and they are prepared to deal with him if he should show up. But, like I said, I think he's had enough of me, gone to greener and more likely younger pastures. The shithead!" she said with a small smile.

"Ain't love grand!" Billy said as the waiter brought their lobster dinners. "Jill?"

"What?" she asked as she broke the claw apart and dipped it in butter.

"You know you could have come back to me at any time... I would have taken you back."

"Yes, I do and I've always loved you for that," she said putting her fork down and staring him in the eye. "But after what I did to you, I was too embarrassed and ashamed of myself. Getting beaten was easier than seeing you."

"If this was a movie or a book it would be my cue to look over at you and say something like 'It's really funny, the way we fuck up our lives.' But you know it's not, I've always been an observer of life and people, I don't think I've ever known anyone who hasn't fucked up their life in one way or another. I'm sure there are those who haven't, but I'd be willing to bet they are probably people who lead such boring lives that they don't even realize that life has just passed them by. Oh Hell, enough philosophy from me tonight," he said with a smile as he tried to lighten up the conversation.

Through the rest of their dinner they said nothing to each other. They both ate their lobsters, occasionally looking at each other and smiling. When the check was placed in front of him, Jill reached across quickly, picking it up. She laid it back down with her credit card. As the waiter was picking it up, he could see that the bill was $145.00.

"Billy Lee," she said as she took a drink of her coffee, the waiter returning her charge slip for her to sign. "When was the last time you went for a walk on the beach. Ocean side not bay side?"

"Geez, I don't remember exactly when, but I know it was before you left me. After that the ocean never seemed quite the same. That's why I've stayed bay side all these years. Sounds corny as hell, but it's the truth."

"Well then, Billy Lee, lets go for a walk on the beach. I think we could both use it," she said signing the charge slip.

As they drove north on the Coastal Highway toward her condo, the sun was setting over the bay. The diminishing light reflected off her golden hair as it blew in the breeze coming through the open car window. Pulling into the parking lot of the Golden Sands, a high rise condominium complex that was loaded with vacationers, they got out of her car, walked through the lobby, then out the back of the building. The sun was down now and it was almost dark as they stood on the deck behind the building looking out at the ocean. Watching as the white caps of the waves were breaking on the shore. Taking off their shoes, they walked down the steps and onto the beach. The sand felt cool on Billy's feet as it oozed up between his toes. He had forgotten how cool it could feel on a warm summer night. Taking his hand, Jill led him down to the waters edge where they played tag with the surf as the waves rolled in around them.

Walking along the ocean's edge, he realized for the first time how alone he had been all these years, that life without someone to share it with was hollow and empty. He was at peace with the world when she was holding his hand. About a mile down the beach they saw the first flashes of lightning off in the distance by the bay. Storms could blow up quickly by the ocean so they both turned and began strolling back in the direction of the condominium. Neither one said anything to each other and he was amazed that the silence didn't have the same feeling of pressure it had earlier. Nearing the condominium they heard the first claps of thunder break over the sounds of the pounding surf. As they reached the steps, the cool strong winds that signaled rain was near, began to gust, blowing clouds of sand down the beach. Stopping by a water faucet they rinsed the sand from their feet and legs before going into the building.

Billy realized he had a smile on his face as he walked through the lobby of the building. As happy as he was feeling it was strange that he also felt sad at the same time. He was just beginning to realize that he had been wasting his life for the past ten years. The rain was pouring down as he reached the large glass doors at the front entrance of the building. Looking around he realized that Jill was not beside him and as he looked back over his shoulder he could see her standing by the elevator doors. She was looking into his eyes, saying nothing and making no movements. A group of people came running through the front doors, wet from the deluge outside, talking in loud tones about the rain. They walked between his sight of Jill and as they moved out of the way he could see her still standing there staring at him. A bell dinged and the group of wet people herded onto the elevator, another ding and the door closed behind them leaving the lobby area quiet once again. The elevator behind Jill dinged and the doors opened, she took a step onto the elevator not breaking eye contact with him until her head moved out of sight. Standing there, he did not know what to do, he was immediately flooded with different emotions and confused. He wanted to get on the elevator but things were happening too quickly. There was no way that he was prepared for this, it was beyond anything he had expected from the evening. Suddenly he knew he could not get on that elevator. He was not prepared to open himself up to the heartbreak and pain that he had managed to put out of his life. He had just barely survived the last time and was afraid of opening up his feelings to anyone ever again. Turning he walked to the front doors and as he was pushing them open he heard the elevator ding behind him followed by the soft sounds of the doors sliding closed.

Standing in the pouring rain in front of the building, Billy realized that his jeep was back up at 144th street several miles away. At first he cursed at himself and then he laughed, it was the perfect way to end the evening, a two mile hike in the pouring rain of a thunderstorm. Fifteen minutes later and ten blocks away, the lightning had subsided. The rain had changed from a tropical downpour to steady showers. Clothes soaked and heavy from the rain Billy kept replaying the latter part of the evening and suddenly realized that the rain that had been in his eyes was now replaced by tears. He felt more alone than he had ever been since Jill left him.

Billy jumped out of the way as a white car pulled off the road onto the shoulder, barely missing him. He saw that it was a white Cadilac Eldorado, as the car came to a screeching stop, Jill opened the door and got out, standing in the rain looking at him. As he stood there looking at her a few feet away, he could see that her eyes were wet and red from crying, much the same as his. She raised her arms slightly and Billy walked into them as they rose to embrace him. Standing by the side of the road in the rain, they kissed deeply, oblivious to the stares from people in the other cars who were slowing down to see what was happening.

Raising her hand to his cheek she pushed his face back, breaking their kiss.

"Billy... Please," she begged so softly that he could barely hear it over the traffic noise. "Please."

Chapter 4
Thursday, July 16

The light of the rising sun woke Billy. For a second he became disoriented and frightened, not sure of where he was. Quickly his memory and senses returned and he realized he was in Jill's bedroom. Looking across the bed he could see that he was alone and turned over to look for Jill. He saw her, standing naked, by the floor to ceiling window watching the sun rise over the ocean. Getting out of bed, he walked up behind her, put his hands on her arms and kissed her shoulder. He was tasting and reveling in the feel of her skin, as he moved up behind her, pressing his naked body against hers. She turned to him and as he was about to kiss her he saw that she had tears in her eyes.

"You OK," he said softly.

"Yea, sure," she smiled as she walked back and sat on the edge of the bed. "What could be wrong? I just spent the night having fantastic sex with my ex-husband, who I practically had to drag into my bed. Yea, great. The world's spinning around and..."

"Hey, hold on, wait a minute, would you? You're not the only one in this, yea, I have some real problems with this too," he interrupted as he walked over and sat next to her on the bed.

"Good, I'm glad I'm not the only one. Listen, I didn't plan for this to happen, well sort of, not exactly, but, SHIT! Why can't I talk right?" she yelled. "Billy, listen, I have to tell you this. When I called yesterday, it was primarily for you to write that story on my shop, but I also wanted to see you again. I know it sounds crazy but listen, this is really going to sound weird, but like I told you before, even after I left you I had feelings for you. I've always had them over all these years. I loved you, I just didn't wake up one morning and say. 'Hey Billy Lee, I don't love you anymore. It's over, I'm out of here.' What I'm trying to say is that I never stopped loving you. After I was sure John was out of my life, there were other men I could have gone out with, I don't look anywhere near as good as I did fifteen years ago, but I'm not some local pig with half my teeth missing and legs the size of telephone poles. There were men who wanted to date me, but I didn't want them!" she sobbed as tears trickled down from her eyes.

"Jill, I..." he tried to break in but she held up her hand to stop him.

"Billy, I wanted to see you and talk with you again. That's part of the reason I called, I just had to find out if there was anything left. I planned dinner, but not everything that happened afterwards. When I woke up this morning, I was as happy as I had been in years, Hell, I was happier. Then I realized that this is not fair to you or me. Billy, we have to stop this. It's not right," she stammered.

"Wait, whoa, hold on, STOP!" he said loudly but with no anger in his voice.

Sitting on the edge of the bed he put his elbows on his knees, then cradled his face in his hands hiding it from view. A second later he stood up and walked around in a circle in front of her.

"Billy, I...," she started but he held up his hand to stop her.

"No!" he said shaking his head as he flopped down in a chair next to the bed.

"I love you," he spoke softly. "I never stopped loving you, hoping that maybe, someday, you would came back to me. Sure after a few years I realized that was all she wrote, but I never stopped loving you," he whispered softly. "I never went looking for another woman or a replacement for you and I carried all the pain inside me, knowing I would never be with you again. It took a lot of time and scotch and whiskey and bourbon, but I managed to harden my feelings and heart enough to function and survive. Over the years I became colder and I hid it deeper within me and was sure I could keep it covered. Last night in that lobby it would have been easy just to come up here and sleep with you, but the tough part would have been being able to go back living with myself once the genie was out of the bottle. Well, here we are, damn it," he said standing in the middle of the bedroom his arms stretched out wide as he turned in circles. "I don't know if I can survive losing you again, but I do know that living life without you in it, is not living at all! Damn, c'mon, let's take a chance, forget about the past and look to the future. We were always good for each other and can be again. Sure we'll have problems but, HELL LET'S GO FOR IT! At least this time if it doesn't work, we can hate each other afterwards and maybe have a life, but damn it, we can't play it safe. This is life, this is real. It's not some book or a movie, you have to take a chance and I want to. I want to take a chance with you and for you to take one with me," he said kneeling before her.

She wiped a tear from her eye. Pushing herself back onto the bed she opened her arms to him. He hesitated for a second then moved onto the bed and then on top of her.

Three hours later they were attempting to get dressed. But every minute or so, one would come up to kiss or caress the other. Earlier, after they had made love, they laid in each others arms for an hour, then made love again. Getting up from the bed they showered together, lovingly washing then drying each other off. It was almost nine o'clock and too late for breakfast. Neither one wanted to leave, but Jill had to open the store. Love was one thing, she told him, but she had too much money riding on the store to take any chances with it. He understood but was not happy about it. All he wanted to do was be with her.

Watching her in the morning sun as she drove him back to his Jeep, parked in front of her store, he couldn't take his eyes off her.

Damn, he thought to himself. The sun seems brighter and the air smells cleaner. It's strange what love can do to you! He shook his head.

"Whatcha thinkin', Babe?" she asked smiling over at him.

"How scared I am of life and living," he shrugged his shoulders.

"Me too, Babe, but doesn't the air smell clean and the sun look bright this morning?"

"I see it's doing it to you, too."

"What's that?"

"Feelings, they seem to open up and change your perspective on life," he said as she began to laugh.

"Billy Lee, you should have been a philosopher. You were never more right about anything in your life."

It was 9:30 as they pulled into the parking lot. They got out of the car. Billy walked over and leaned against his Jeep. Jill walked around her car, leaning against it, she was facing him.

"I was supposed to go to New York on a buying trip tonight, but I think something's coming up later, so I'll put it off till tomorrow."

"What's coming up?" he questioned not sure of what she was talking about.

"That thing between your legs, I hope," she said with a smile as she pulled her sunglasses down over her nose and gave him a sexy smile.

"Very funny, very funny, maybe you should have been a philosopher or at least a comedian," he smiled softly.

"Babe, I wish there was some way I could get out of here this morning and we could spend the whole day together in bed, but I have to reconcile the check book, get the cash drop from the bank, make deposits, etc., etc. I'll switch things around with the girls. The earliest I can get out of here will be around one or two, can you wait to have sex till then? Ooops, I meant that to be lunch, I guess you can see where my mind is," she sounded embarrassed.

"Wait, tell you what, how about this? I'll meet you in the parking lot of Giovannis Restaurant around two, if you have to be late, don't worry about it. I'll wait. We'll have some lunch, light lunch, then go back to the trailer."

"Oh Christ, the trailer! I can imagine what it looks like now," she cut in with a laugh as she put her hand up to her mouth.

"We'll go back to the trailer and whatever, then later, I know this sounds stupid as hell, but would you like to go fishing like we used to? You were good at it," he said timidly not wanting to ruin anything.

"I'd love to Billy. It's a date. See you in the parking lot around two," she walked up to him and gave him a big kiss.

Pulling back from her, he looked into her smiling face then kissed her back again. She stood there watching as he climbed into his jeep. As he sat down on the front seat, it made a loud squishing sound and Billy felt his pants immediately soak through with last night's rain. He looked at her and smiled sheepishly as he started the Jeep.

"Billy Lee, you have got to stop riding those damn topless Jeeps!" she said with a smile. He smiled, backed out and pulled away.

He didn't want to go to work today. What he really wanted to do was spend the day with her, but he understood why he could not. He decided to make the best of it and handle as many calls as he could this morning before he met her for lunch. It was still early in the morning as he drove down the Coastal Highway, the beach worshipers just beginning to drift in. Soon the roads would be clogged with people attempting to find places to park, the people dangerously milling around the streets on their way to the beach, not paying attention. They would always say later, after they were hit by a car, that they thought nothing bad could happen to them while they were on vacation.

Finding a prime spot on Somerset Street next to the newspaper's offices, he got out, walking to the door. Across the street he could see Jonathan Banks repairing the broken down front door of one of the restaurants.

"Yo, Joe-nathan," Billy yelled across the street to Jonathan who looked up and waved to his old friend.

"Billy Lee, looks likes it's goin' to be another fine day, hot as Hell. How are you this fine morning?" replied Jonathan with a wave and a smile.

"Feeling young again! Hey, Joe-Nathan want to hoist a few tomorrow night?"

"Why wait till the last minute, how about tonight?"

"Can't, got things to do, what about tomorrow night?"

"Damn, Billy Lee, why don'ts you let them flounders alone. What'd they ever do to you anyway?" he shook his arm at Billy.

"No, really, I can't tonight. How 'bout tomorrow night?"

"Ok, where?" asked Jonathan.

"What say we meet at the Paddock Night Club around eight. Watch some rich old men dance with those pretty young girls and make fools of themselves."

"Sound like a fine time to me. See you then!" Jonathan yelled back as he went back to work on the door.

Billy walked through the office door, then sprinted up the flight of steps to the offices. He walked quickly past Bev and back to his desk where he sat down and flipped on his computer. As soon as the machine was initialized and the word processing program was working, he started typing Jill's story. It was a rearrangement of the usual dribble he wrote for everyone else and within twenty minutes was done. Printing out a copy, he proofed it and then went back, rewriting most of it, giving it a more polished, professional look, then printed out another copy to give to Jill.

"Hey Janet," Billy yelled over to the girl who did the page composition for the newspaper.

"Yea, Billy, what's up?" she yelled back not taking here eyes from her monitor.

"Got a Page One story, can you fit it in for tomorrow's edition?" he asked making it sound more like an order than a question.

"Sure, Billy, why not just put a stake in my heart and get it over with. I've got more cover stories than I can handle for tomorrow. Eli's been selling his ass off, unfortunately promising everyone the front page."

"OK, can you fit me in for Page One on Friday?" this time making it sound more like a request than an order.

"Sure, no problem, Friday's great. What's the file name?"
"KMA717."

"Hey, Billy," she said as she took her eyes off the monitor and looked over at him. "I hate to be nosy, but I've been working here for five years, you always name your files KMA and then a number to show the date. But what's the KMA stand for?"

"Kiss My Ass," Bev blurted out before Billy could speak. "It's his way of communicating with Eli."

Beverly placed the messages he had failed to pick up when he came in the office on Billy's desk along with a thick FedEx envelope.

"Billy, guy name of Oliver, probably the same Oliver that's on that FedEx package, called you three times this morning.

Each time he gets angrier and angrier when I tell him you ain't been in or called in for your messages. Billy, I ain't talkin' with this ahole anymore. He calls in again, you talk to him. I don't have time for this," Bev ordered as she was walking away.

Looking at the clock, Billy could see it was 11:00 a.m., he still had time to write some more copy and then make a few calls before meeting Jill. A half an hour and four stories later Bev called back to him from the front desk.

"Hey, Billy, your ahole friend is on line 3."

"Hi, Oliver. What's happening?" Billy asked pleasantly into the phone.

"What's happening, you shithead, I've been calling your office all morning. I know you got my FedEx, why the hell didn't you call me back? I picked up a little more info on your guys."

"Oh yea, give it to me," Billy said, already bored with the conversation and watching the clock as he worked on another story.

"Did you read the stories in the FedEx pack about St. John that research dug out?"

"Oh yea, good stuff." Billy lied as he looked at the unopened FedEx pack.

"On a hunch, I called the prosecutor on the case. He told me that this guy St. John's a real sociopath. Seems like the nicest, friendliest guy you'd ever want to meet but has about as much feeling for you as a common house fly. Absolutely no conscience. He told me that if he hadn't been this incredibly nice, sweet talking, friendly sort of guy, he'd have done five years along with that Dr. Ling in the slammer. He warned me to be extremely careful around this guy, said he could be as dangerous as hell. Billy you there?" Oliver barked into the phone.

"Yea, Oliver, sure, just making notes that's all," Billy lied again as he continued with the story he was working on.

"So, what's the status on this, where are you, what'cha got? Can you tell me just where you are with this?" Oliver asked making it sound more like a command than a question.

"Gee, Oliver, to tell you the truth, look's like I was wrong on this thing, all the way around," Billy said as he slowly opened the FedEx pack.

Pulling the contents out, he saw an article about Dr. St. John with his picture in it and immediately pushed the papers back into the FedEx pack. "Yea, look I'm sorry about this, there must have been some mix up. The guy in the picture is not the guy I've been talking to. Also, it turns out I was wrong anyway, what I thought might be going on isn't, so, looks like there's no story. Listen, thanks anyway for your help, I really appreciate your sending this information down to me," he was saying as Oliver cut in.

"Listen you cocksucker! What the fuck are you doing? You blowin' me off after I got you all the information? I talked to that District Attorney guy, he told me he heard St. John had something going on near Ocean City, but it was out of his jurisdiction, so he could care less what was happening with him. Now damn it, Billy, somethin's goin' on down there and you owe it to me to let me be in on it," Oliver yelled.

"Oliver! Come on, calm down. There is nothing. I was wrong. No story. Nada! Zip. Give me a break. If there was, I would gladly let you in on it," Billy said with as much sincerity as he could muster.

"You know. I never liked you, you prick. Don't you ever, EVER! call me again. You understand?"

Billy heard a loud click as the phone went dead.

"Well, that sure was nice," Billy said sliding the FedEx envelope on its edge between his desk and the wall.

"Billy, your ahole friend is on line 4 again. Tell him to stop calling, please," Bev called back dryly.

"Yea, Oliver," Billy said as he picked up the phone.

"and, FUCK YOU!" screamed Oliver. Billy heard the loud click as the phone was slammed down again and the line went dead.

"Nice talkin' with you Oliver," Billy said as put the phone in its cradle and went back to work. "Hope we can do it again, real soon!"

Fifteen minutes later Billy had finished writing more than his quota of stories. He decided to make a couple of quick calls before going to meet Jill at Giovanni's to keep ahead of his work, just in case his new love life started to eat into the amount of time he needed to spend on work.

Rushing quickly through three interviews Billy was making sure he would get to the restaurant with time to spare. Driving North on Baltimore Avenue toward the restaurant he saw a policeman had pulled a car over and was writing the unhappy vacationer a ticket. As Billy got closer to the car he could see the policeman was John Eastwick and he began to feel nervous, as he reflected back on Jill. Driving past the police car, he didn't turn his head to look at Eastwick, but did glance at him through his sunglasses, looking out the corner of his eye. Pulling up even with Eastwick, he could see that Eastwick was watching him as he drove by. Shifting his eyes to the rearview mirror when he was past, Billy was relieved to see that Eastwick was no longer looking in his direction, but had returned to writing the ticket. He couldn't help wondering, thinking to himself, did Eastwick have any idea that he was seeing Jill, did Eastwick even care?

Ten minutes later Billy pulled into Giovanni's parking lot at five minutes before two. To his surprise, Jill was waiting for him sitting on the front fender of her car, her feet resting on the top of the front tire, elbows propped on her knees.

"Hi, been waiting long?" asked Billy as he pulled up beside her.

"Nope, got here about five minutes ago. I knew I would be a little early so I called ahead for a pizza to go and picked up a bottle of wine."

"Great, I'm sure you remember how to get to the trailer. It's still parked in the same place it's always been. A block that way," he said pointing south down the highway.

"Oh yea, I remember. Billy, listen why don't we go back to my place? It's larger and a lot more comfortable, we can come back later to go fishing," she replied sounding a little uneasy about going to the mobile home.

"The trailer's just a few minutes that way. Go to the condo, this time of day with traffic, it'll be an hour before we get to your apartment. C'mon, trailer's closer," he said with a large smile as he got into the Jeep, started it and drove away.

Jill got down off the car, raised her eyebrows and shook her head as she got into the Cadilac.

"My God, Billy," she said pulling into the driveway behind him. "It looks almost the same. Just a little more faded and a whole lot more rusty."

Billy walked up the two steps to the door ahead of her, opened it and went into the mobile home. Jill took a deep breath, shook her head, then followed him in, carrying the pizza and wine.

"AHHHHHH!, My God!" she exclaimed as soon as she walked in. "Billy, this place looks exactly the same. Christ, I remember buying those curtains! The paint on the cabinets is the exact same color of green. BILLY! What is this, a home or a shrine? Nothing has changed since I left, nothing, except maybe it is a little neater, no it's a lot neater and a whole lot cleaner."

"No! I just liked the way it looked and never got around to changing anything. I mean, if you like something the way it is, why change it?" he was saying as if it were perfectly logical.

"Oh Billy Lee, Billy Lee, you are an enigma," she said as she walked around the living room looking at things and running her hand across an old vase on the end table.

Walking over to the telephone she could see that the little light on the answering machine was blinking. Reaching down, she hit the rewind button and then the play button.

The mechanical drone of the voice from the machine came on. "You have one call. One thirty P.M."

"Hey Billy. Just had to tell you one more time. FUCK YOU! You Schmuck!" Oliver's voice bellowed over the answering machine followed by the sound of him slamming the phone down again.

"Sounds like you're still making friends. Anybody I know?" asked Jill with a surprised look on her face.

"Naah," Billy replied. "Just another phone solicitor trying to sell me some life insurance. They're getting so much more aggressive these days!"

"OK, Billy, get a couple of glasses and we'll break into this bottle of wine. I had them uncork it at the restaurant.

Knowing you, you probably don't own a cork screw, do you?" she questioned with a smile.

"Good thought, well, yea, you were right about that one. I'm afraid I'm cork screwless! Here's a glass," he responded as he handed her a glass, which she filled half way with wine and put it down on the end table next to the old couch. "Next glass, Babe," she motioned with her hand.

Billy stood there looking at her sheepishly and then got a twisted look on his face. Jill seemingly understanding his body language got a blank look on her face.

"Billy, my God, is this the only glass you have in this house?" she exclaimed.

"Well, yea sort of, you see I don't entertain much and well... it was sort of this thing between me and the dishes. Kind of a contest to see which one of us could outlive the other. I seem to be winning. I'm down to a plate and a glass and a cup," he stammered shyly trying not to look at her.

When he did finally look over at her, she had a warm look on her face that turned to a smile as she unbuttoned her shorts and let them fall to the floor. He stood there looking at her, thinking she was just as beautiful as the last time he had seen her naked in the trailer all those years ago. When she was undressed she walked up to Billy, reached out, took his hand and turned leading him back into the bedroom.

"Why don't we try the wine and pizza a little later," she said turning her head, smiling at him as they walked down the cramped hallway. "You know, Billy, it's a little intimidating. After all these years, this place is cleaner than I ever had it!"

Two hours later they were sitting naked on the bed eating pizza. Jill drank wine out of the glass, Billy out of the coffee cup.

"Can I borrow an old pair of pants when we go fishing? I don't want to get my shorts dirty," she said taking another drink of wine.

"Actually," Billy replied. "there's an old pair of shorts you left behind. I washed them. They're in the drawer over there, if you can still fit into them."

"That was the unkindest cut of all," she smiled as she leaned forward to pick another piece of pizza out of the box. "I'll have you know that I am actually five pounds lighter then when I last wore those pants. This bod may be old, but it's still to size. Oh, and listen when we go fishing, you cut the squid and put it on my line. I spent a small fortune on this manicure and I don't want to ruin it with the smell of squid. OK?"

"But of course, M'lady. I would never, ever think of letting you damage that beautiful manicure. I'd rather be drawn and quartered than let that happen," he said in a mock British accent.

Putting her glass down on the night stand she turned looking coyly at Billy with a sexy grin on her face. "Hey, Billy Lee, what do you say to one more time before we kill some fish?"

"Well, I'm game but I'm not sure about my friend down there. He's been getting more than a little work out lately and I'm not sure if he's up to it, so to speak."

"You just come over here. I'll take care of him. Don't you fret, Babe. I'll take real good care of the both of you," she said softly with a large grin on her face.

The sun was about an hour away from making its dive into darkness. Jill and Billy were up near the Thoroughfare by Ocean Pines, along with a number of other fishermen, chasing flounder or anything else that would bite. Instead of trolling like the serious fishermen, Billy and Jill were sitting in the boat, side by side, their lines in the water, drinking wine, making small talk and generally not giving a damn if a flounder or any other form of fish below great white shark took the hook. They watched the sun as it began slowly sinking into the Bay.

"You know, we should do this again," Billy said.

"We will, Babe, but next time, could you remember to bring the squid? I know you're a good fisherman and all that, but Billy, it's a hell of a lot easier with bait on the hook," she replied.

"One would think! C'mon, it's time to go back," he said as he sat up, starting the old Mercury engine.

The trip back took about ten minutes and they arrived just as it was getting dark. Billy was tying the boat up to the dock as Jill sat on the edge of the dock, dangling her bare feet in the waters of the bay.

"I wish, I didn't have to go to New York tomorrow," she said sadly. "I haven't had a day like this in many years. Wish we could try for another one like it tomorrow."

"We will, when you get back. Look, I don't want you to go either, but it is business, you have to. I understand it and so do you," he said making it sound like a matter of fact.

"Yea, Billy, but it doesn't make it easier. I already miss you and I'm not gone yet. Listen, would you mind if we go back to my place, I need a shower and a great back rub like you used to give. You know. allllllll over my body! That damn mobile home is just too small, I can't believe we actually lived in that little thing?"

"Yea, I know what you mean. Seems small to me too. I'm flattered you still remember those back rubs after all this time, I'd be honored to give you one, my dear."

"Billy there were a lot of things about you I wanted to forget, but those back rubs weren't one of them. You animal you!" she said coyly with a smile on her face.

"OK, but listen, I'll follow you over. That way you don't have to worry about getting me back here tomorrow."

"No, Ah..., ride with me babe. You have to have a permit to park there, you might get towed. I wouldn't want that to happen."

During the drive to her Condo, Billy was amazed at how much he was beginning to like riding in an Eldorado. The only thing he didn't like was that it had a top on it. Three blocks away from the building, he suddenly saw blue and red lights from a police car flashing just behind them and felt fear slip quickly into his body.

"Were you speeding, Jill?" asked said calmly as he looked over at her not wanting to show how alarmed he was.

"Yea, damn it, I was more than ten miles over the limit. Great just what I need a ticket," she said testily.

Billy turned and could see the police officer walking up beside the car. The officer leaned over and shined his flash light into their faces and then back on himself. Billy froze in fear as he saw it was John Eastwick.

"Well now, isn't this an amazing predicament. Just think about it, the husband pulls over the wife and ex-husband as they were speeding along the highway. You know, that's one of those little story things you see in the newspapers. Hey, Billy boy, you ought to think about writing that one down and putting it in that rag of a paper you work for," Eastwick said in a calm and suprisingly pleasant voice. "Well, Jill, it has been a while. Nice car, when did you get it?"

"Couple of months ago. What do you want John?" she replied coldly.

"I honestly did not know it was you. Son of a bitch. Just goes to show you how funny life can be. Of course, I'm not going to write you a ticket, you being my wife and all. Just keep it slow, and Jill, I can't fix any more tickets for you, so slow down, keep it in the speed limit. OK?" his voice still sounded pleasant and it was un-nerving Billy.

"Yea, thanks a bunch," she replied.

"Take care, y'all have a pleasant evening," Eastwick said as he casually walked back and got into his car. Turning off the flashing lights he slowly pulled back onto the highway and drove away into the darkness.

"Well, that sure as hell was fun," Jill said as she put the car in gear and pulled back onto the highway. "You know, I've got to tell you. I think it was just dumb luck that he pulled me over. I know him Billy, a lot better than you do. If he was interested in causing trouble for us, he would have started it back there. Please, believe me. Everything is all right."

They were silent the rest of the way back to the condo. When they got up to Jill's apartment and she turned the deadbolt on the front door, Billy finally breathed a sigh of relief.

"Hey," Jill said to gain his attention. "Bath and backrub time. Remember?"

"Yea sure," he replied feeling a little more secure that she was not upset by having seen Eastwick.

After the bath and a long, sensuous back rub, they made love again. Later they were both laying naked on the bed staring out at the moon as it was rising just above the ocean. The lights from a freighter were twinkling in the night as it slowly made its way up the coast heading towards New York.

"Shit," Billy suddenly blurted out.

"What's wrong," Jill said as she sat up suddenly.

"I wrote that story and brought it home with me. I forgot to show it to you."

"Hey babe, it's OK. I'll see it tomorrow when I take you home. You ever going to try to write another book?"

"Nah, I tried to a couple of times after that first one, but I just don't seem to have it in me yet, but I will one of these days. The time just has to be right. When it is, it will flow, no matter what, when or where. At least that's what all the guys I've talked to who've written books have said."

"It'll come babe! You working on anything else? Any big scandals in Ocean City or projects you can talk about?"

"I wish, of course Eli would never let me write about them if I had one, unless it involved the opening of a restaurant or candy store," Billy said as he laid his head down on the pillow. Why was Jill asking about what he could be working on? The thought bothered him.

Chapter 5
Friday, July 17

Billy could just barely smell the aroma of fresh brewed coffee as he began to open his eyes. The first thing he saw was Jill sitting naked, cross legged on the bed drinking a cup of coffee.

"Good morning, Mr. Sleepy," she said reaching over to the night stand. Picking up a cup of coffee, she handing it to him.

"God, fresh brewed coffee in the morning. It's better than sex," he said with a smile.

"Hey, I happen to represent that remark," she said smiling as he took a big drink. "All right then, be that way. See if coffee does the same things to you I do, or did." she stuck her tongue out at him.

"What time do you have to leave?" he asked pulling a pillow up as he leaned back against the wall.

"I'm not on any time table, probably leave when I get ready. I just have to see this one guy who's in New York for two days and buy some black coral jewelry from him. Stuff's beautiful and expensive as hell but sells quickly, so I hope to make some big bucks on it. Listen Billy, I know this sounds like I'm pushing things, but I'm not. I want to give you a key to my place. I'll be back tomorrow morning. I'd like you to be able to meet me here after I get back and not have to wait outside for me. Really, it's OK with me."

"Yea, sure, that's fine with me. I understand, it's not any type of commitment. I'd like to be able to just come up if we're meeting here. I'm not too wild about hanging out in lobbies, it sounds great. Well then, so let's get going. I've got some work to do today so I can take off part of tomorrow and you have to go to New York," he said as he started to get up.

"Whoa, Billy Lee, it's not that easy. We have a few things to do before we leave. First you have to completely satisfy me, then bathe me and give me a shampoo annnnnnd there's a couple of things I'd like to do to you..."

Billy walked into the newspaper offices just after one o'clock. He was already missing Jill as he tried to picture her in his mind, driving to New York. Her blond hair flowing in the breeze coming through the open car window. The one thing he was happy about, was that he had been able to knock out a lot of work yesterday. Taking the morning off had not put him behind in Eli's scheduling and the people he had interviewed yesterday afternoon would allow him to take off early on Friday to be with Jill.

Sitting at his desk, he looked out the window at the weathered wood siding on the building a few feet away, as he was daydreaming about the things Jill and he had done, just a few short hours ago. As he slowly came back to reality, he picked up the FedEx pack that Oliver had sent him. He was going to read what was inside but then realized he didn't really care anymore, even if there was a story, Eli wouldn't let him print it, and he was sure Oliver was no longer on his "old friends" list. He was about to throw it in the trash, but at the last minute changed his mind and slid it back between the wall and his desk where it had come from. Billy spent the rest of the afternoon working on stories. It was torture but he knew he had to write as many as he could now, in order to have time with Jill tomorrow and next week.

By six o'clock, he was the last person left in the building. He decided to go out and get something to eat before meeting Jonathan at the Paddock Night Club. Walking out of the building and up the street to his Jeep, he decided to grab a sandwich and walk along the boardwalk, something he had not done in years. Walking down Talbot Street and up the walkway to the boardwalk is like being in a scene from a movie. You walk down between old wooden, decaying buildings up a wooden walkway then wham, you're on the boardwalk. Straight ahead is a beautiful sandy beach. It's late afternoon, several umbrellas still up with a few people sitting and talking under them. At this time of day it always had the look of an impressionist's painting by Cezanne or Renoir. To your left the boardwalk runs on for miles, you can stand there watching it diminishing in perspective. Thousands of people were walking the boardwalk now that it was in season, tens of thousands will be on it in just a few hours.

Billy used to hate to stand here looking at the people. There was nothing lonelier than to be in a huge crowd of people, knowing you had little or no chance of ever seeing anyone you knew. He was smiling now as he looked around at the people milling about. It always amazed him, all these people come here on vacation, get sunburned, then put on the ugliest clothes that they had purchased just for their vacation. Clothes that they would never wear at home. Outlandish prints and colors that didn't even come close to matching. They would all descend on the boardwalk spending every night of their vacation walking from one end to the other. Sometimes it too would take on the look of an impressionistic painting, but most of the time it looked like something out of a horror film.

The area seemed to change by the way the wind blew. If the wind came off the ocean you would get the aroma of salt and suntan oil from the beach, if it blew up the beach along the boardwalk, you could smell the french fries and sweat from the people as they walked the boardwalk. When the winds turned to blow up from the bay, you got the smells from the restaurants and dead, decaying fish from the bay.

He felt out of place as he stood by one of the food stands. Wearing a pair of jeans and a white shirt, getting ripped off to the tune of five dollars for a coke and hamburger, he didn't look like the typical tourist. Walking back through the crowd and across the walkway he took a seat on one of the benches. He enjoyed the whole scene that was playing out in front of him as he ate his dinner. It was pure theater. As good as any play in New York.

A large blond woman in her thirties, who had a pretty face but was way too heavy for the hot pants and belly shirt she was wearing, pushed her young son's stroller down the boardwalk She was hoping and looking to see if she could still catch the eyes of men as they walked by. On his left, a fat balding man, in his thirties, smoking a long, fat cigar and wearing black Bermuda shorts with sandals and black socks was wiping ice cream from his son's shirt while yelling at him for not being more careful. A few feet away from him were two young men in their late teens or early twenties. They had closely cropped hair and were wearing baggy shorts that hung so low on their hips that the ends of the pants legs almost touched the ground, defeating the whole purpose of wearing shorts. They were nervously waiting for a guy to show up and sell them some drugs. A few feet away from them was a group of six girls in their mid teens, fashionably dressed, their hair looking like it was styled. They had probably spent the whole day indoors preparing to walk the boardwalk tonight, hoping to see and be seen by Mr. Right or better yet another group of their friends. Walking in front of him was a group of tanned, wrinkled little old ladies in their sixties, complaining about how unsafe it was to walk the boardwalk at night.

Losing track of time, Billy realized he had been sitting there for over an hour watching the dramatic sideshow unfold in front of him. It was just after seven-thirty and the sun was beginning to set. The gaudy neon lights were already lit and the boardwalk was coming alive as thousands more people were emptying onto the boardwalk from the hotels and restaurants. Looking at his watch, Billy realized he had to meet Jonathan at the Paddock in five minutes. Hurrying to his Jeep, he drove up to 18th Street and Coastal Highway. The Paddock Night Club had been a popular night spot and drinking hole in Ocean City for years. Billy didn't know exactly when it was first opened, but knew it must have been at least 40 years old. He had his first legal drink there and had been in and seen some of the best fist fights of his life on the dance floor. The place was always crowded with young people but still seemed to attract a group of rich old men looking for pretty young women, who would be more than eager to help them spend their money. Pulling into the parking lot Billy could see it was not crowded yet. A large group of burly bouncers was stood outside, smoking cigarettes and talking among themselves. Within the next few hours the place would be loaded to capacity with a line of people that would run the length of the building, waiting to get inside.

The sound of the band hit Billy like walking into a wall as he opened the door. The room was crowded but by no means packed yet. Looking back along the wall he saw Jonathan sitting at a table waving at him to come back. Carefully he began weaving his way through the crowd.

"Hey Joe-nathan, what's happening man?" Billy yelled above the music as he sat down. Looking around he saw a waitress a few tables away and signaled to her to bring a couple of beers.

"Not much Billy Lee, not much. The band's rockin' but there's not much happenin' yet. Why thank you, Bill Lee," Jonathan said as the waitress arrived with two beers, Billy sliding one over to Jonathan.

"My pleasure, Joe-nathan, my pleasure. What you been up too?" Billy asked loud enough for Jonathan to hear over the noise from the band.

"Been real busy, Billy Lee. Had to fix that restaurant door you saw me workin' on yesterday. Had a fight in there between two motor cycle gangs. Couple guys hit that door and tore it off its hinges, couldn't screw it back up, stripped the holes for the screws, they musta really banged into that door. Spent all day today cleanin' that Mr. St. John's boat. Filled it with gas, emptied the head, they's takein' off tomorrow. Don't know where they's goin'. I asked him if he wanted me to pick him up some bait from my brother and fill his ice chests but he said he don't need none, not to worry about it."

"Oh yea," Billy said not really caring anymore about Dr. St. John. "I missed it last night, how'd the Orioles do?"

"Took both of them from the Yanks. Great games three to one in the first game and believe it or not nine to two in the second. It was just soooo sweet."

"Been up to see the Shorebirds play in Salisbury, this year?"

"No damn it. I keep meaning to go but never get the chance. What say we go up there next week if they're not on the road?"

"Damn, I'd love to, but my time's a little tight these days. I'm seeing someone."

"GOD DAMN! BILLY LEE! You and a woman. Hell, if I didn't know better Id've thought you was one of them faggots. You finally over that bitch after all these years. Congratulations, who is she? I gots to know," Jonathan exclaimed with a large smile on his face.

"It's that Bitch!" Billy yelled across the table.

"Get outta here, Billy, you can't mess with Eastwick's wife?" Jonathan said looking at Billy with a very concerned gaze. "She may have been yours first, but man he catches you with her, he'll kill you man. You know that asshole's nuts... Don't YOU?"

"Yea, he's a crazy fuck, but they split up about six months ago, he's living with someone else now."

"You sure, Billy Lee? You know I hears most of the dirt on all the locals round here and I ain't never heard nothin' 'bout that one," Jonathan said with a puzzled look on his face.

"Trust me, it's OK. Yo, can we get another round of beer here, hey make it a double round please," Billy yelled to the waitress. "Damn, that's what I hate about this place, get's too crowded, takes too long to get service and you have to double up on your orders."

"Billy Lee, I know you been carrying a torch for that bitch, excuse me, lady, all these years. Damn, why not find someone else? You playin' with fire."

"Hey, Joe-nathan. I can take care of myself. Thanks for worrying 'bout me. But I'm a big boy," Billy replied sarcastically with a touch of anger in his voice.

"Billy Lee, for as old as you are, you shoulda learned by now that a man in love can't take care of himself or anything else. Hey, look over there. It's Steve and Mike. YO, STEVE AND MIKE!" Jonathan yelled across the room to their friends. The two men saw them and waved back. Making their way through the crowd, they came over and sat down at the table with them. After ordering a few more beers they all launched into a heated discussion about the best place to fish for flounder in the bay at this time of year.

As the night wore on, the band got louder and the building grew more crowded. Conversation became more difficult due to the noise. At about 11:30 and too many beers later Billy said goodnight to his friends. The three people had stopped arguing about the best place to fish an hour ago and were now arguing about who the starting pitcher should be against the Yankees tomorrow night. They broke off their conversation as Billy rose to leave, saying their good-bye's, then immediately went back to their animated arguments about the Yankees and Orioles.

Stepping out into the night air, Billy's ears were still ringing from the music. There was a large crowd of people waiting to get in the building that stretched back and around the corner, just as he had known there would be. Walking through the parking lot, he found his Jeep and climbed in the front seat. Taking a deep breath of air he could almost taste the salt that was in the air. Instinctively, he knew it had been carried in by the wind blowing in off the ocean. Pulling onto the Coastal Highway, he just missed hitting a car as he pulled over into the fast lane. A few seconds later he noticed the flashing blue and red lights of a police car come up behind him. It beeped its siren once. Billy tried not to panic as he pulled the Jeep over to the side of the road. Watching intently in the rear view mirror, he breathed a sigh of relief when he saw the police car door open and that it was not John Eastwick who got out. Instead, he recognized the police officer as Dave Johnson, an old friend of his, as he came walking up to Billy's Jeep.

"You almost hit that guy back there, Billy," Dave Johnson said in a stern voice.

"Yea, I know. Look, Dave, I'm sorry. I wasn't watching where I was going and..."

"Billy, you smell like a brewery and I don't have to give you a roadside breathalyzer test to tell you been drinkin'," Dave interrupted.

"Hey Dave, listen. I'm sorry. Look. Promise I'll go right home, you can follow me. You know where it is, it's just a few more blocks up the street. I can.."

"Can't do it this time, Billy. Got you twice in the past month. Can't let you keep doin' that. Warned you last time. This time I'm gonna have to take you in," Dave said shaking his head.

"Hey, Dave, I've never been arrested before, come on be a bud," Billy pleaded.

"Bud's the problem Billy, as always you had too many of 'em. C'mon now, climb on down out of their. Got to take you in. Sorry, but I warned you," Dave said sternly.

Billy felt embarrassed as he was handcuffed and placed in the back seat of the cruiser while car loads of vacationers passed by gawking at his arrest, wondering amongst themselves what vile deed he might have committed. On the way to the station he was trying to think how he was going to get out of jail. There was no one he could call, except Jill and she was out of town. He could possibly call Eli and get an advance on his meager salary, but he would rather rot in jail than have to be grateful to Eli for bailing him out.

"Great, really great!" he said to himself as the car pulled into the station.

Dave opened the back door and helped Billy out of the car. As they walked into the building, Dave held onto his arm to guide him and make sure he didn't fall. Once inside, Billy could see it was an average night. Several young people were scattered around the room being processed for various crimes and misdemeanors. Dave took Billy by the arm and led him into one of the back rooms.

"Have a seat there, Billy, I'll be back in a minute. I just have to get the paperwork on this. When I get back I'll take those cuffs off of ya," Dave said disappearing out the door.

Billy sat there completely disgusted with himself. After all these years of drinking and driving, now just when things are looking up for him he gets busted. A few minutes later Dave came back into the room He unlocked Billy's handcuffs. Taking a seat on the other side of the table, Dave began filling out the paper work.

"OK, Billy, here's what's going to happen. I'm going to charge you with have'n just over the legal limit of alcohol. You've had a lot more, and if I take blood or give you a breathalyzer test, I'm sure you'd be high, I think you know that too. You understand," he said continuing to fill out the paperwork, not looking up at Billy.

"Thanks, Dave. I appreciate that," Billy said sincerely.

"You are welcome. Like I said before, I am just doin' my job. Nothin' personal. OK. After I finish the paperwork. I am going to take you for prints and pictures. Got to do it. Anyone charged with anything gets prints and pics. Then I'm goin' to release you on O.R., you know what that means?"

"Yes, Own Recognizance."

"That's absolutely correct. You will be notified when the trial date is set. You bein' a local and not one of them asshole vacationers, guarantee you'll get off lightly," Dave said as he finished up the paperwork, placing it in an envelope as he stood up.

"Billy, I got to take care of something. I'll be back in about an hour. I have to lock you in this room here. People know you are here, so don't go panic and think you have been forgotten. You understand? Just sit here and be comfortable and don't cause no trouble. You cause any trouble and you'll spend the night and possibly tomorrow night in lock up, you understand me?"

"Don't worry Dave, I promise. I'll sit here and be good. I don't want anymore trouble."

"Great, that's what I wanted to hear. You have to take a leak, there's a toilet through that door over there. I'll be back as soon as I can," Dave said as he closed and locked the door from the outside.

Billy stayed seated at the table, he knew he was getting a fair break from Dave and was not about to cause any trouble to mess things up any more than they already were.

Sometime later he was beginning to get a little worried that he had been forgotten. It was an hour and a half since Dave had left, and he had told him he would only be gone an hour at most. Finally, Billy heard a key in the door lock and was relieved to see Dave come walking through the door.

"C'mon Billy, let's get them prints and pics and get you out of here. Sorry that took a little longer than I thought, but it couldn't be avoided."

Billy followed Dave out the door and down the hallway into a small room. Another man had just gotten his finger prints and picture taken and was being led out in handcuffs by another officer.

"Hey Fred, how's it goin' tonight?" Dave asked to the officer escorting the prisoner.

"Not bad, Dave, How 'bout you?" asked the officer.

"Tell you Fred, would a felt a lot better if the O's hadn't lost to them Yankees tonight. That's for sure."

"Yea, me too, Dave. Sure wasn't pretty, was it. See ya later," the officer was saying as he closed the door behind him.

"Phil," said Dave to the other officer in the room who was standing by the camera. "I'll take care of this one. Why don't ya take a break."

"Thanks, Dave, don't mind if I do, be back in twenty," Phil said quickly. He left before Dave could change his mind or find something else for him to do.

"Billy, I'm pretty damn sure you don't have AIDS. But, since it's my life and an order from above, I have to wear these gloves whenever I touch you," he said slipping on a pair of plastic gloves.

"Hey listen, it's all right. I'd do the same," Billy said.

"Damn it! Phil didn't readjust the camera. I'll be right back, have to find somethin' to adjust it. Shouldn't have sent Phil out like that before I had him do it."

Dave was gone for less then a minute. When he came back in he was carrying a long rod that was bent at one end and looked very much like a lug wrench.

"Damn, Billy, you think this isn't your night. Well, it's not mine either. Hold this for a second," Dave said as he handed Billy the piece of metal. "Watch out. Oops, sorry, you got it. I accidentally knocked some paint over on it when I was in the store room. Sorry you got it on your hands. Here hand it to me. I'm ready to loosen this thing now."

Dave moved behind the camera and out of sight for just a second. Billy heard him make a small grunt and then stand up.

"That should have her," Dave said walking back out of the room. Coming back a second later, he picked up a paper towel and handed it to Billy.

"Sorry 'bout that paint, here wipe it off with this towel, Then come over here and have a seat while I put your name on the picture board," Dave said as he sat Billy.

Reaching into a box filled with white plastic letters, he began placing them one at a time into the black placard in front of Billy. Eventually the letters spelled out Billy's name, the date and his arrest number. Moving back behind the camera, Dave took a left, center and right picture of him. Billy wanted to make a small joke about getting copies for his Christmas cards but decided against it, thinking he had better play the whole thing straight.

"Billy, I'm afraid I owe you an apology. Looks like I got some of that damn paint on your shirt. If it doesn't come out, you let me know and I'll replace it for you. I'm really sorry 'bout that. Like I said, this just ain't our night is it," Dave said shaking his head.

"Dave it's just a cheap white shirt. If it doesn't come out, I'll make it a cheap white fishing shirt. Don't worry about it."

"OK, Billy, but if you change you mind later, you just let me know. Now, let's get them prints and we'll get you out of here," said Dave.

Taking Billy by the arm he Dave walked him the few feet to the print section. Dave put a drop of ink from a tube on a glass plate, then smoothed it out with a roller until it looked like it was a flat black stain on the plate. Taking each one of Billy's fingers, Dave rolled them across the ink. He then took each finger and carefully rolled it across the card. After he was finished, Dave took what looked like a red inked rag out of a plastic baggy. Placing the red inked rag on a small section of Billy's left hand he then placed his hand on the paper making a small red palm print.

"This's somethin' new the FBI's have'n us try out. Got to do with DNA or some such stuff like that. Probably a waste of time but since the FBI wants to pay the department to test it, we test it. OK, Billy, that's it. Here's a rag to take the ink off. Your car had to be towed. We can't leave it on the side of the road, could cause an accident. You can pick it up tomorrow at the impound lot near the 90th Street bridge. I'm goin' to have an officer drive you home, if that's all right with you?"

"Yea, sure, Dave. Listen, I'm sorry I gave you a little trouble about arresting me earlier," Billy said apologetically.

"Billy," he smiled "believe me, that wasn't trouble. You should see some of the stuff I have to go through with drunks."

"Well, I wanted you to know I appreciated it anyway."

"I thank you, Billy," Dave said as he picked up the phone. "Got a cruiser out front to take Mr. Lee home? Good. We'll be right up. All right, Billy, let's go. I'll walk you out."

Billy felt like he was being released from prison as he walked out of the station. The warm breeze blowing in his face felt familiar and reassuring. Dave walked down the steps ahead of him and opened the rear door of the cruiser. Billy climbed in and waved thanks to Dave, then jumped back in a panic when he saw that it was John Eastwick who was driving the car. Dave walked around the car and stuck his head in the open side window.

"Everything went clean. There will be no problems on this end. I'll take care of everything here." Dave said to Eastwick before he turned and walked back up the steps.

"Billy Lee, what a surprise," Eastwick said in a cold voice. "It's so nice to see you again,"

Billy said nothing, he was locked in the back of a police car with no way out. At least Dave had seen him get into the car, so if anything happened, he could verify that he was with Eastwick.

"Billy boy, before we take you home I have to stop off at Tenth Street. Seems something happened a little earlier tonight and they're in the middle of an investigation, only take a minute or two. You got the time, don't ya?" Eastwick asked with a laugh.

Eastwick said nothing as they drove down to the lower end of Ocean City. Billy sat quietly in the back, not wanting to give Eastwick any excuse for starting something. He wanted no confrontations of any kind with this man and during the drive. He was praying that Eastwick had been telling him the truth about where they were going and that he really didn't care about Jill anymore. When they got down to 10th Street, Eastwick made a left turn on 10th, following it down to North Atlantic Avenue. He could see the flashing police car lights and a large crowd of people in the distance as they came up to North Atlantic. Eastwick honked the horn twice, an officer cleared away the people, then lifted the yellow police tape so they could drive through.

A few hundred feet before you get to the boardwalk, there is an alley that runs behind the row of hotels that face the ocean. There were several police cars parked at the entrance to the alley and two policemen stringing more yellow tape to keep people back from the scene. Eastwick pulled into the alley. Billy could see a group of police officers standing around in a circle just ahead of them. The area was lit by headlights from cruisers on either side of the officers and the flashlights they were shining at the ground. Eastwick pulled up beside the officers, got out of the car and walked over to the group of men who stepped aside to let him in. A few seconds later Billy could see more flashing lights as an ambulance pulled into the alley and up behind the police car. Two men got out of the ambulance, walked behind it and opened the rear doors. They rolled a stretcher out of the back, wheeling it up to where the police officers were standing. As the men moved aside to let the stretcher through Billy's mouth dropped open in horror. There on the ground lay Jonathan Banks. His eyes were wide open looking up at the night sky. He had a terrible frightened look on his face as if he had known he was about to die. The side of his head looked misshapen as if it had been caved in. The body was resting in a pool of blood that looked almost black in the limited light coming from the police cars. Billy sat staring at the body of his old friend, barely believing that this could have happened. Eastwick walked back around the car, got in and drove on up the alley way. Billy turned, watching the horrid scene disappear behind him into the night as Eastwick slowly drove through the crowd of people in the alley. Turning left onto 11th Street, he drove up another block to Baltimore and then right on Baltimore heading back in the direction of Billy's trailer.

"You know, Billy," Eastwick said calmly as they drove along. "Some people think I'm an idiot, not too bright. Hell, I'll even bet you're one of those guys. But what I did tonight was brilliant, and the unfortunate part is, I'll never get any credit for it. But I guess life's like that, you know! Let's face it you really lucked out tonight. That should have been you laying by the side of the road instead of Banks. Hell, I wanted to do it, but Dr. St. John talked me out of it."

Billy's mind suddenly snapped to attention at the words, St. John. This had nothing to do with he and Jill seeing each other.

"Yep, I wanted to take you out all by myself, I was really looking forward to it, but Dr. St. John was afraid, you being a reporter and all. I tried to tell him that rag you work for is not even really a newspaper, but Hell, he wouldn't listen to me. He was afraid you might have made some notes or had tripped onto some information about him that you had written into a story that could cause him some problems in the future. So he left it to me to take care of you. I must say, he was delighted with my plan when I told him what I was gonna do. Yep, gettin' a big bonus for this one. You remember when Dave left you alone in that office. He came down and picked up the lug wrench I used to kill Banks with and a sample of his blood. He handed you the wrench in the camera room, remember.

Welllllll, it's the tire iron out of your Jeep. That's the murder weapon. Guess what! It's got your finger prints *ON* the blood, that's a tough one to beat. Your mug shot, that little bit of paint on you shirt is Banks' blood. Shows up real good in the picture. Course you can't tell it's blood, but it'd be part of the chain of evidence the District Attorney would use to convict you. When you were finger printed, little bit of that niggers blood was put on your palm and then printed on the finger print card. DNA can prove it's Banks' blood. Hell, they can even tell how long it's been there. Billy your ass is mine, ain't this just great? Bank's was just an old nigger, nobody will miss him. I got to tell you it was fun takin' him out, not as much fun as you would a been, but it was enjoyable. Couple days from now, when the case isn't solved, no one's going to care one way or the other about him. Hell, they're all asshole vacationers anyway and they'll be gone home in a few days, not be able to find out or even care if the case was ever solved. It'll just be another part of their great adventure vacation to remember. All the locals are going to think it's just another dead nigger, probably killed by one of their own in a fight over drugs or a woman. Hell, they won't even care if the case isn't solved. So here it is Billy, and this is from Dr. St. John not me. As of this minute, you no longer work for that rag of a newspaper, you do nothing, you write about nothing, you investigate nothing, you just exist. That's all. Find a job bagging groceries or flipping hamburgers at McDonalds. He don't care what you do as long as it don't concern him in any way and you don't go anywhere near his plant. If for any reason, we find out you are looking into anything about Dr. St. John or his associates, or even try and talk to them on the street or any of their friends or people who work out there, the murder weapon of Jonathan Bank's is going to be found next to your mobile home. When they check back they'll pull your mug shots and prints from tonight. They'll find the blood on the print card and see it on the mug shots. They'll run a DNA test and match it as having come from Jonathan Banks. There's no way you can beat this one. It'll look like you killed him after a drunken argument. You were seen at the Paddock Nite Club arguing with him earlier in the evening, then got picked up for drunk driving. Billy, there's no way you can beat it. I've got you tied up so tight, you can kiss your ass good-bye. At your age, ten, twenty years is a life sentence, that's the least you can get, if you get off light. Well, here we are. You are home," Eastwick said as the car pulled up in front of Billy's trailer.

Eastwick got out of the car, opening the door for Billy. He slowly got out, without saying a word. He started to walk away as Eastwick reached out and grabbed his arm, squeezing it hard.

"Funny thing, Billy. As mean and nasty as you think Dr. St. John is, he said you can keep Jill. Me, I don't like it. I mean, hell, I don't want her anymore, but I don't want anyone else to have her either. But, Dr. St. John said to leave you a little something in life to live for, so that you don't try and do anything stupid. Unfortunately, that means you get a free ride on my wife, so to speak. Have a nice life, Billy. You see me again and you know you're in big trouble, BOY," Eastwick said with a vicious smile.

Billy opened the door to the trailer and walked in as Eastwick was driving away. The air-conditioning was not working again and the old trailer felt like an oven. He sat down on the couch looking out into space, then glanced down at his hands and could see that they were shaking uncontrollably. He felt something deep in his stomach and knew he was about to throw up. Running for the toilet he made it just in time. Retching several times, he rolled over onto the floor crying loudly like a small child who had been hurt.

Chapter 6
Saturday, July 18

The sun was about two hours away from its scheduled rise over the ocean as Billy sat alone in the darkness of his mobile home drinking a glass of ice water. An ocean breeze was blowing in one of the small windows on the side of his trailer then out through the screened door. It was carrying with it some of the heat being generated by the still very warm aluminum and steel parts of his mobile home that had been baked in yesterday's hot sun. When he returned home last night the temperature was in the low 100's but had dropped into the mid 80's by 4 o'clock in the morning.

Wiping a few beads of sweat from his forehead, Billy took the final drink of ice water from the glass. Standing up he went back to the refrigerator. He reached in and grabbed a handful of ice cubes from the freezer. Refilling the glass with water from the tap, he sat back down at the table.

Billy was not sure how he felt about being dead. In the quiet of the early morning as he sat contemplating the events of last night and past week, he felt he should have been a little more outraged. Screaming out into the darkness of the night in terror at his impending doom or cowering in a corner crying in fear. But he had always considered himself a realist about life. Over the past years, living a life totally alone and with no family, he had often laid awake in the night contemplating his death and sometimes, out of abject loneliness, even considered taking his own life.

He was fucked, there was no better way to explain it. No better choice of words from his vocabulary could better define his predicament. There was absolutely no way out. If he left town and ran away in fear, they would set him up and have him charged with homicide in the death of Jonathan Banks. Having little or no money he could not travel far or even have much of a chance at covering his tracks. Finding him and bringing him back to face justice would be easy. Eastwick had been right, at his age any sentence over fifteen years would probably be a death sentence, and that was the best he could expect if he got a light sentence. However, he could not be sure that they might not have some other surprises in store for him that could land him in one of the crueler prisons, like the main prison in Baltimore City, aptly know has the "the house of pain." A place that was worse than death itself. He could do what Eastwick had ordered, stay in Ocean City and do nothing, making an existence working in a McDonalds or bagging groceries in a super market. After a few months, when they believed he was no longer a threat to them, he would receive a visit one night and the next day he would be found in his trailer an apparent suicide. He was definitely fucked and out of some perverse sense of humor he even saw the beauty of it. There was no authority he could report it to and no one would believe or even listen to him if he tried, including Jill. She had not been spared from his thoughts in the past few hours. Looking back over everything, it seemed a hell of a lot more than just a coincidence that she appeared at just this time, after all of these years, sweeping him off his feet and taking his mind from everything but her. He was feeling a mixed bag of emotions about her that ranged from embarrassment over the way he had acted in this whole situation to happiness. It hurt to admit it but, yes, he was glad that for one last time in his life he had felt the warmth and tenderness of love, something he had believed he would never find again in his lifetime. In some macabre way, he even felt that what he was about to face might have even been worth this whole thing.

Sweating in the dark at 4 o'clock in the morning, there was one thing he did know for sure, he was going to fight back. It was his life and as miserable as it might be, he was not about to sit back and give it up without a fight. Before he could begin to fight, he had to know just what and whom he was fighting and that immediately led back to St. John. He had to somehow find out what was going on, without them suspecting he was investigating them.

At this hour of the morning there would be no one on the streets and this was in his favor. There was a good chance that they would be watching him closely, and if they followed him on the empty streets he would be able to spot them. He knew he had to get to the office to get the FedEx pack that Oliver had sent him and find out what the story was on Dr. St. John and friends. Writing a letter of resignation, he put it in his pocket. If they caught him going into the offices at this hour of the morning, he could explain it away as going in to resign when no one was around to question him. Walking to the door, he switched on the old air conditioner and was happy to hear the compressor kick in, blowing out some cool air.

"Things might be looking up, not a bad omen!" he said to himself as he closed and locked the door behind him.

Walking to his Jeep his eyes scanned the darkness looking to see if there might be anyone watching him. Seeing nothing he climbed in his Jeep and headed for downtown Ocean City. The wind blowing off the ocean and over the town was cool and damp, leaving small patches of fog. He could taste the salt in the air as it blew around his head, leaving a slimy residue on his face as it mixed with the sweat and oils on his skin. The sodium vapor street lights lit up the small town making the vacant streets look more like an inner city project than one of the premier tourist traps on the east coast. During the trip to the office, he was constantly looking in his rear view mirror but could see nothing on the street behind him. When he reached the end of Ocean City by the inlet, he circled the several blocks around his office to make sure no one was around the corner waiting for him.

Sure that he was alone he pulled up in front of the newspaper offices. Jumping out of his Jeep, he headed for the front door. Attempting to put his key in the lock he was surprised to feel the door open. Noticing marks and scrapes on the side of the door, he could see that it had been pried open. Standing there, out in the open, he contemplated for a few seconds what to do. There were no lights and he could hear no sounds of movement inside. Sure of his story about the resignation, he slipped in the door and up the steps. The offices were dark but the street lights outside the windows were giving off more than enough light to see that there was no one there. Silently he moved through the dimly lit office and back to his desk without turning on the lights. Taking the letter out of his pocket he was about to place it on his desk when he noticed that all of his desk drawers were open, their contents gone.

"Shit!" he said quietly to himself. "These guys aren't missing a thing. They didn't want to take the chance of not finding a piece of information so they stole everything in the desk. Smart, very smart!"

Reaching down between the desk and the wall, he closed his eyes as his hand searched in the darkness for the FedEx pack. He breathed a sigh of relief as his fingers touched the package. Pulling it out, he stuck it under his shirt and ran from the offices. As he was about to open the front door, he gently pushed at it to see if anyone might be outside waiting for him. Seeing no one, he jumped in his Jeep and drove back to the trailer, all the while checking for headlights in his rear view mirror.

Locking the door behind him he felt a momentary feeling of elation in the darkness of the trailer. He was back safe in his home. Walking into the bedroom he switched on the light. Closing the curtains, he wanted to make sure no one could see what he was doing. Methodically he pulled everything out of the envelope, grouping the articles by date in separate piles on the bed. When everything was arranged, he picked up the first article and began reading.

Two hours later, he felt he was no closer to figuring out the mystery of Dr. Will St. John from the newspaper articles. Dr. St. John, Dr. Ling and Dr. Jackanock had a very successful, if not enterprising OB/GYN medical practice in Washington, D.C. That was their problem, they were too successful. Over a five year period they had taken in over 35 million dollars in Federal and District of Columbia Medicaid money. Bells and whistles started going off in the Federal and Washington D.C. city offices when they figured out there was no way they could have had a practice that made that much money. The District of Columbia investigated and naturally botched the investigation. There were some allegations of bribery concerning city officials but no one was able to prove anything. The Federal government had to step in and take over the investigation from the city. After three months of investigating they released their findings, concluding that all the moneys were justly earned by a group of hard working, professional medical practitioners. A nurse who lived in Maryland and had been fired by the doctors a few years before wrote a letter to her Congressman complaining that the doctors were crooks and had not been providing even routine medical care for the poor people they treated. The Congressman, who was coming up for re-election, contacted the General Accounting Office and strong armed them into launching an investigation on their own into the affairs of the doctors. Again, there were allegations of bribery but no charges were ever placed against anyone. However, it was found that there was no way the doctors could have made that amount of money from their practice and were defrauding the Federal government out of tens of millions of dollars in services never performed. The doctors were tried and found guilty. Drs. Ling and Jackanock each received fifteen year prison terms of which they eventually served five years. Dr. St. John apparently managed to charm the jury and for some reason was found not guilty, something that horrified the prosecutors. They were out to get him and retried him a year later on new charges related to the moneys the government attempted to get back from the doctors that could not be located. Again, he charmed the jury and they found him not guilty. The judge chastised the jury for the verdict in such an open and shut case. The Federal government, having nothing else to go on, gave up the case and Dr. St. John vanished from sight. The Federal officials who had originally investigated Dr. St. John and found he had run a "hard working and professional" practice, naturally received promotions for their good work. All three of the doctors were subsequently barred from ever practicing medicine again. The last article was a strange one, it concerned a Dr. St. John, but didn't mention if it was Will St. John. It was an announcement about a non-profit organization, operating out of New York city called <u>HelpMed</u>. The article, dated last year, stated that a Dr. St. John was appointed Chairman of the Board and CEO. That was all, it didn't mention his first name, anything about who he was, where he was from or what the company was engaged in.

The morning sun was up and blazing over the ocean as Billy was going over the articles for the fourth time, looking and hoping that he had missed something. Sitting on the bed thinking, he suddenly recalled something that Jonathan Banks had said last evening. He had cleaned St. John's boat and filled it with diesel fuel but that he hadn't wanted any bait or ice for today's trip. Getting up from the bed, he went to the window, staring out, trying to figure what Dr. Will St. John might be up to today. Then he saw it, several houses down, on the next street over. He could just barely see between the houses and make out the emergency lights that sit on top of a police car. There was no way he could be sure if they were watching him but could not assume otherwise. The phone rang and he jumped suddenly, tensing up as he listened to the noise of the phone, awaiting the answering machine to answer it.

"Billy, this is Eli. What do you mean you quit! Pick up the phone, damn it. Billy, I know you're there, pick up the phone, damn it. Billy, call me please when you get in. RIGHT AWAY I HAVE TO TALK TO YOU!" the machine then beeped and clicked off.

Reaching under the bed, Billy pulled out a small and very old portable typewriter. Removing it from its case, he sat it on the bed. Searching through the trailer he found a small pack of paper and sat back down. He typed everything that had happened since he had seen St. John's boat, including the Asians, the murder of Jonathan Banks, who did it and why. An hour later he was finished. Proofing it, he made corrections in the margins instead of retyping. He picked up a large manila envelope from the book case next to the bed and emptied the contents of it on the floor. Picking up all the articles he placed them in the envelope along with the letter he had written, closed the envelope and sealed it, licking the flap and then placing tape over it. Walking to the window, he could still see the police car in the same place it had been earlier, as he shoved the envelope under his shirt and down the front of his pants. Picking up his checkbook from the kitchen counter, he left, locking the front door behind him. He walked the several blocks down to the Bank of Ocean City office on Coastal highway. He could feel his body sweating against the envelope, sure that the very baggy short sleeved shirt he was wearing would hide it.

For the first time in his life, Billy was glad to see the long lines that were always in the bank. It was a small branch that had only two tellers, unfortunately for them, but fortunately for him. At this time of the morning shop keepers and store owners were coming in to pick up their cash bags that would have their opening money for the day. As Billy stood in the line he kept watching through his sunglasses at the reflection of the front door on the security glass in front of him. A few minutes later, he was watching as a blue police cruiser slowly pulled by the front door, then slowly backed up out of sight. The front door opened and Billy could see Dave Johnson, the police officer from last night, in the reflection of the glass. Billy stood there, his check book in hand, looking like he was waiting to get a check cashed as another person walked in and got in line behind him. After a few seconds Dave left. The line moved quickly. When he got to the front, he wrote a check for twenty dollars, asking the teller to notarize the sealed envelope he was holding. Giving him the cash she told him he would have to see the assistant manager, the only notary in the bank. A few minutes later he had the envelope notarized and left.

Walking home, he would occasionally stop and look in a store window to see if he was still being followed. He needed to make a call but was afraid to do it from home. Although he doubted that his phone was tapped, his life was depending on it, so he had to act as if it were. Walking up to a phone booth on Coastal Highway he looked in the reflection of the Plexiglas door. He could barely see the police car a block away sitting on the side of the street. Closing the door behind him, he reached into his pocket and took out a handful of change, along with a phone number written on a small piece of paper. Making sure his back was to the car he dropped a quarter in the box and called the number.

"Coast Guard Station, Ocean City. Good morning. May I help you?" announced the young voice on the phone.

"Lt. Early, please," Billy said quickly, already beginning to suffocate in the enclosed box of the phone booth from the heat of the sun.

"Lt. Early," the voice said crisply.

"Mike, it's Billy Lee. I need to speak to you, can you talk?"

"Just one minute, Sir," Billy heard him say as the phone clicked, putting him on hold. It was followed by another click a few seconds later as Lt. Early came back on the line. "Billy, how've you been? I heard about Jonathan this morning. I couldn't believe it. Who could have killed him? The radio made it sound like a drug deal gone wrong. Christ, you and I both know he was as straight as an arrow. No way he'd be doin' drugs. Somethin' stinks!"

"Mike, I know," Billy cut in. "Look I only have a minute and I need some help quick."

"This concern Jonathan?"

"Mike, I'm not going to get you involved in this. I need to know something. Can you help me?"

"Shoot!"

"There was a ship loaded with Asians that was stopped off the coast of New Jersey several days ago. Can you tell me anything about it? Did it come close to here or was it way out to sea?"

"Billy, there's a whole hell of a lot I could tell you about that boat, but it's going to take more than a few minutes. Yea, it came within a few miles of here then went further on back out to sea, just like the one last night."

"Last night!" Billy said as he felt his heart beating faster.

"Yea. I just read the reports a few minutes ago. We've been following several of these boats. One came up the coast last night, veered in like the last one, then back out a couple of miles. Our guys are out there right now and are going to intercept it in about an hour off the coast of New Jersey. They're waiting until then, so they can get some good coverage in the press. It will probably be on the news tonight, should be a big story. We're always watching a bunch of ships like that. This'll be the last one for several weeks. The rest are spread out on the West Coast working their way to Panama. What else do you need to know?"

"That's it, Mike. Listen. Thanks for your help and please do not mention to anyone I called or that you talked with me, understand?" he whispered in the phone.

"Won't tell anyone, Billy. Listen, you need any info or if there's anything I can do, let me know. Jonathan was my friend too!"

"Thanks, Mike. I will," Billy said as he hung up the phone. His back was still to the police car. He was watching it in the reflection of the glass as he put another quarter into the phone and dialed.

"Hello," Jill answered cheerily into the phone.

"Hello, welcome back. How was the trip?" Billy asked trying to sound sincere.

"Not bad," she replied. "I picked up some great merchandise. I just got home a few minutes ago. How soon can you come over? I've missed you?"

"It'll be a little while. I have to get cleaned up first. I'll be over in a couple of hours."

"You sound funny," Jill said sounding concerned. "Everything all right?"

"Yea, I just walked down to the bank and cashed a check. I'm baking in a phone booth right now."

"Several hours is a long time, Billy. Can you get over any sooner than that? I missed you," she whined into the phone, then with a very sexy voice. "I'd like to show you how much I missed you."

"Sounds great, but I can't. I've got some stuff to take care of. I'm taking a little leave of absence from the office and I have to get everything straight."

"Taking a leave of absence? Billy, you can't afford to take time off. Is everything OK?

"Yea, sure, everything's just fine. It's just hot as hell in this phone booth. See you in an hour or two, as soon as I can get there. OK?" Billy said as he recalled the immortal words of Marion Barry, the Mayor of Washington D.C. 'The Bitch set me up!'

"Great, see you then!" she said as she hung up the phone.

Opening the door to the phone booth Billy stepped out of the oven and onto the sidewalk. He was sweating profusely as he bent over trying to catch his breath. Dave Johnson would probably report back that he made a call, and if his hunch was right it would be checked out against the time of his call to Jill. No one would suspect there had been a second call to Mike Early at the Coast Guard Station.

Opening the door to his trailer he was greeted by a blast of cool air as he walked inside.

"Still a good omen," he said to himself as he walked into the bathroom to take a shower.

Walking into the bedroom after his shower, he picked up a screw driver from the night stand and bent down, prying a piece of plasterboard away from the wall. He slid the envelope behind the wallboard. It sank deep into the insulation as he began pushing the wallboard back into place. Standing there thinking for a minute, he knelt back down and pulled the wallboard back open again. Taking out the notarized envelope, he placed it on the floor. Walking over to the bed he picked up the FedEx envelope. Making sure that the Washington Post return address was still on the envelope, he shoved the empty package in behind the wallboard then pushed it closed again. Moving over to the window, he looked out to see that the police cruiser was still there watching him. He shoved the notarized envelope under his shirt and down into his pants. Picking up a second envelope, he placed a handful of junk mail in it. Going into the kitchen for his tool kit, he picked it up and walked out of the trailer. Taking his time, he walked slowly to his boat. Climbing in he took the housing off the old Mercury engine. He placed it carefully on the dock. Undoing the fuel lines he began methodically cleaning them out. It was something that he had been doing for years in order to keep the old engine operating smoothly. Picking up the engine housing after he was finished, he moved it back across the dock knocking his tool kit over and into the boat. As he reached over and began picking up his tools, he pulled both envelopes out from under his shirt and shoved them up, under the aluminum seat. The envelope with the junk mail was facing out to protect the other envelope from the elements. Placing the housing back on the engine, he gave the starter cord a good pull. She sputtered a few times, put out a small belch of white smoke then, as always, began to purr like a brand new engine. Listening to the sound for a few seconds, he smiled, then turned it off. Picking up his tool kit, he slowly walked back to his trailer. Once inside, he walked to the bedroom window, looking out to verify that the police cruiser was still there.

Twenty minutes later he had showered and was sitting naked on the edge of the bed. Trying not to think, he wanted to keep his mind clear and ready. He felt his fingers begin shaking, followed closely by his hands and arms. He was beginning to have trouble breathing and realized that he was in the middle of a panic attack. He rolled off the bed and sat shaking on the floor, tears welling up in his eyes. Closing his eyes he tried to concentrate on the things he had to do. A few minutes later he began to feel more in control of his emotions. Getting up from the floor, he got back up on the bed, his body wet with perspiration.

"Damn, I am so fucked!" he said to himself as he stood up and dressed.

Walking out of his trailer to his Jeep, he looked out the corner of his sunglasses and saw that police cruiser was back in the same position it had been earlier. Driving up Coastal Highway to Jill's he watched in the rear view mirror as the cruiser followed him a block away. A few hundred feet away from the entrance to Jill's condo, he was stopped in traffic waiting for the light to change. Out of the corner of his eye he spotted a police cruiser driving across the parking lot. As it came into view, he could see it was Eastwick that was driving. Pulling into the parking lot, he was wondering what fun they might have been planning for him. Walking to the front entrance of the condo he saw the car that had been following him make a U-turn. It pulled into the small parking lot of a shopping center across the street.

Opening the front doors to the building, he was greeted by a blast of cold air that seemed to roll out the door, drying his perspiring body and helping to clear his head. During the elevator ride to Jill's floor he kept concentrating. He had to make it seem like nothing was happening, just like they wanted him to act. It was very important, if he tried to act differently than they expected him to, they could move in and end this game too soon. He needed time, more time than he knew he had.

Standing outside her door, he was about to knock, then thinking for a second, reached in his pocket for the key she had given him. Hesitating for a moment, much like an actor preparing to go on stage, he took a deep breath, placing a smile on his face as he unlocked the door and walked in the apartment. He expected her to jump in his arms as he walked through the door and was surprised not seeing her in the living room. Walking a few steps, he heard a muffled sound then looked into the bedroom. Jill was laying naked on the bed face down.

Oh great, let's play it to the hilt. God, it's embarrassing, these guys really do think I'm this stupid, he was thinking to himself as he walked toward her bed.

Watching her intently, it hurt to see the beauty of her nakedness, knowing that she had betrayed him. He watched as her body twitched slightly on the bed as he walked over to sit down next to her. As his body touched the bed, Jill jumped up and screamed. Diving off the bed and onto the floor, she was cowering in the corner. Crying hysterically and shaking with fear, she extended her arms as if to fend him off.

"NO MORE! PLEASE NO MORE!" she yelled.

Her screaming scared Billy. He jumped up off the bed and stumbled backwards. Looking at Jill, sitting in the corner, he was shocked. Both her eyes were swollen and black, as was the side of her cheek. Her lips were also swelling, the upper lip split open and bleeding profusely. He could see red finger marks around her neck and bruises all over the top portion of her body. Looking out the corner of his eye, he could see that her pillow was drenched with blood.

"Jill!" he said as he took a step towards her.

"Noooo!" she whined as she put out her hands in front of her to stop him. He could see a piece of rope dangling from each wrist. She had been tied up.

"Jill, it's me Billy," he said moving closer to her, taking her in his arms. She began crying hysterically again as he held her gently, cradling her in his arms.

Those bastards. Damn them, they're going to pay for this, he said to himself as he continued to hold her.

Half an hour later, Billy felt her stop shaking and move slightly. Her arms were still wrapped around him, holding him tight. Suddenly he felt her push him away and she looked at him angrily.

"You son-of-a-bitch, how could you do this to me? He told me this was all your fault. That he was doing this to me because of St. John, that you know or have something on them, it wasn't about me," she was saying angrily as tears streamed out of her eyes. "Billy, I'm scared. What's going on? What are you doing? What do you have on them? TELL ME!" she yelled.

Billy sat back on the floor looking over at Jill. His heart was breaking as he looked at the cuts and bruises all over her body. He bowed his head slightly then looked back up at her.

"I can't," he said softly, shaking his head.

"My God, Billy. Look what John did to me. He was here for over an hour. Billy, God damn it an hour. Tell me what's going on. Why am I mixed up in this? What do you know? What's going on?" she whined and then with a fierce look in her eyes yelled. "WHAT'S HAPPENING?"

"I can't Jill, it could get you in trouble," he said softly again, his eyes now avoiding hers.

"Get me in trouble? Get me in trouble? Billy! I am in trouble. Look at me, damn it," she yelled as she crawled over and took his head in her hands. "Look at me, God damn it. I would call this trouble. Billy! I'm scared, what's going on? You have to tell me! What do you have on them?"

"I can't Jill. I can't. It's the only way I can protect you," he said shaking his head.

"Protect me? Protect me? Yea, looks like I've been protected all right. LOOK AT ME! Look what that sick fuck did to me! Billy I want out of this and I want out now! You want to protect me, tell me what's going on and I'll protect myself."

"Jill, believe me. I want to tell you, but if I do you could get into more trouble than this. Believe me I know these guys and what they are capable of doing. I can't tell you or anyone else anything!"

"Thanks, Billy, thanks a lot. I thought you loved and trusted me. If this is all I mean to you then get out, out of my apartment and out of my life. LEAVE! NOW!" she yelled.

"I'm sorry, Jill. It's because I love you," he said as he walked to the door and out of the condo. On the elevator trip to the lobby he stood staring at the doors, not wanting to think. He glanced to his side at the mirrored wall on his left and saw Jill's blood all over his shirt. Walking through the lobby, he could feel the eyes of strangers looking at the man with the blood all over his shirt, wondering how it had come to be there. Pulling his Jeep back onto the Coastal Highway and heading home, he wanted to jump it over the curb on the other side of the street and slam it into Dave Johnson's car as it sat there waiting to follow him. During the drive back to his trailer, he tried to clear his thoughts. Was he wrong about Jill or could it have been another part of the set up? Entering his trailer, he felt a hot blast hit him in the face as he walked in, the air conditioner was not working again.

"So much for good omens!" he said as he opened the windows to the trailer. Walking to a chair, he pounded hard on the air conditioner as he went by, surprised to hear the compressor click on. Flopping into the chair he brought his hands to his face, interlocked his fingers and started to think about what he could do next.

Contemplating his options, they all ended the same way, either he was dead or in prison for the rest of his life. He realized there was only one thing he could do, he had to go back to the factory. Desperate times required desperate acts. They would expect him to do this eventually, but would they be expecting it so soon? Again, his life was depending on the decisions he was making. The lug wrench with his finger prints on it had to be there, Eastwick would not leave it at his home. It would be too unprotected there, easy for him to steal back. If he was going to go on the attack, it had to be done and it had to be done soon, while they were not expecting it. Walking around the trailer he began picking things up, throwing them in a pile on the center of the floor. A large loud Hawaiian shirt; a long sleeved black T-shirt; a pair of bright red Bermuda shorts; a pair of black exercise pants; an old red baseball cap; black sneakers, all lay in the floor in the center of the living room.

"Let me think, there were two, no four security cameras at the front of the building and one covering the roadway entrance. The concertina was thick around the top of the fence, so that lets out going over the fence," Billy said as he walked to the cabinet. Reaching between several bleach and detergent bottles, he grabbed a heavy pair of wire cutters and threw them on the pile of clothes.

Looking at the clock on the counter, he could see that it was just 3:30, he would wait to leave until 7:30. Sitting in his chair by the TV, he looked at the answering machine light blinking. Reached across the table, he hit the rewind button, then the play button.

"You have two calls. 3:25 p.m." droned the answering machine.

"Billy, it's Eli again. Why haven't you called me? Billy, please. Please call me," the machine beeped signaling the end of the call then beeped again to begin the next call.

"Billy it's Jill. Look I was wrong. I'm sorry I shouldn't have said those things, please call me Billy, please," the soft sound of her voice was followed by the beep signaling the end of the message.

For the next hour he sat there, replaying the answering machine, listening to the sound of her voice over and over again, mesmerized by it.

Chapter 7

At 4 o'clock Billy showered and shaved, refreshing himself for the tasks that lay ahead. He put on his red Bermuda shorts, followed by the long-sleeve black T-shirt, pulling the sleeves up high on his arms so it would not be seen under the Hawaiian shirt. Pulling them as tightly as he could, he wrapped his black exercise pants around his chest so that they would not be seen. He slipped the red baseball cap next to them and taped them all down with duct tape. The heavy wire cutters were positioned vertically just below his armpit and also taped down with duct tape. Putting on the loud plaid Hawaiian shirt, he walked over and looked at himself in the mirror. He looked like he had put on a few pounds but the articles under his shirt were not readily visible. One thing was for sure, wearing that shirt he could be seen a block away. It was just seven o'clock, he turned on the TV for the CBS Evening News. Dan Rather's top story was about a boat load of Asians that was intercepted off the coast of New Jersey. There were helicopter shots of the men on board the boat as it was being escorted into New York harbor. Other shots showed terrified passengers, caked with dirt, being escorted off the boat and into custody. Flipping the TV off, he walked to the front door, stopped and turned, surveying the place that had been his home for the past twenty years. Feeling anxious and afraid that he would never come home again, he felt the first tinges of fear creeping into his body. Emotions welling up inside him as he left the trailer, he began walking down Sunset Drive and across Philadelphia Avenue in the direction of the boardwalk. Waiting for the traffic light at North Baltimore Avenue he casually turned surveying the traffic and could see Dave Johnson out of the corner of his eye waiting to cross North Philadelphia. When the light changed Billy walked across the street, then down 27th Street and up on to the boardwalk.

Weekends during July and August in Ocean City are renown for their crowds. Hundreds of thousands of people will crowd onto the little sand bar creating monstrous traffic jams that start early on Friday night and last until late Sunday afternoon. It is a study in waiting. You wait to cross the bridges to get into the town. Once there, you wait in traffic until you get to your motel, hotel or condo where you wait to check in. You wait for everything: food, gas, parking and service of any kind, all to spend a few hours laying on the sand while a hot sun fries your body crispy brown.

The crowds were what Billy was counting on, and he was more than rewarded when he walked onto the boardwalk. A sea of bodies milled around the walkway. Slowly walking down the boardwalk, he was giving Dave Johnson a chance to catch up to him. At 26th Street he stopped and waited in line to get a Coke. It was a fifteen minute wait and he was sure Dave had been able to catch up to him by now. He turned once, while in line, and casually looked at the crowd, but there were too many faces to pick out just one person. Walking down the boardwalk, he drank his Coke, carried by the speed of the crowd. He was about a mile and a half from the lower end of town and did not want to get there too quickly, his timing had to be perfect. Stopping suddenly he turned and walked back fifty feet to throw his empty cup in a trash container. He hoped that this would make Dave nervous, keeping him further back in the crowd. Forty-five minutes later he reached Thirteenth street, the crowds growing larger, making it more difficult to move around. Unbuttoning his shirt, he reached in, pulling the duct tape off the pants wrapped around his chest, then casually unraveled them as he walked along. He hoped that Dave was far enough behind him to not see what he was doing. Billy was surprised that no one around him seemed to think that it was odd for a man to be walking down the boardwalk unwrapping a pair of pants from his chest through an open shirt.

It was now 8:30 and the crowds were just beginning to reach their peak as night began to fall over the city. The sweating group of people moved like the sea, drifting to and fro, speeding up and then slowing down. When he reached Sixth Street, the boardwalk was illuminated by neon lights from stands, vendors and amusement rides brighter than the day itself. Making a sudden movement sideways, cutting across a group of people, he bent over quickly, putting his baseball cap on his head and taking off his Hawaiian shirt, letting it fall to the ground. Pulling the sleeves of his black T-shirt down over his arms before standing back up, he quickly moved back to his left across the crowd about twenty feet, practically crawling on his hands and knees. A number of people grumbled at him to watch out or get out of the way as he excused himself, not trying to create a commotion.

Standing up slowly, he put on a pair of sun glasses and kept moving casually with the crowd down the walkway. He was hoping Dave Johnson was still looking for him and his Hawaiian shirt on the other side of the boardwalk. Moving more to the left, against the flow of people coming up the boardwalk, he picked up speed as he moved amongst the people. A few minutes later he walked off the boardwalk and down onto Caroline Street. Crossing Baltimore Avenue he turned and waited on the street corner, watching the crowds of people, looking to see if Dave Johnson was still behind him. Five minutes later when he was sure no one was following him, he turned and walked down the street to the Route 50 Bridge. Traffic was backed up across the bridge with cars waiting to get into Ocean City. As usual there were a few die hard people fishing off the bridge, but no one noticed him as he slowly walked along, heading out of town. Half way across the bridge he stopped and looked down the inlet, seeing St. John's boat 'Bow Wow' was tied up to the dock. He thought briefly of his friend Jonathan and wondered to himself if the boat had been out to sea today as Jonathan had said it would. Once off the bridge, it was a one mile walk along Route 50 to Steven Decatur Highway.

At nine o'clock he turned left and began walking down the highway, knowing that he still had about four more miles to go. Stopping for a second, he slid into the black athletic pants he had been carrying then continued on his way. Walking down the edge of the road, he could feel cool air being pushed out of the groves of trees by the changing evening temperatures. The air no longer smelled of french fires and sweating people. It had been replaced with the scent of pines and cut grass that was carried on the breeze that got cooler with every step down the road. A number of cars were still traveling the road but not as many as had been on Route 50. Groups of people were gathered at small convenience stores and gas stations along the way, stocking up on ice, soft drinks, beer, food and bait, oblivious to anyone walking down the road.

At nine-thirty he was standing at the corner of Stephen Decatur Highway and Keel Drive. He could see the lights from the plant several hundred yards away, surrounded by ten acres of corn field. Occasionally a car would come by, and he would step back away from the road into the trees, out of sight. He decided it would be best to just cut across the cornfield that bordered the complex and move to the fence behind the building. Walking about ten feet into the cornfield, he looked around and realized he was lost. The corn was almost ready to be picked and the stalks were at least seven feet high. From within the cornfield he could see nothing but cornstalks. He could be lost for days, walking in circles and never reach the fence. Slowly he backed out and breathed a sigh of relief as he exited the field near the same spot he had entered. He had no other choices, he would have to take a chance and move down closer to the building. When he was about one hundred yards from the entrance to the complex he entered the cornfield once again. This time walking in laterally, following a line of corn down the row. The leaves on the corn stalks were sharp, occasionally cutting his face. Raising his arms, he tried to protect himself.

Hidden in the cornfield, Billy could barely see his hand in

front of his face as he tripped in the darkness down the rows of corn. Counting out three hundred paces, he made a right turn and began walking crosswise to the rows at a ninety degree angle. Counting his paces again, he stopped at one hundred, figuring he was within several feet of the fence. Slowly he began moving across the rows again, following a little light that was shining through the rows. Pushing through the next row he found himself up against the fence looking into the rear of the parking lot. Looking off to his right he could see he was too close to the side of the building to enter the back lot and began walking down the fence and around the corner towards the rear of the building.

He was now at the center of the fence. There were two flood lights on either side of the end of the building barely lighting the loading dock area. His guess had been right, there were no cameras on this end of the building. The only things behind the building were a dumpster, small loading dock and the same truck with the words 'wish me' barely visible on the back, parked next to the dumpster. Reaching under his shirt he pulled at the duct tape holding the wire cutters. He wanted to scream as the tape pulled at the hair on the side of his chest. Bending down he cut an opening in the fence. As he was cutting the last of the wire he stopped. A piece of the wire was not the same thickness as the others. Inspecting it closer, he realized that it was a security wire set to sound an alarm when cut. A precaution to prevent him from doing what he was about to accomplish.

A few minutes later he had cut enough fence so he could squeeze through to the loading area. Taking one last look, making sure no one was watching, he slipped through the fence and ran the one hundred feet to the loading dock. Walking up the steps to the back door, his heart pounded in his chest and perspiration poured in rivulets down his face. For all of his planning and scheduling on how to get here, he had no idea what to do next. He didn't know if he could get in the rear door or even break it open, or how long he would have once inside before he was spotted.

Blinking his eyes twice and taking a deep breath he reached out and gently pulled at the door. He felt the door open slightly and it scared him. He let go and jumped back. Cursing at himself, he reached out and gently pulled at the door again, opening it just enough to let the light shine out so he could see what was inside. It was the back of the building as he had remembered it from his tour with St. John. The area where cans of dog food were placed in boxes and loaded onto trucks. The place looked empty and there were only a few lights on in the building. He could not see or hear anyone, but was sure someone had to be there, they had spent too much money on security to go away for the weekend and leave the back door open.

Taking another deep breath, Billy opened the door and slipped into the building, hiding behind a stack of boxes. Listening intently, the only sound he could hear was his heart beating rapidly. Raising his head, he looked over the boxes. The first thing he could see was the door to the research area. It was open. Crouching down, he walked along the row of boxes and towards the research area, constantly watching the door, hoping no one would come walking out. When he was about ten feet from the door he stumbled, the lights seeming to glare brightly. He felt himself stumble once again, the lights flashing a bright white. Looking to his left, he saw a pair of legs and looked up to see John Eastwick. He had a policeman's baton in his hand and was swinging it at Billy's head.

The baton glanced off Billy's head and Eastwick grabbed him behind his neck. The light from the door kept coming closer as Eastwick drug him into the research area. Billy looked up to see that they were in a hallway that ran about fifteen feet, opening into a large room. Standing at the end of the hallway was Dr. Will St. John, arms folded in front of him and a large smile on his face. Billy watched carefully as St. John walked down the hallway shaking his head.

"Billy Bob, Billy Bob, Billy Bob," he said softly. "I had hoped it would not come to this. Well, at least not this quickly. I must say you seem to be a lot brighter than I suspected."

Walking up to Billy, St. John knelt down and took Billy's head in his hands, examining it.

"John, I don't think it was necessary to hit Mr. Lee that many times. Once should have been sufficient. You could have damaged him," St. John said in an almost jovial voice.

"Damn right I wanted to damage him, the son-of-a-bitch," Eastwick said angrily.

"Now John, we don't have to sound so serious. Billy's had a rather tough week, haven't you Billy?" St. John was saying in a friendly tone as he turned to Billy.

Billy, his head still reeling from the beating by Eastwick, said nothing as St. John stood up and faced Eastwick.

"John, we seem to have a problem here. We paid quite a bit of money on your recommendations to put in this security equipment. Had this been a thief who knew what he was doing and not Billy here, we could have had a very embarrassing incident. Why don't you go see what went wrong, and while you're at it, Billy's Jeep's probably parked somewhere around here. Find it and do something with it, so it's not traced to us. OK, John?" St. John said in a very pleasant voice, with no sign of displeasure or anger.

"Yes sir, Dr. St. John," said Eastwick as he turned and quickly walked away.

"Oh! John!" St. John called after him. "I think it would be wise if you were to go over to Billy's trailer and check the place out. Ahhh, better yet, tear it apart, see if there is anything in there that might pertain to us."

"Yes sir," Eastwick said with a smile. "Consider it done!"

St. John reached down, picked up Billy by the arm and walked him down the hallway. Walking into the room, Billy felt disoriented as if he had just walked into a hospital ward. He began shaking his head to clear his thoughts, not sure of what he was seeing.

"It's OK Billy, here, have a seat on the bed and I'll get you a sedative for your head. Make you feel a lot better," St. John said walking over to a table. He picked up a syringe and came back giving Billy a shot in the arm. "There Billy, that'll take the headache away and make you feel better. I take these myself when I need a little escape. It's great shit! Really! It's a horse tranquilizer, same type of stuff they use on humans, just a little more concentrated. You would not believe how easy it is to get this stuff. If I ordered a quantity of that as a doctor," St. John said holding up the small brown and green bottle, "I'd have to fill out a bunch of forms, give them my BND number and be generally checked out on how the drugs were administered and to whom and in what quantities. A real pain in the ass. Now, if I go to the farm supply store in Salisbury, I walk to the refrigerator case, pick up a box full of this stuff and can give them cash and walk out without anyone questioning or caring how I use it. God, I love this country. Only in America! Eh, Billy?"

Almost immediately he began to feel better. His headache was gone in a few seconds. The only problem was that he felt weak and began to lie back on the bed.

"Be back in a minute Billy, I have to check on something. Please don't try to walk away, or even walk for that matter. That shot's gonna put you on your behind for quite a while. It will all be fine in just a bit," St. John said pleasantly as he turned and walked away.

"Son-of-a-bitch, why do you have to sound so damn pleasant all the time?" Billy muttered as he surveyed the room again.

He had not been hallucinating, the room did look like a hospital ward. There were two rows of hospital beds, each row with seven beds in it. Nine of the beds had patients in them and as he looked around he could see that they were all Asian.

St. John was right, it was 'good shit,' he was feeling no pain. Laying back in the bed he found himself looking up at the ceiling, smiling as if he didn't have a care in the world. Hearing a door open he managed to turn his head slightly and see St. John coming back in the room carrying what looked like two saline bags for an IV. Walking up to where Billy was laying, St. John hung the bags from a pole next to the bed, hooked the two bags together with a tube then connected Billy to them via a needle in his arm.

"I'm sorry that took so long Billy. We were making arrangements for the departure of one of the Chinese gentlemen. Dr. Jackanock is just about ready to go to the airport with him right now to fly him to New York and then down to Tulsa."

"Let me guess, you're making plans to fly me somewhere too," Billy said smiling, as if it were a joke.

"Yes we are Billy Bob, we have big plans for you. But first, I'd really like to know all about what you may or may not have uncovered about our little operation here," St. John said. Billy began to laugh loudly.

"That's funny," Billy said smiling. "Bet you didn't know I was scared to death of flying did you?"

"Very aptly put Billy, I think you've pretty much described you next flight."

"Tell you what. Let's make a deal. I'll tell you everything I know, and you tell me everything you're involved in with these people. OK? Huh? OK?" Billy laughed as if it were a joke.

"Sure, why not. Billy you start, and I want you to tell me everything you know or think you know."

"Will!" Dr. Ling called from the door at the end of the room interrupting St. John and Billy. "Jack's ready to leave for New York. Can you give me a hand with this guy?"

"Sure Dr. Ling, be right there," he called back. "Billy, got to go for a few minutes. I'll be right back, please don't try to go anywhere."

St. John stood up and adjusted the IV bottles by Billy's bed. They slowly started dripping together into a single tube that led to his arm. Billy was still feeling high from the drug that St. John had given him but was beginning to feel some strength coming back into his body. Not capable of lifting his arms yet, he began turning his right arm against his body. He could feel a little pain from the needle in his arm as he turned it against his body, trying to dislodge the needle. The pain suddenly stopped. The needle was no longer in his arm. Turning his arm again, he tried to hide the needle against his body so no one could see that it had been removed. Twenty minutes later he was feeling much stronger and his head was beginning to clear as St. John came walking back into the room. St. John walked to each one of the beds, looked at the occupant and checked the IV bottles connected to them. Billy knew he was in big trouble. He had to think of some way out of this situation.

St. John casually walked up to the bed, checked the drip of Billy's IV, smiled and sat down. Crossing his legs as if he had all the time in the world, which at this moment he did, he put on his best bedside smile as he looked down at Billy.

"Hell, I'm sorry about that Billy. There are just too few of us, so we have to work twice as hard. But I'm sure I'm boring you with my problems, so let's get back to yours. Just before I left, we had agreed. You would tell me everything you knew about us, and then I would tell you all about our little operation here. So, go ahead, please begin."

"Well, gee Will," said Billy trying to act as drugged as he had felt an hour ago. "I don't think you're gonna like my little story."

"Oh, sure I will Billy, I'll bet it's going to be a cracker jack one too," St. John interrupted.

"Nope, there you go Will, see, you're wrong about that one, you know why?"

"No, I don't Billy, suppose you tell me why." St. John said with a warm smile.

"Because there isn't one. Didn't find a damn thing out

about you. Not one little thing. Oh, I checked, but you guys are slick. Couldn't find a thing about you. So tell me what's going on here. Looks like a hospital?"

Billy's heart was beating fast, he could feel the adrenaline pumping through his body. He had just laid out the bait, now would the flounder, St. John, take it.

"Really, Billy? Nothing? Wow, I find that hard to believe. You seemed so much smarter than that!"

"Guess I'm not," Billy said with a happy smile on his face, while his stomach was churning. "So tell me, what's going on here?"

"Aw gee Billy, you see, I have this one small character flaw. I really don't like to talk about it much, but it is a flaw none the less," St. John said leaning over to whisper in Billy's ear. "I lie."

"Awwww Will, you mean you're not going to tell me about these guys," Billy said slowly now closing his eyes slightly.

"No, Billy, I'm not. But, hey, listen, in a few hours it won't make any difference anyway, now will it?" St. John said with a smile as he gestured with his hands.

"Damn, I wanted to hear all about that HelpMed operation," Billy said quietly as he set his hook in.

He knew he was grasping at straws, but this was the only thing he had, the obscure little article from the Washington Post that might not even have been about St. John at all. It was admittedly an act of pure desperation. Billy turned his head slightly and watched as St. John got up, walked over to the bed next to him and sat down without saying a word. Breathing a sigh of relief at seeing St. John thrown off, Billy laid there nervously watching him and waiting, hoping to be able to make the next move.

The silence was broken a few minutes later as the cell phone in St. John's smock began to beep. Startled by the noise, St. John jumped to his feet.

"Hello!" He barked into the phone. Billy noticing that it was no longer a friendly and calm voice.

St. John stood up and began pacing nervously in front of Billy's bed. Occasionally he would grunt out "yea," "huh," or an "OK" as he paced looking very worried.

"John, think! You found a FedEx pack from the Washington Post dated the fifteenth with nothing in it. Do you really think that it would be hidden somewhere else in there? Yes, that's right. If it were there... Yes, John good thought, he probably did hide it somewhere else, but probably not there John... Because he would not want someone to find an empty envelope and keep looking for something else. Right? John! John... JOHN! Listen John, just torch the fucking place. Yes John, the whole thing! If it's there it'll burn, but I've got a hunch it's not there. So just do what I say. Yes, John. Right," St. John was talking to Eastwick as if he was speaking to a small child. Clicking off the cell phone he sat down on the bed with a bewildered look on his face.

"What a fucking moron," St. John muttered.

Not sure of what to do, Billy continued to lay there with a smile on his face, eye lids half closed, head occasionally moving slightly from side to side. A few minutes later, St. John stood up and turned off the drip into Billy's IV, then walked out of the room without saying a word.

Half an hour later, Billy could lift his arm and reached across his stomach. He felt the prick of the IV needle against his finger as he searched between his body and his other arm. He tried lifting himself up on the bed. Slowly he managed to sit up, but he knew his legs were not ready to walk yet. Massaging his legs with his hands, he began to feel better and attempted to stand up. His legs buckled slightly as he braced himself against the bed to stop from falling down. Trying again, he managed to stand up, using his arms for support on the foot board of the bed. Slowly he walked around the bed, hoping no one would come into the room. He took a chance and walked toward the wall.

Barely making it, he helped support himself with his hands against the wall. Slowly inching his way down the hallway toward the warehouse door. Feeling much better and able to walk without support, he stumbled into the dimly lit warehouse. The door to the loading dock seemed like it was a mile away as he slowly walked the fifty yards to the exit. Stopping by the door, he grabbed the handle to support himself, breathing heavily. It had taken all the energy he had to get this far. As he walked out of the door he heard an Asian accent behind him. He put his hand on the rail to the loading dock steps.

"No, No. Stop!" yelled Dr. Ling. Billy turned to see the doctor run across the warehouse towards him.

Dr. Ling caught up to Billy and wrapped his arms around him, pulling Billy away from the stairs. Billy was too weak to fight him off. Standing at the edge of the loading dock, Billy had no choice but to push himself backwards off the loading dock, pulling Dr. Ling with him. Dr. Ling yelled as they both began to fall. Their bodies shifted as they fell, and Billy felt Dr. Ling's body under him as they hit the asphalt lot some four feet from the top of the loading dock. Dr. Ling's arms sprang open, and he gasped as if all the air in his lungs was being pushed out of his body. Billy felt his body bounce off of Dr. Ling's, their heads smashing against each other with a thud. A large gash ripped across Billy's forehead. Rolling off of Dr. Ling and on to the asphalt, he immediately tried to get up and run. Two steps later he fell down crashing against the ground scraping the skin off his chin. Again he tried to stand up. Looking like an animal, he ran across the lot on his hands and feet, constantly trying to push himself upright. Looking up, he searched for the pole in the middle of the fence. He lost his balance, fell down again and rolled across the asphalt ten feet from the fence.

Gasping for air, Billy laid on the ground for just a second, then lifted his head to look around. As he looked back at the loading dock. Dr. Ling's body lay on the asphalt. Out of the corner of his eye he caught a glimpse of light. A police cruiser pulled around the corner onto the road that led to the back of the building. Bright lights shinning in his eyes, the cruiser picked up speed as it raced toward him. Not sure if the cruiser was attempting to catch him or run over him, Billy rolled over, pushed himself back up with his hands and stumbled the ten feet to the hole in the fence. As he reached the fence, he heard the scraping of metal against metal. The car was traveling against the side of the fence, throwing up a shower of sparks that lit up the night. The car was now just a few feet away from him now. Billy pushed his body through the fence, awaiting the pain of the car crushing him. To his relief, the car continued past him screeching as it ran along the chain link fence. The police car squealed to a sliding stop and then began moving backwards in a cloud of smoke. The tires were screeching as they rotated in reverse leaving the smell of burning rubber in the air. Moving to the left on his hands and knees, Billy dove between the rows of corn. Trying to stand and run, he tripped over a cornstalk falling back to the ground. Engulfed in darkness he rolled over on his back gasping for air. He was lost. Looking up he saw the small sliver of the moon above him. Two shots fired from a pistol.

"No! John, NO! STOP! Don't go in there. Stop shooting! STOP!," St. John shouted in the distance.

Billy rolled over as he heard a car door slam and the sound of muffled voices. He thought he heard the sound of another car or was it Eastwick's car driving off? Either way he was safe for the moment.

Twenty minutes later he was sitting up listening to the sounds around him. Several times he thought he heard police sirens and once or twice he was sure he heard gun shots. His strength was back now, but he didn't want to move. He was at least one hundred yards from the complex. He couldn't go tripping around in the dark. The noise would draw too much attention. Believing he was in the safest of all places at the present time, he decided to stay where he was and wait.

An hour later his adrenaline levels dropped and he was in pain, his body reacting to the past few hours. Reaching up to his throbbing head, he felt the wet blood. The palms of his hands were sore, ridged with cuts from sliding across the parking lot. Reaching down to his knees he felt rips in the knees of his pants and a moistness that he assumed was blood. His elbows were also sore and his shirt ripped to shreds. Feeling light headed, Billy realized he was going into shock. Laying back on the cool ground, his body began shaking slightly. He felt cold and clammy. Knowing there was nothing he could do, he rolled over on his side in a fetal position. To distract his mind and body, he tried concentrating on fishing in the bay.

"ZZZZZZZZZZZZZZ," the high pitched sound rang in his ears.

He frantically brushed at the fluttering of wings against his face. Patting his face with his hands, he could feel and barely hear the crushing of insects. His face was covered with mosquitoes. Sitting up he began rubbing his hands across his face trying to brush them away. The Ocean City area is known for having some of the largest mosquitoes on the East Coast. Wing spans as large as two inches. Once the bugs were brushed away Billy tried to cover his face with his arms, but could feel them attacking the open holes in his clothes, especially his knees and elbows. Keeping his face partially covered with one arm he swatted at the bugs with his other. The relentless high pitched whine invaded his ears. Exhausted from swatting mosquitoes, he rolled down onto the ground, falling into semi-consciousness.

When he opened his eyes, he could see that the sun was up. Feeling disoriented, he sat up looking around in all directions. The green corn stalks surrounded him. A deep blue sky was above him. He could just barely feel the warm breezes moving among the corn stalks. The wounds from last night were still throbbing as he looked at his hands and knees caked with a combination of dirt and blood. His hands, knees, and arms, were covered with small welts that began to itch from the mosquito bites. Every muscle in his body ached from the beating his body had taken, not to mention spending the night sleeping on the hard ground.

Closing his eyes, he concentrated on the sounds around him. He could barely hear the sound of cars off in the distance. He had no clue as to just where he might be in the cornfield.

He could distinguish the sound of a Piper Cub taking off from the airport. The sound was very familiar to him. Piper Cubs pulled signs up and down the beach, every hour, every day, all summer long. He reached down and picked up several rocks then placed them in a row pointing to the aircraft sound. That would be the direction to the airport and possibly the first and only reference point on his position. He tried to calculate the position of the sun and which way it was moving. Being surrounded by cornstalks, the shadows changed too unpredictably to be sure. He was hoping he could get a fix on the sun around noon and get a better feel for his position.

Beginning to feel a little better now that the sun was up, he surveyed his environment. Billy was sure they would be looking for him. St. John had told Eastwick to torch his trailer, so he was pretty sure his home was gone. Except for Jill, he had no friends or relatives that he could go to and expect help without asking too many questions. Because they knew about Jill, he could be sure that they would be watching her too. The only safe place to hide was right where he was. With the sun up, they would assume he had escaped from the cornfield. The cornfield would be the last place they would look for him. The next question was how long to stay. He decided to spend all day and leave just before first light the next morning. By then, he was hoping, they would not be searching so hard for him. They would be concentrating on people who would hide him. Billy realized that a lot was riding on his assumptions, but he knew he would have to handle this on a common sense basis. His only hope was that he wasn't too paranoid or going over the edge. His life depended on it.

He crossed his legs as he sat on the dirt and smiled. A few

seconds later he became aware of a new problem. He needed to relieve himself. Oh Christ, he thought to himself. They never cover this in books or movies!

Standing up and walking around, he realized the problem would not go away and began looking for something he could use to dig a small hole. Finding a long flat rock, he moved several rows over and dug down a couple of inches then squatted down over the hole. When finished he went back to his spot and sat down feeling embarrassed at what he had done. Five minutes later he was wondering if he had turned into little more than a wild animal surviving in a corn field. Feeling depression beginning to slip into his body, he immediately tried to shake it off. He had to keep his mind sharp and clear.

He passed the day away, scratching at his mosquito bites and looking up waiting for the noon time sun to help him gauge his position. To his dismay, clouds rolled over. Tears welled up in his eyes and he brushed them away with his dirty hand, angry at himself for letting his emotions surface so easy.

The clouds parted briefly. The sun was overhead. A second later more clouds covered the sun but as he watched the clouds go by, he began thinking that on normal days clouds drift from West to East. If that was correct then the direction he had picked out for the airport was wrong. It was south and not north as he had deducted. Pondering the situation he tried to swallow. His throat was dry.

"Damn, now I need water! What next?" he said dejectedly.

Knowing he would need water eventually, he decided to leave his position and search for the end of the cornfield. Heading south toward the airport, away from the complex, there was a chance he could find some water in a drainage ditch beside the field or next to the road.

Walking along the row of corn, he had traveled only ten feet when he saw a highway in front of him. Staying back under the cover of the corn he moved a little closer and realized that he was just a few rows away from the corner of the complex. His heart racing with fear, he retreated back into the corn and began moving quickly back down the row, crouching down, trying to make as little noise as possible. Forty minutes later, his knees and thighs aching, he came to the end of the row. Another row of corn heading out at an almost ninety degree angle went off to his left. Knowing he was now deep in the corn, he decided to take a chance and stand up, stretching his legs. The wound above his face hit a large ear of corn, and he flinched in pain as he reached up and grabbed his head. He hit the ear of corn with his fist, knocking it loose from the stalk, as he fell to his knees and began crying.

"You stupid son-of-a-bitch, you couldn't find food or water when it was right in front of you. How in the Hell are you ever going to beat these guys?" he cried.

From his kneeling position he reached up and picked the ear of corn he had dislodged from the stalk. Shucking the green leaves from the ear, he sunk his teeth deep into the kernels, sucking out the juices. An hour later, his stomach full and his thirst quenched, he felt better and stood up to explore the end of the cornfield. This time he walked down the row of corn slowly much like a breeze creating just the slightest movement of the green stalks. What he presumed was about two hours later he came to the end of the cornfield. He was about ten feet from the edge and could just barely see a road in the distance. Crouching down low, he moved forward a few feet and recognized Stephen Decatur Highway. By the angle of the sun, it was probably after three in the afternoon. His eyes shifted left and right. Seeing nothing he slowly pulled back out of sight into the corn field. Not wanting to be too close to the edge of the field, he moved back approximately one hundred yards and sat down.

There was only one way out of his situation. Late tonight after leaving the corn field he would take a chance and go back to Jill's, then he would go to the boat and get the envelope. The following morning he would have to take a chance and go to an attorney he knew, tell him the story and let him contact the State Police instead of the local Ocean City Police. They could work out an arrangement for him to safely surrender. He knew that he was taking a chance on a murder charge but either way he was dead. At least this way he could take them down with him. His key would be the HelpMed Corporation, whatever that was.

Turning suddenly, he thought he heard a noise. Tensing up he lowered his head slightly and concentrated on the direction of the sound. A few seconds later he heard it again but could not quite make it out. It was another minute until he heard it again, this time he recognized it as a boom.

"Shit, It's a thunder storm! Christ, just what I need!" he said to himself as he sat back dejectedly once again.

There was no place he could go, no place he could hide. He could only sit there and wait as he listened to the thunder growing louder in the distance. Looking up, the clouds were still white and fluffy. The booms were slowly being replaced by the sound of rolling thunder as it moved unimpeded along the flat eastern shore landscape. The clouds above were now becoming black and he could feel the cold winds blowing through the corn just ahead of the torrential rains.

The sky became a light show as the clouds opened up. Billy felt refreshed by the cold rain as it washed the mud and dirt off of his wounds. Reaching out he grabbed a leaf of corn and pulled it up to his lips. The rain ran off the leaf and into his mouth, quenching his thirst. He jumped several times at the cracks of lightning that seemed to hit nearby. In the midst of the worst part of the storm he began to wish he was back in his office, writing boring copy and bantering with Bev. The rain continued falling and his appreciation of it turned sour as he felt his body shaking from the cold, wishing the rain would stop. An hour later the rain turned to a light mist and Billy found himself standing in the middle of a large puddle of water, his arms wrapped around his body trying to get warm.

Stepping out of the puddle, he felt his feet sink up to his ankles in mud and realized he would leave large foot prints behind him, a trail that could lead anyone who might still be searching for him, right to where he was standing. Deciding not to move, he remained standing by the puddle feeling the humidity and heat growing around him. Slowly the puddles began to dry up as the water was absorbed into the arid earth. Billy could feel his clothes beginning to dry, but he was still shivering. Looking at his exposed arms once again he saw that the welts from the mosquito bites last night had grown large and sore. Knowing that the mosquitoes would be back again tonight he reached down and picked up a handful of mud, spreading it over the exposed areas of his skin. He realized he must have looked like a monster standing there caked with mud but it was the only protection he could get from the mosquitoes.

Billy passed the rest of the afternoon nervously pacing

around his little spot in the corn field, scared, reflecting on his future or the possibility of one. Late in the afternoon he decided to eat another dinner of corn and then head out closer to the edge of the corn field. Billy didn't want to take a chance of getting lost in the field later in the night when he was trying to get out. The corn tasted delicious, there was nothing better in the world than fresh, bright white, Silver Queen corn. Starting in early July and up into September, Billy would eat dozens of ears a week. Hot, steamed, buttered corn and fresh flounder was Billy's favorite meal. Although the corn was not steamed or even close to hot, he voraciously ate a dozen large ears in just a few minutes. Dinner finished he slowly walked along the row of corn towards the edge of the field. He decided to look out and see if there might be someone waiting for him. Not seeing any people or cars, he slowly backed into the corn field about one hundred feet and sat down to wait until night fall.

As the sun began to set he heard a rustling in the corn field. Turning to see what the noise was, he saw a small raccoon about ten feet away from him, pulling over a corn stalk and grabbing at an ear of corn. Slowly the raccoon pulled the green leaves back and began eating the ear as he looked over at Billy. He heard another rustle off to his left and looked over to see another raccoon doing the same thing. On his right he saw another and another. They seemed to be invading the corn field from the woods on the other side of the road. Hearing more rustling, Billy stood up and moved deeper into the field not wanting to have a confrontation with an angry raccoon. The sound of a gun going off made him jump. Looking around quickly, he saw a raccoon laying on the ground about twenty feet in front of him, it's head blown away. Running back deeper into the field, he could hear people talking, their voices getting louder as they got closer to him. A volley of six shots rang out and Billy dove to the ground covering his head with his hands. A second later he jumped back up to his feet and began running, again looking behind him to see where the shooters were. Running at full speed, Billy took six steps and ran face first into a body, bounced back and fell down on the ground. Looking up, he expected to see a man holding a gun, instead he saw the hind quarters of a deer running down the row of corn.

"Damn Walter, you see that buck. Sum bitch almost got me with his horns, must a been a ten pointer," a voice said off in the distance just barely audible.

"Damn right, I did and I'm gonna get him this fall too, his heads gonna look good on my wall," said a second voice.

"Shit Walter, where you goin' to get the money to get a head stuffed? Look there's one," the first voice said and was followed by a rifle shot.

"Stuff it yourself, Fred! I'll kill 'im, just you wait and see. Look over there!"

Billy tensed, afraid he had been seen. He heard another six shots ring out but couldn't feel or hear any of them come close to where he was laying.

"C'mon, let's move on down here a little bit. I saw a couple of 'em scurrying down that way," said one of the voice. "Got me six of 'em so far."

"Six, my ass, four of them's mine, you missed, usin' a damn rifle, hell why didn't you bringing a shot gun?"

"It ain't sportin', Fred. Any asshole can kill 'em with a shot gun. Hell, If I was usin" a shot gun. I'd had twenty of 'em by now, not that measly four you think you got."

"Think I got? Damn, Walter, they's mine, and I didn't bring you out here for sport. I want to get rid of these damn coons. Don't give a shit about sport."

Hearing the voices trailing off in the distance, Billy stood up, deciding to move a little deeper in the corn field and take his chances on finding his way out later. He could hear gun shots off in the distance and began moving in the opposite direction across the rows of corn.

As night began to fall the shots stopped and Billy sat down again, awaiting his time to leave, as the high pitched whine of mosquitoes began to take over the night. Trying to stop the incessant sounds they were making, he put his hands over his ears. Several hours later he decided to try and work his way back to the edge of the field. Walking down a row of corn he emerged from the field twenty minutes later. He could see that he was still on Steven Decatur Highway, and he backed into the field a few feet to allow him to look out without being seen. As a number of cars were still traveling up and down the road, he had no intention of walking down the highway until very late at night when just about everyone would be gone.

An hour later, he could see some flashes of light off in the distance, it was another thunder storm. Giving a sigh, he watched as the light show began building off in the west. Billy usually loved thunder storms but with the coming of this second one, he was growing weary of them. The only bright spot was that it would get rid of the mosquitoes for a while and stop them from making that horrible high pitched sound in his ears. Ten minutes later the storm was upon him. Unlike the storm of the afternoon, the lightning and thunder were not as fierce. The rains hit heavy and hard but lasted only about five minutes, then stopped. Although it had been a brief storm, the rain still left him shivering and cold, his clothes heavy with the weight of the water. Minutes later he began to hear the high pitched sound ringing in his ears and could feel the flutter of wings against his face. The mosquitoes were back again. Brushing them away with his hand, he realized that the rain had washed off the protective mud. Reaching down he grabbed a handful of mud and rubbed it over his face, arms and legs. Then placing his hands over his ears, he managed to block out the maddening continual high pitched whine.

The number of cars traveling the road began to diminish as the night wore on. There was the occasional car on the road now. Billy was going to wait another hour before setting out, but having no idea of what time it was, he decided that the time to leave had arrived. Standing up, he walked out of the corn field and stepped into the middle of the highway, he could see no car lights in either direction. Looking back to his right, he could see the lights of the complex, barely visible above the corn field glowing in the night. Cautiously he began walking down the road, trying to keep an eye out, for oncoming vehicles.

Chapter 8
Sunday, July 18

Occasionally Billy would see a car light in front or behind him and would step off the road, into the trees, waiting for it to pass by. There were several convenience stores and gas stations on the road, not wanting to be seen, he would circle in the woods or fields around them and then back to the road. Some time later in the night he came to Route 50. It was late on a Sunday night and the road was practically vacant. Waiting for a spot between traffic, he crossed the road and into the brush on the other side. Following Route 50, he walked approximately one mile down the road and then crossed through the heavy undergrowth to the beach of the Sinepuxent Bay. Looking the half mile across the bay he could barely make out the lights of Ocean City through the fog that had formed. Knowing there was an old dirt road that followed the edge of the bay, he walked forward a hundred yards through the brush until he came across it. Following the old road, he fought a battle with a swarm of mosquitoes that kept getting in his eyes making it difficult to see. Finally he came to what he was looking for, the closest point of land to Ocean City across the bay. From here on up, the bay would begin widening until it reached its widest point of about two miles at low tide. From where he was he knew that it was just about a half mile swim and walk across the bay to Twentieth Street in Ocean City.

The night air was warm and felt damp from the humidity. Stepping into the salty waters of the bay he was rejuvenated, much like bathing in the Fountain of Youth. Sitting down in the water, he felt as if he had returned home. He washed the mud and dirt from his body and splashed around like a child making his first visit to the beach. He had not realized how depressing it had been spending that much time in the corn field living and behaving like an animal. Tired but refreshed, he began swimming across the bay. Constantly on watch for boats that might be out, he swam slowly not trying to tax his remaining strength. Approximately half way across the bay he knew he had come to a place that at high tide would usually be out of water. Suffering from exhaustion, he stopped and felt for the bottom with his foot. The sandy bottom was just a few feet below him. Kneeling down, his head just above the water, he relaxed trying to rebuild his strength for the next quarter mile of swimming. From here on he knew he would not be able to stop until he reached the shore, if he ran out of strength he would drown in mid stream.

Refreshed enough to try the swim for the other side, he looked across and saw the fog had become thicker. Through the haze he could still make out a few reference points that would lead him to shore. He heard a rumbling sound behind him. Turning, he waited for a few seconds and over top of the fog by the shore he saw a flash of lightning, another thunder storm was building behind him. He would have liked to rest a little longer, but knew that storms on the bay were easily capable of kicking up two and three foot waves, more than enough to take down a good swimmer, let alone one who was tired and nearing exhaustion.

Quickly, Billy set off swimming for the shore. He could hear the thunder growing progressively louder behind him as he reached a fog bank. That meant he was getting closer to the warmth of the land. Watching a light on the shore he swam towards it as the torrential rains opened up. Nearing complete exhaustion he began to feel his hands hitting the bottom of the bay. Rolling over, sitting on the sandy bottom with his head just above water he gasped for air. This time he was thankful for the cold rain that washed over his head, refreshing him. Looking back over the bay, the fog now blown away by the wind before the rain, he could see the waves he had worried about. It frightened him to think that if he had left the corn field a half an hour later, he would never have made it ashore.

The rains ended as quickly as they began and Billy could see stars twinkling in the night sky as the dark rain clouds moved out to sea. Turning back towards the shore he saw a lot of tall sea grass and waded up a hundred yards to a spot where he could walk easily up the bank and on to ground. Once on land he sat down, smiling that he had beaten the elements and was still alive. Fog was beginning to form again, this time pushed on by a light sea breeze blowing cool moist air in off the ocean. Standing up he walked off the bay beach and down the street by a block of houses. Walking under a street light he could see that his black athletic pants were now little more than shreds of cloth hanging from his waist. Not wanting to take the chance of attracting attention by looking like a flasher, he ripped at the waist band, tearing apart the piece of elastic that held his pants up. Quickly he pulled them off and balled them up, leaving only his bright red Bermuda shorts. When he was out from under the street light, he dropped the worn pants beside a car.

Standing by the Coastal Highway, he felt he had been gone for years. There were just a few cars on the road. Crossing at Twentieth Street, he walked the two blocks to the Boardwalk, deciding to follow the Atlantic beach up the two miles to Jill's condo instead of trying to walk the street. Taking off his shoes he walked from the boardwalk, down the beach towards the oceans edge. He could feel the cool wet sand sift up between his toes and around his feet. When he reached the ocean he stood in the water, letting the cold waves wash up and over his legs. Walking up the beach he decided to take his time so as not to attract any attention. Billy would look like a tourist on an early morning beach walk, awaiting the sunrise. Over the ocean he could see the sky beginning to lighten, the sun would be up in an hour.

Walking up the steps to the Golden Sands, the sun was just minutes away from rising above the ocean. People were beginning to come out, walking the beach, awaiting the magnificent sun rise. Washing his feet off under the spigot by the rear doors, Billy waited until the hallway was clear and slipped into the building and up the emergency steps. He knew he should have walked around and checked out the front of the building first to see if anyone might be watching but the sunrise forced him to change his plans. Finally reaching the eleventh floor, he sat on the steps to catch his breath. The exhaustion from the past days was catching up to him, and felt weak and light headed. Laying back on the cement, he closed his eyes for a few seconds that quickly became a few minutes.

C'mon sport, he said to himself. Pass out now and you're a dead man.

Forcing himself to his feet he staggered to the door way and leaned against it. He looked through the glass to see if anyone was keeping vigil outside in the hall. Seeing no one, he slipped through the door and down the empty hallway. He was about to knock on Jill's door but didn't want to take the chance of attracting attention. Reaching in his pocket he found the key he had placed there several days ago. Slowly he inserted the key in the door and turned the dead bolt. It slid across the lock making practically no noise. From the apartment door next to hers, Billy heard voices and the sounds of someone opening their door. Billy managed to slip into Jill's apartment just as the door to the next apartment began to open. Closing the door behind him, he put his head against it to listen to the voices. A vacationing couple was trying to get down to the beach for the sunrise. Hearing the ding of the elevator door closing, he quietly latched the dead bolt locking the door, then turned around in the dark apartment.

He had to know if there was anyone else besides Jill in the apartment. Reaching up he turned the light switch on and breathed a sigh of relief, seeing the apartment was vacant. No one else was there. Laying back against the door, he closed his eyes and tried to regain some more strength. Feeling a little better he walked toward the bedroom. As he passed by the mirror on the living room wall he looked at himself and jumped. He thought he had seen someone else in the reflection. Billy turned back to the reflection of the mirror. His mouth dropped open in disbelief. There was a large cut above his head that was hanging wide open. It was about three inches long with a large piece of skin flopping down. His face was covered with insect bites and massively swollen. There was not a white piece of flesh to be found. The mosquito bites had all melted together making a large red lumpy mask. He had not realized that his eyes were practically swollen shut. There were dark lines from the dirt of the corn field all over his face that the waters of the bay had not washed away. His lips were split open in several areas and badly swollen with pieces of skin hanging down.

The image of himself left him feeling light headed. Reaching for a chair, he sat down, letting his head rest back, trying to keep from fainting.

"Who's there?" he heard Jill's voice speaking from the bedroom.

She must have heard him collapse in the chair. He tried to speak but could not get his lips together properly to form the words.

"WHO'S THERE?" she asked again.

"Aaaas me Bi ye," he mumbled trying to get the words out through his swollen and cut lips.

It took all his strength to push himself up and out of the chair. He could hear her getting out of bed as he took a few steps toward the bedroom door. He saw the barrel of a pistol coming out the door and tried to lunge for it but managed only a small forward movement as he fell on the gun. He pulled it down with him as he fell to the floor. In his peripheral vision he could see that it was Jill but he was too exhausted to prevent himself from falling. Hitting a chair by the door, his body turned slightly and she fell down on top of him, her pistol knocked loose, bouncing across the rug.

"Ahhhh," she screamed as she reached out to pick up the pistol.

The gun was close to his hand and he beat her to it, her hand landing on top of his. Rolling over and away from her with the gun, he lay on his side looking up at her.

"BILLY!" she exclaimed. "My God, Billy is that you?"

"Yeth, help me," he muttered in broken English.

"God, Billy, what happened to you? Where have you been?"

"Help me," he said slowly.

"Billy, do you want me to call an ambulance?" her voice was anxious and full of fear.

"NO. Get thum stuff and help banda me up," he was saying as he gripped the pistol and held it to his side.

She jumped up and ran into the bathroom, coming back a minute later, hers arms loaded with medical supplies. Carefully she pulled out a large wad of cotton and poured a large amount of alcohol from a bottle directly into it. Reaching out she carefully wiped around his face. Alcohol from the cotton dripped down his face and onto the open cuts in his lips. Screaming and wincing from the pain he clenched his fist. The contraction of his index finger resting on the trigger of the 22 caliber pistol caused the gun to go off. There was a loud pop, the pistol jumped in his hand as a bullet went flying across the room. It came to a rest inside a white leather chair leaving a hole about the size of a dime in the side of the cushion.

"AHHHHHHH," Jill screamed as she jumped back in fear. "God damn it, Billy! Put that pistol down before you kill someone!"

"Thit Jill. I thorry," Billy stammered.

"You're sorry!" Jill yelled again. "Billy! I'd be dead if I had been standing in front of that gun!"

"I'm thorry. I'm thorry. Pleathe. Water I need thome water," he said slowly, attempting to get the words out, as he sat up against the chair. The pistol still in his hand.

Jill immediately got up and went into the kitchen. A moment later she came back holding a large glass of ice water. Reaching up with his free hand he took the glass and drank down the water, holding the glass up high so that the ice would rest against his cut and swollen lips.

"Mowa Wawer," he stammered.

Taking the glass from his hand she jumped up again, running back into the kitchen and coming right back with the glass refilled with water, along with a pitcher filled with ice and water. Taking the glass again, he drank the water as he did before, this time letting the ice rest longer on his lips. The coolness of the ice helped numb some of the pain in his lips, which was immediately replaced with pain from other parts of his body.

"Hel me up. Help me into bafroom," he said putting out his arm for Jill to help him up.

Grabbing his arm, she got him on his feet and hobbled to the bathroom. Stepping into the shower with his clothes on he took the hand sprayer from the shower head and sat back down in the tub. Placing the pistol in the shampoo tray, he held onto the hand shower with one hand as he adjusted the water temperature with the other. Jill, not sure of what to do, sat down on the toilet, watching him. Temperature of the water adjusted to tepid, Billy leaned his head forward, adjusted the spray to a fine mist and began spraying the wounds on his head. His stomach turned slightly as he watched chunks of dirt run down into the tub, mixed with dried and fresh blood falling from his face into the shower. Closing his eyes, he began spraying his face. He would stop periodically to check the water that was in the tub to see if his face was getting clean. Reaching for the bar of soap he ran his hand over it and then over his face, loosening the last of the dirt.

"Can you give me thome gauze or a towel pleathe?"

Jill got up and came back with a large pack of gauze pads. Pulling several out, she unwrapped them and handed them to Billy. Carefully, he wiped his face as Jill sat back down on the toilet lighting a cigarette. His face dry, Billy looked at the residue from the pads and nodded his head. Picking up the sprayer again he repeated the procedure cleaning out his knee caps, then his hands and elbows. Turning the water off he sat back in the tub resting to regain more strength. He felt a little better but was by no means well.

"Billy, I think we should go to the emergency room or something and get some stitches for your head and lips, they look awful," Jill said sympathetically.

"No, ith too late. The wounds are over twenty-four hoursth old, too old for sthitches. Get me a mirror and tape and thissors. I'll bandage them," he said reclining back in the tub.

Jill came back into the bathroom carrying a small face mirror on a stand, a large roll of tape and a small pair of scissors. She set the articles on the edge of the tub and sat back on the toilet lighting another cigarette, puffing on it as vigorously as she had done with the last one. Reaching up, Billy adjusted the mirror so he could see his face, then picked up the scissors and sat back in the tub again. Carefully he cut off pieces of tape about an inch long and one inch wide. Cutting a triangle out of each side of the tape he made butterfly bandages that he carefully placed on the edge of the tub. After he cut out the fourth piece, he adjusted the mirror again. Picking up a piece of tape, he placed it on the piece of skin dangling down from his face, then pulled it across, taping it back onto his head. Picking up two other pieces, he taped up his lips. Not needing the fourth he crumpled it up and threw it on the floor. Sitting back in the tub, Billy looked over at Jill.

"I look like hell, don't I?" he asked with a sigh.

"I'm not going to lie to you Billy, you do look like shit. What happened, where have you been?" she asked.

"I'll tell you later, but you haf to help me and underthand what I am doing. OK?"

"Billy, I'm not sure I like the way you said that," she said wearily.

"I haf to get some sleep. I am thorry I can take no chances now. Thingth ah movin' to quikly. You hef to underthand. I'm go to lock you in bafroom while I thleep."

"Billy, you've got to be kidding. I want to help you not hurt you. Please, don't do this," she pleaded.

"Thorry, get what you need for few hours while I thleep. I will clothe bafroom door and sleep out thide it so you can not get out."

"Billy, no plcasc. I don't like that. Please I don't want to bc."

"Thop," Billy said holding up his hand interrupting her. Standing up he stepped from the tub. Taking off his clothes, he let them fall to the floor in a wet heap. Stepping back, he pulled a large soft towel from the rack and wrapped it around his body as he reached over picking up the pistol.

"Pleath Jill, get what you will need for a few hours. I don't want hurt you, this will help protect you. Pleath do it."

"Shit, Billy," she said with a touch of anger in her voice. "OK, God damn it, I will, but when I get out, I want some explanations," she said as she walked out of the bathroom. A few minutes later she came back carrying a large cup of coffee, a pack of cigarettes and a portable TV.

"I jeth need some thleep, please understand. I'll try and esthplain when I wake up," Billy said wearily as he walked out and closed the door.

"OK Billy, but I want to hear it all when I get out. ALL OF IT!" she yelled through the closed door.

Taking the sash from Jill's bathrobe that was hanging on the door, he tied it around the door knob. Laying down on the rug against the door, he pulled the sash tight under him. If Jill tried to open the door, it would pull him over, waking him up. Within seconds he was in a deep sleep.

Chapter 9

The canopy created by the branches of the weeping willow tree kept the hot humid air at bay as small streams of sunlight filtered through the long thin leaves. Billy was sitting with Jill in his Boston Whaler, laying back in her arms as the fingers of her hand gently combed through his hair massaging the back of his head. Fishing rod in his hand, the small boat was gently being nudged back and forth by light breezes barely disturbing the surface of the water. Slowly he began reeling in his line and with every crank of the reel the rod would bend. The rod was bent into the shape of an inverted U as Billy continued to gently crank the reel. The water began to bubble and churn as his line finally broke the surface of the water, his hook attached to a dark blue police officers uniform. Looking over the side, he could see that it was John Eastwick's body and as he slowly turned to Jill, he saw the horrified look on her face as she began to pound on his back with her hands.

"Billy! Billy! Damn it. BILLY! WAKE UP, BILLY!"

The thumping of the door against his back woke him from his dream and he sat up, wincing in pain and disoriented. He quickly looked around and when he could see he was safe, began to calm down.

"Billy, open the door... BILLY, PLEASE OPEN THE DOOR!" Jill was yelling from behind him.

"OK. OK, just a minute." Billy rolled away from the door.

Jill pulled against the door but with the cord tied around Billy it wouldn't open. She pulled hard against the door one more time. The door flew open hitting her in the shoulder with a loud thump as the cord, still tied to Billy's hand, pulled him over.

"AHH, Damn it Jill," he yelled.

"Oh Billy, I'm so sorry," she said walking out of the bathroom, both hands together at her mouth as she looked down on him. "Are you all right?"

"Yea, Geez. I'm OK. What time ith it?" he was asking as he rolled over, propping himself up with one arm.

"It's three o'clock you've been asleep for a little over eight hours. I'm sorry. I didn't want to wake you, but I ran out of cigarettes, I'm tired of sitting on that toilet watching TV, I'm hungry. I have no idea what's going on and I am scared," she blurted out, breaking into tears as she finished talking.

"Jill, Jill, it's OK. Please calm down."

"Billy, what is it, what's going on? Please tell me," she pleaded.

"Jill, I tell you everything later when I can talk better. It hurts talk. I hungry too, can you fix some foo."

"I've got some eggs but not much else. I was going to go shopping this morning. I...."

"Eggs, fine, please go fix," he said interrupting her as he waved at her to go fix the food.

Jill got up and walked into the kitchen. It was an open kitchen with a counter separating it from the living room. As Billy watched her, she opened a pack of cigarettes, pulled out one and lit it. Standing in the middle of the kitchen, she took several angry puffs as she paced about nervously, mumbling to herself. Walking to the stove, she reached up and took a frying pan from the rack next to it, slamming it down on the stove. Yanking open the refrigerator door, she grabbed a carton of eggs and a stick of butter. Looking at Billy, she opened the stick of butter and squeezed off a small section with her fingers, throwing it into the pan. Grabbing two eggs she smashed them hard against the edge of the frying pan and held them six inches above the pan, letting the slimy ooze drip from the shells and her hands. Plopping them into the pan, she stood there staring at him. Realizing he was naked, he walked into the bathroom and picked up his bloody clothes from the floor. Going back into the kitchen, Jill was still standing at the stove watching the eggs frying to a crispy brown. Looking around, he saw a washer dryer combination next to the sink and placed his clothes in the washer. Closing the door he turned it on, stood up and leaned against the counter with one hand.

"JESUS CHRIST, BILLY! You're not going to get those clothes clean that way. MEN!" Jill said walking over to the cabinet. She took out a bottle of laundry detergent, measured out a cup and poured it in with the clothes. "That's what you have to do to get clothes clean. It's called soap! You idiot!"

"Aw Jeez, I know that attitude, you'll be like this all afternoon," Billy was muttering as he walked into the bedroom and came back wearing one of Jill's bathrobes.

"Hey, cute Billy. Going for the old Homo look are we? Thanks for asking. Sure, wear anything I've got. Want some panties, maybe a bra, how about some panty hose?" Jill asked sarcastically.

Shaking his head, Billy walked over to the bathroom door and picked up the pistol laying on the rug. Looking at it he turned it in his hands a few times then placed it in the pocket of the bathrobe. Walking back to the counter that separated the kitchen from the living room, he pulled out a stool and sat down. Eggs finished Jill angrily pulled a plate from the cupboard and placed it on the counter in front of him. Walking back to the stove, she picked up the frying pan and went back to him. Turning the frying pan upside down the eggs flopped and dripped falling onto the plate as she vigorously shook the pan.

"You're hungry, there eat!" she said angrily.

"Glad I still have the gun," Billy said under his breath but, unfortunately, just loud enough for her to hear.

"Oh yea, great. Just what we need right now a little laughter. Billy, you eat your fucking eggs and then we're going to talk." Jill had a mean look in her eyes.

Although slightly mangled, the eggs tasted great to him. After shoveling the eggs into his mouth, he got up and walked over to the edge of the counter where there were several liquor bottles. Running his fingers over the tops of the bottles very lightly, he grabbed a bottle of bourbon, unscrewed the top and lifted it to his lips. Tilting the bottle up, he took three large gulps and then put it down. Wincing slightly as some of the alcohol ran into the cuts on his lips, he opened his mouth as if to scream but no sounds came out. Taking a deep breath, he walked over and sat down on the sofa in the living room.

"Come, thit down," Billy waving his hand for her to sit on the sofa with him.

Strolling very slowly, she walked over and sat down at the furthest edge of the sofa, crossing her legs and looking away from him across the room.

"John, Thaint John and thome others are bringing illegal aliens into the country. Thaint John's also Prethident and CEO of a New York Company called HelpMed. I have the information on them that will bring down the orgaizthion. They have me framed for the murder of Jonathan Banths," Billy said quietly.

"Oh my God, Billy. What are you going to do? Where's the information you have on them? Is it safe?" Jill asked sounding concerned.

"It's thafe for now. They burned the trailer down, hoping they would get it. But I had put it thome place else."

"Where Billy, where is it?" she asked quickly.

"Thafe. When I am throng enough. I'll get it."

"What will you do when you get it?"

"I have some planth. Hasth anyone been by here looking for me?"

"That explains it! John was here twice. He barged in like he owned the place. Walked around and left. The last time he was here, last night, I told him I'd call the police and file charges against him, that he had no right to burst in like that. He just looked at me and smiled, then he left." Jill looked off, nodding her head as if everything that had happened was now making sense.

"I don't want to get you in trouble. I better leave," Billy said as he tried to stand up.

"Sit down, I don't think he'll be back," Jill reassured reaching over to push Billy back down on the sofa. "If he does, I won't open the door. We'll just stay here and be quiet. He'll think no one is home."

"No, I better leaf now. You could get in trouble for harboring a fugitive." Billy tried to stand up again.

"Stay there Billy, you aren't going anywhere. I'll take my chances. You're going to need my help sooner or later, whether you want it or not." Jill pushed him back onto the sofa.

"I don't have the strength to try and get up again. OK, you win. I'll get thome rest and maybe we can get the stuff later tonight. I'm feeling a lot better." Billy looked exhausted.

The phone rang and they both jumped, Jill giving a small scream. She looked over at him and laughed nervously, then got a serious look on her face. The answering machine clicked on and Billy heard Jill's voice saying she was not at home and to leave a message. The phone clicked off, no message was left. He sat back and rested his head on the sofa as Jill lit another cigarette.

A few minutes later the phone rang again and like before they both jumped. This time the caller left a message.

"Hi Jill, It's Sarah at the store. Taking the day off again are we? Must be nice! It's kind of quiet today. A guy named John called a few minutes ago. He said he was looking for a piece of jewelry you were holding for him and that he'd call back later. Give me a call and let me know which piece it is. OK? Take care and bye!"

"Eathwick?" Billy said looking at her angrily.

"Whoa, settle down," Jill said putting up her hands. "There are more Johns than Eastwick around, it is somewhat of a common name. Yes, it was a guy named John but he wanted me to hold a piece of that black coral jewelry for him, you know, the stuff I went to New York to buy. That's who it was and all it is, settle down Billy. Stop being so God damned paranoid."

Picking up the phone, Jill quickly called back to the store.

"Sarah, yea, it's me. No, I'm not going to be coming in today. Listen that piece of Jewelry is under the counter. It's in a little box and has the name J. Jones on it," Jill said making a face at Billy and sticking out her tongue. "Yep, that's the one. Right. Eighty-five dollars and don't take a check. I told him it's cash or credit card. OK, yea, great. You too. Bye!"

Standing up she walked across the living room and grabbed a cigarette out of a pack on the counter, as she was lighting it she looked up at Billy.

"See, wrong John, get some rest Billy. Look, why don't you go into the bedroom and lay down," she said shaking her wrist, extinguishing the match.

"No, I am fine here. I'm justh going to clothe my eyesth and get thome rest. Don't open the door or leaf wifout telling me. OK?" he looked at her sternly.

"Billy, you just get some rest. I'll sit here on watch. Get your strength up, so we can get that envelope tonight. OK?"

Laying his head back on the sofa and closing his eyes, he was soon asleep. It was a semiconscious sleep and he was somewhere between a dream state and awake most of the time. He thought he heard Jill talking once but did not want to open his eyes, he just drifted back deeper in sleep. Later he thought he heard her talking again and began to wake himself up. Shaking his head and yawning, he sat up watching Jill come in from the bedroom.

"Who were you talking too?" he said putting his hand behind his head and rubbing his neck.

"No one. I was just singing to myself in the bedroom. I put your clothes in the dryer and they're ready to wear. Billy, you really need to get out of my robe. It disturbs me to see you in that thing, just a little too frilly for you," she said changing the subject in mid sentence.

Standing up, he walked over to the dryer and took his clothes out. After he put his shorts on, he reached for the long sleeve black shirt he had been wearing. The arms were ripped to shreds and there were holes in the front and back of it. Holding it up, he stuck his fingers out of the holes in the front of the shirt and wiggled them at Jill.

"I don't have any of John's old clothes. He took everything when he left. I have an old, large sweat shirt that might fit you," she said walking back into the bedroom.

Coming back, she held out a white sweat shirt then she threw it over to him.

"Great fit," he said pulling the sleeves up high on his arms. "Might be a little warm in this weather, but it's definitely better than that old one."

"Billy, what are your plans, after you get the package?" Jill asked softly.

"John Bishop, Bishop, Bishop," Billy repeated the name as he moved his lips and turned his head. "Hey, the swelling is going down. I can almost talk normally."

"What about John Bishop?" Jill asked.

"He's an attorney I know, or knew in Salisbury. I'm going to take it to him and let him broker a deal with the authorities. That's about the only chance I have." Billy put his hand on his jaw and opened and closed his mouth.

"What about trying to work a deal with St. John?"

"Naah, no way. St. John wants me dead, that's the best deal I can get from him," he said quietly, thinking about his dismal future.

"You could try, Billy. You never know. Give him a call. Maybe you can cut a deal with him," she prodded.

"No, believe me, it is not possible. I have talked to the man and seen the look in his eyes. I know what he wants and it's not a deal."

"Billy, you.."

There was a knock at the door and they both jumped up looking at each other.

"If it's Eastwick, he'll only come back," Billy said walking quickly toward the bedroom. "I'll hide in the bedroom closet, if it's him, you let him in, but don't let him back in the bedroom. I know him, he'll only come back later if you don't answer the door. Just get him in and get him out as quickly as you can."

Jill walked to the door and looked through the peep hole. Turning around she shook her head yes to Billy and pointed to the bedroom. Standing by the bedroom door, he walked over and into the walk-in closet. Taking the pistol out of his pocket he closed the door behind him. Straining to hear, he could just barely make out what Jill was saying as she opened the door.

"I told you not to come back, John, and I meant it," she said angrily.

"Just came for a little visit, you know, to see my cute little woman," Eastwick said with a touch of anger in his voice.

"Get out. That's it, I'm calling and making a complaint against you," Jill said loudly.

"Shit you are," John yelled.

Billy could hear a commotion in the living room ending with the sound of something hitting the floor. He wanted to walk out and just shoot Eastwick, but that would definitely make matters worse. Looking at the light seeping through the bottom of the door he saw a shadow pass by it and raised the pistol, determined that if Eastwick opened the door it would be the last thing he ever did.

"Yes, I'd like to report a prowler," he heard Jill talking on the phone, followed by the sounds of foot steps running out of the bedroom. "Yes, it's a policeman who is the prowler. His name is John.."

There was the sound of movement in the living room followed by a noise, as if something fell on the floor again.

"Bitch, you just better watch out, or one of these days I'm going to come back for a long visit," Eastwick snarled angrily.

"You sick son-of-a-bitch, I've had it! Come back here at all, ever again, and I'm going to place harassment charges against you. I mean it. I even hear you've been in this building for something other than doing your duty, and I'm placing charges against you. It ends today. Go on, push me one more time tough guy. Let's see how you like it from the other side of the law!" she yelled angrily.

"Get out of my way," Eastwick yelled.

Billy could hear the sound of the front door slamming closed. Still watching the light under the door, he saw a shadow move in front of it and lifted his pistol again. Staring down the barrel, finger on the trigger, he was ready for whatever might happen. The door opened and light began flooding in, squinting at the bright light shining in his eyes, he could see it was Jill.

"Ahh," she yelled as she jumped out of the way. "Damn it Billy, will you put that gun away before you kill someone."

Breathing a sigh of relief, he walked out of the closet. Going over to the night stand by the bed he opened the drawer, dropped the gun in and closed it. Turning around he saw Jill in the bathroom, putting a wash cloth over here eye. Walking up to her, he pulled her hand down and could see that she had been hit in the face again. It was swelling and would undoubtedly turn black, like the one that had just healed. He could also see that her chin was red and swollen too.

"That son-of-a-bitch. Damn, I wish he would just lay down and die," Billy said angrily.

"If it's any consolation, I'm sure he will someday, but as mean as he is, it'll probably be after we're both dead. Come on, I have to get some ice for this," she said walking out of the bedroom, Billy following close behind.

Opening the freezer door, she grabbed a handful of ice cubes out of the tray and put them into the wash cloth she was holding. Folding the ends of the wash cloth over the ice, she placed it up to her face, wincing as she rested it back down against her eye. Walking back across the room she sat down on the sofa and pulled a cigarette out of a pack on the table.

"You mind, I only have one hand," she said putting the cigarette in her mouth.

Walking across the room Billy picked up a plastic cigarette lighter, flipped the end piece down with his thumb and held it out for her to light her cigarette. Satisfied that the cigarette was lit, he walked over to the counter and poured himself a straight bourbon.

"You OK, anything I can do?" he asked feeling helpless.

"Shoe's on the other foot, isn't it? Now you're trying to help me," Jill gave him a small smile. Reaching into the wash cloth she pulled out an ice cube and dropped it into his drink. "I'm OK. I've been through this before. How you feeling?"

"Mmmmm, thanks for the ice, actually, I'm feeling pretty good. I can feel the swelling on my lips has gone down and my head stopped hurting some time ago. May look like hell from the mosquito bites, but they don't hurt any more either. Overall, I'm doing pretty good." Billy stood there smiling at Jill with a little look in his eye.

"Billy, now! Are you crazy?" she said with a giggle.

"Yea, my face may be messed up but that's all," he said a large grin still on his face.

"Well, OK then, if you're sure you're all right," Jill said with a giggle as she walked over and took his hand, leading him into the bedroom.

The sun was beginning to set, the room was turning dark as Billy rolled over. Jill was naked as she walked into the bedroom carrying a tray of sandwiches and two bottles of beer.

"Want a sandwich?" she asked with a smile as she put the tray down.

"Yea, don't mind if I do," he said rolling over and crawling up to where Jill had put the tray on the bed.

Running his hands over the sandwiches, he picked pieces of bread off the top to see what was under them. Picking one up, he changed his mind, put it back, then picked up another and took a big bite. Grabbing a bottle of beer he washed the sandwich down and looked over at Jill.

"Good sandwich! Having one?" he asked sheepishly, knowing he had been acting like a glutton.

"Gee Billy, I don't know. I don't think you've examined enough of them yet," she said with a sly smile as she sat down on the bed and picked up a sandwich, taking a big bite.

"OK, OK, I'm sorry for acting like a pig, satisfied?" he asked apologetically.

"Yes, thoroughly," she said giving her head a flip.

"How's the eye?"

"Now you ask, after throwing me all over the bed," she said sexually. "Not bad, how about your infirmities?"

"I feel in great shape."

"You were a little while ago," she interrupted as she stretched out next to him on the bed.

"No, I mean it. I'm in great shape. I feel good... and I also think I should be leaving soon."

"Not a chance, you still need my help!" she said quickly.

"I told you, I don't want to get you in trouble. You could get killed hanging around with me. I'll be leaving later, by myself," he said emphatically.

"Billy," she whined. "You still need me. How are you going to get around, and what are you going to do when you pick up your package? You're still going to need some wheels to get to Salisbury. You need me Billy, like it or not, I'm going."

"You may be right," he was angry for having to put her in a dangerous position. "Look, let's just wait and see. It's a while before we leave."

After eating, Billy got up from the bed, put on his shorts and walked through the darkened living room to the sliding glass doors that lead to the balcony. Sliding the door open, he stepped onto the balcony. A humid sea breeze was blowing in his face and the night air felt warm and soft. Looking out over the ocean he could see a freighter about half a mile off shore heading towards New York. Standing in the darkness of the balcony, he wondered to himself if there could be a storage hold filled with Chinese aliens heading for New York in that ship. He heard the door slide open behind him, feeling her presence, as she walked up and pressed her naked body against his.

"What'cha thinkin' Babe?" she asked wrapping her arms around his chest.

"That boat out there, what's on it, who's on it. Where's it going, could it take me with them? Am I as royally fucked as I think I am?" he said forlornly.

"It'll be OK Billy, you'll see," she said biting playfully at his ear.

"It's a nice thought, but it won't be OK. I've been thinking, you are right. I do need your help, but that doesn't mean I have to like it."

"What do you want me to do?"

"We'll leave about three or four in the morning."

"Where we going?" she asked.

"I'll let you know later," he said as he kept staring out to sea, thinking and contemplating his future.

Fifteen minutes later he walked back into the bedroom, picked up the clock radio and set it for three a.m.

"You better get some sleep," he said to Jill who was lying on the bed. "We'll be leaving at three."

Laying down on the bed naked next to her, he fell asleep.

Chapter 10
Monday, July 19

The Rolling Stones were belting out their version of *Brown Sugar* on the radio. Billy, laying awake in the darkness, rolled over to look at the clock, watching the seconds ticking away wondering if there might only be a limited number of them left for him.

"Jill, come on. We have to get up," he said giving her a little shove with his arm.

"Yea, Yea, I'm up. I'm up. Stop pushing, what the hell time is it anyway?" Jill asked wearily as she sat up.

"Come on, we have to go," he said rolling out of bed.

Jill got up and walked into the bathroom and began washing her face. Billy walked over to the night stand and looked back at the bathroom door. Pulling open the night stand drawer he reached down, picked up the pistol and put it in his pocket. Jill came walking out a few minutes later, slipped into a pair of light brown shorts and a white knit pull over top.

"OK Billy, where we going?" she asked wearily rubbing the sleep out of her eyes.

"Seventeenth Street. Take a right towards the bay and get on Teal Drive. Also, we'll take the steps down the back and walk around to your car. I don't want us to be seen leaving by the front door." Billy walked into the kitchen and took a trash bag from the cabinet. folding it, he slipped it down the front of his pants. Coming out of the kitchen he walked towards the front door, Jill following close behind, grabbing for her keys and purse as she quickly looked around to see if she had forgotten anything.

Once out the front door, Billy looked around to make sure no one was watching. He walked over to the emergency exit door and down the steps. Jill followed close behind him, her hand nervously touching the back of his sweatshirt. When they reached the fourth floor landing he had to stop to catch his breath. Bending over, he put his hands on his knees as he tried to breath. Looking up at Jill, he found himself starring at her bruised eye. She smiled nervously, wanting to get moving again. When they got down to the ground floor, he held up his hand to slow her down and they casually walked out the door. Billy talking softly, saying nothing audible and occasionally laughing lightly as they walked out the rear entrance, acting like vacationer's heading out for a late night walk along the beach. Once outside they hurried around to the front of the building. Finding her car, they got in and drove out the front entrance, making a left onto the Coastal Highway at the light. Billy constantly looked behind them as they drove down the highway, checking to see if there were any headlights following in the distance. Five minutes later, no trace of anyone following them, they made a right at Seventeenth Street, drove back several blocks, then made another right onto Teal Drive.

"Stop the car here," Billy said curtly as he turned, checking in all directions to see if anyone else was around.

"What now?" Jill asked as she turned to him.

"You wait here, I'll be back, but it's going to be a little while. Don't leave. I'll be back. I promise. You understand?" He said gently reaching out to touch her arm.

"OK Billy. I'll wait till you get back, you know you can count on me," she said nervously, her voice cracking slightly.

"Just in case, if a lot of cops or other people start showing up at this hour of the morning take off and don't come back. Don't come looking or asking about me. If I get away with this, I'll be back for you." Billy bent across the seat and kissed her. "If I don't, just LET IT GO. Understand? Let it go." His voice turned soft.

"All right," she said a tear drop falling from her eyes.

Walking away from her car, he proceeded down the street and around the corner. There was a small space between some houses and he slipped between them, down to the bay. Looking across the waterway and up the beach several hundred yards he could see just about where his trailer had been. Walking into the warm waters of the bay, he began swimming, following the shoreline, trying to stay about one hundred feet off shore. Like the night before, he was constantly on watch for boats. Being close to the shore the chances were slim that one would be by that section of the bay, but he had to keep an eye open anyway. There was a small sliver of a moon. The night was dark but he was still able to see fairly well from the lights on the shore reflecting off the water. There was no fog yet and hopefully there would be none. As he swam up and around the point where his trailer used to be, he tried to look for it under the street lights. He could just barely see it off in the distance. The windows were broken and the door ripped off. It made him feel sad that his beloved old home that had served him so well for so long was gone. Once up and around the point, he turned and headed down the channel to where his boat was docked. As he swam he began imagining all the creatures of the water that were swimming with him and it made him a little nervous as he wondered if one might be stalking him as he used to stalk them. He felt a stinging feeling on his hands and realized he was touching a jelly fish. Cursing at himself, he shook his hand under the water as he kept on swimming.

Reaching his boat, he pulled himself around to the dock and stopped, searching the night to see if anyone might be around. Carefully he put his hands up on the dock and tried as quietly as possible to pull himself up onto the top of the dock. Once there, he looked around as he got up and walked the few steps to his boat. Climbing onto his boat, he reached under the aluminum seat and put his hand on the envelopes. He gave a sigh of relief to find that they were still there. As he was running his hands across the envelopes, about to pull them down, he saw the dock in front of him move slightly. Hesitating for a second he thought he heard the creak of one of the wooden planks behind him. Reaching up, he pulled down the protective envelope, stood up and turned around. Behind him on the dock he could easily make out the figure in the dark it was John Eastwick.

"Billy Boy, I am feeling stupid. I should have checked here. I can't believe I didn't," Eastwick said pleasantly.

"I can John, a stupid fucking moron like you. That's why I hid it here. I knew you would be too stupid to look here." Billy's voice equally pleasant.

"Billy boy, I am going to take so much pleasure from what I'm going to do to you. You cannot believe how much fun I'm going to have with you. St. John wants you back, but shit. What could I do? You resisted," Eastwick said, his voice not as pleasant as it had been.

"I don't think so, John. Fun with me? Haven't you heard by now? John, I'm not a flaming faggot like your are," Billy said as he put his hand in his pocket.

"Get out of the fucking boat, Lee!" Eastwick ordered.

"Gee John, I don't think so. I really kind of like it where I am. Think I'll just hang around here for a while."

"That was a direct order from a police officer. Get out of the boat," Eastwick ordered again.

"No, it was a direct order from an asshole. What are you going to do? Pull your gun and blast away at me? It's gonna be kind of difficult explaining why you were down here at this time of the morning, killing me. St. John won't like it either, and you know that. So, go ahead, show some initiative, shoot me. I'm a dead man anyway, right? Go on, do it now asshole. You're hesitating. Hey, I must have hit a nerve. Oh that's right you're just St. John's little flunky, aren't you? Can't do anything St. John does not approve, can you, Johnny boy?"

"I told you to get out of that boat, and I mean it, Mister," Eastwick said angrily walking down the dock toward Billy.

"Bite me, dick head," Billy watched Eastwick come up beside the boat.

Eastwick reached into the boat and grabbed Billy by the shoulders, one hand squeezing hard on each shoulder. Billy felt him begin to pull him towards him and dropped the envelope as he reached out and grabbed Eastwick by his shirt, just below his chin. Eastwick let go of Billy's right shoulder and reached for the hand that was pulling on his shirt. As Eastwick's hand grabbed Billy's, Billy put his foot up on the dock, braced himself and pulled back.

"Uoah," was all he could mutter as Billy pulled Eastwick's body towards him into the boat.

Falling back, Billy continued pulling Eastwick to him with all the strength he had. Eastwick was stepping into the boat trying to maintain his balance to keep from falling over. As Billy continued to fall over the edge of the boat backward into the bay, Eastwick had no way of regaining his balance and followed him into the water. As he felt his back hit the water with a large splash, Billy pulled the pistol from his pocket. Releasing his hand from his grasp of Eastwick's shirt he reached his arm up and wrapped it back around Eastwick's head. Eastwick, who had been trying to prevent himself from falling into the water, had no idea of what was happening as he felt Billy's arm coiling up and around his neck. By the time he realized what Billy was doing, it was too late and his body was over the edge of the boat, on top of Billy's when he hit the water.

Billy could feel their bodies sinking deep into the water as he pulled his body up close against Eastwick's, their heads next to each other. Placing the barrel of the pistol against Eastwick's stomach, he started pulling the trigger. Under the water the popping sounds the pistol made were barely audible. Billy did hear the muffled sounds of Eastwick's screams. Holding on tight, Billy kept pulling the trigger. The gun was empty, but he couldn't stop himself. Feeling Eastwick's body go limp in his arms, he realized he needed air. Disoriented in the darkness of the water he began kicking his feet, hoping he was heading to the surface. He felt the side of his head run into something hard and realized he had been swimming down towards the bottom of the bay, turning his body around he pushed off the bottom up towards the surface, brushing against Eastwick as he flew by. Billy broke the surface of the water gasping for air. Seeing his boat just inches away, he grabbed the side of it and pulled himself up against the rail, breathing hard, forcing oxygen into his lungs. He felt something brush up against his legs and a few seconds later Eastwick's body broke the surface of the water. Still gasping for air, Billy reached out in the darkness grabbing Eastwick's lifeless body and pulled it over to the side of the boat.

Holding onto the side of the boat he rested for several minutes until his breathing returned to normal. Letting go of Eastwick's body, he pulled himself up on the rail of the boat, reached in and grabbed his mushroom anchor. Easing himself back into the water he stretched out his arm and grabbed hold of Eastwick's shirt, pulling him back over to the boat. Carefully Billy began wrapping the anchor rope around the body until it was tight from his shoulders too his feet. Letting go of the boat, he wrapped his arms around Eastwick's waist, placing his hands together, he squeezed them hard listening as the bubbles of air came up to the surface as they excited his lungs. Treading water, Billy turned the body around and tied the heavy anchor to Eastwick's belt. Guiding the body as it began to sink under the weight of the anchor, Billy pushed it under the dock next to the retaining wall and it sank the eight feet to the bottom of the channel. Taking hold of the rail of his boat again, he waited, thinking about what he should do next as he caught his breath. At best he figured he had three days until the gases from the decomposing body would make it buoyant again, bringing Eastwick to the surface. Reaching into the waist of his pants, Billy pulled out the plastic trash bag and placed the envelope that was laying on the bottom of the boat into the bag, tucking it back into his pants. Before leaving he reached under the seat to make sure the other envelope was safe, then pushed himself back into the water and began swimming back toward Jill's car.

The return trip was pure drudgery. He was tired and weak from his fight with Eastwick. Coming around the point and heading back to the place he had first entered the water, he swam through a section of dead fish that had gathered into a floating scum patch. The smell was horrible and some of the water got in his mouth as he swam through, leaving a foul taste that almost made him throw up. His energy depleted, he tried to touch bottom for a rest about one hundred yards from shore. His feet could not touch the bottom and his head went under. Taking in a mouth full of water, he began choking, kicking trying to stay afloat and breathe. Just as he thought he was going to go under again, he felt his toes barely brushing against the sand on the bottom of the bay. Pushing off with his feet, he bounced up and down on the soft bottom, just enough to keep his head above water and allow him to breathe as he attempted to propel himself forward towards the shore. Half an hour later he managed to drag himself up on the shore, rolling over on his back, panting and gasping for breath. Finally when he had enough strength to get up, he stood and began staggering down the street like a drunken man. Jill saw him when he walked by the light of a house. Starting the car, she pulled up beside him. Exhausted, he braced himself against the car for a second as Jill got out and ran around to help him.

"Hurry, we've got to get out of here," he told her, exhausted, barely able to speak.

Grabbing him under his arm, Jill guided him to the door and seated him in the passengers side. Billy managed to drag his feet in and close the door as Jill ran around to the driver's side. Throwing the car in reverse she backed up, leaving a patch of rubber, as she sped into a drive way, then throwing the car in gear, she pulled away into the night. Once they were on the Coastal Highway, heading back towards Jill's condo, he checked out of the rear window to see if there might be anyone following them.

"Did it go all right, Billy? Did you get it?" she asked anxiously, sounding nervous.

"Yea, I got it but it did not go all right. Eastwick was back there. I just barely got away from him. He was chasing me out around the point as I was swimming away. A few minutes later and he might have caught me. Either way, he knows I got the envelope and will really be looking for me now. I don't think it's safe, my staying with you. I should take off on my own, right now," he said as he looking out the rear of the car again.

"No way Billy, we're in this till the end. Let's go back to my place. We'll be safe there. John will know you've been hiding some place else. There's no way he'll come back looking for you. You are safe with me, stay at my place, all right. I'll drive you to Salisbury tomorrow," she said emphatically.

"I think you may be right," he sighed as he slumped back in the seat and turned his head, staring at her with a blank expression on his face.

Pulling back into the Golden Sands parking lot, Jill managed to get the same parking space she had before. Getting out of the car, they walked around to the rear of the building, slipped in the back door and up the emergency stairs. Exhausted from the trip, he had a great deal of trouble making it up the steps. They had to stop several times and she had to help him up the last flight of stairs. Once in the apartment they walked over and sat on the sofa, not sure of just what to do next. Billy reached down and pulled the plastic bag from his waist, then pulled the envelope out of the bag, throwing it on the coffee table.

"That's what it's all about," he said kicking the envelope across the table with his foot.

"So, everything's in there, right Billy?" Jill questioned.

"Yep, that's all of it, and there ain't no more," he said with a sigh.

"Well at least it's safe for now," she smiled.

"Wow, what a night," he said wistfully. "But then on the other hand, I've been saying that every night for a week. Christ will it ever settle down, and if it does, will I be alive to enjoy it?"

"Don't worry Billy. I think things are looking up for us now. Listen, why don't you go in and take a shower. I'll make us some drinks and we can try and unwind a little."

"Damn, that sounds great," he said barely able to move.

"Come on Billy, get up," Jill pulled him to his feet. "Shower's in that direction, remember? I'll make us some stiff drinks."

Billy walked off to the bathroom as Jill headed for the kitchen. Taking off his sweat shirt, he waited for a minute then walked back to the kitchen. As he walked around the corner he saw Jill pouring something into one of the glasses from a small brown and green vial. She jumped at seeing him and turned smiling.

"Wow, that was a quick shower, Babe," she said nervously.

"I, ahh, just wanted to throw these... in the, ahh, washer. Drinks, great. I'll have mine before I take a shower," he said stammering but with an uncertain smile of his face.

"Here, Billy," she said as she handed him the glass she had poured the liquid in.

"Ahh, on second thought, I think I'll wait until after I take a shower," he said putting down the glass.

"No come on, cheers, let's toast to a successful evening," she said holding her glass in the air.

"What's that little thing you've got in your hand there Jill?" he asked with an edge to his voice.

"Oh that," she shrugged. "It was just a little liqueur I added to our drinks. It's really great, I have it all the time with mine."

"Oh great, let's see it, what is it?"

"It's creme do cacao," she said holding up the little brown and green bottle. Smiling nervously, she threw it in the trash. "It's great. Taste it. Go on. One drink and you'll be hooked on it like I am."

Walking over to the trash can he reached down and picked up the vial as Jill was fidgeting nervously.

"Hey this is really good shit," he said with a smile. "St. John gave me some the day before yesterday. Yea, it's great shit. Knock's you right on your ass. Jill, It's a horse tranquilizer. Gee whiz, how did you get it, Jill?" he questioned with a smile.

"Billy, why are you acting like this? I don't know what you are talking about, I don't think I like the way you're acting! That's not what I put in your drink. John must have left it here when he came by this afternoon!" she said cautiously, her voice sounding a little fearful.

Walking over to the coffee table, Billy picked up the envelope and walked back into the kitchen. Ripping the top off, he turned the envelope upside down and the contents fell onto the floor. Bending down, he picked up one of the pieces and stood up in front of Jill.

"Hey, look. We're in luck, we can get ten free CD's if we send this in right away. usually it's only eight. Drink my drink Jill," he said calmly holding out his glass.

"I've got a drink, Billy, you're scaring me." she said nervously.

"No, don't drink your drink, here, I want you to drink mine," he said softly.

"Please Billy, I don't want..."

"Drink this one!" he interrupted as he knocked Jill's glass out of her hand and onto the floor where it smashed to pieces.

"Great, now look at the mess I have to clean up!" she said with a touch of anger in her voice, trying to change the subject.

"Fine, clean it up, but after you drink this drink. Here drink it. All of it!" Billy commanded.

Jill struck out with her hand in an attempt to knock the glass out of Billy's hand, but he was too quick for her and moved his hand just in time. Catching her arm with his other hand he pulled her close to him.

"DRINK IT!" he commanded.

"ALL RIGHT!" she yelled. "Is that what you want?"

"Yea, that's what I want. Drink it," he said calmly.

"You really want me to drink it?" she asked again.

"Yea, I've said that several times now, Jesus Christ, Jill, quit asking me if I want you to drink it. I WANT YOU TO DRINK IT!"

"NO!" she yelled as she attempted to walk out of the kitchen.

Placing the glass on the counter, he grabbed her by the arm and gave her a hard shove that sent her flying across the living room, onto the sofa. Looking up at him with fear in her eyes, she quickly reached for the phone on the end table next to the sofa. Billy was on her a second later, grabbing the phone from her hands and taking it away, pulling it out from where it was connected to the wall.

"You betrayed me. How could you do that? To me?" he asked softly as he looked down at her.

"You wouldn't understand, I didn't want to," she said quietly.

"It was all a set up and a lie. Everything from when you first called me till now?" he said softly again.

Nodding her head yes, he could see tears forming in her eyes.

"Tears? I can't believe it. I should be the one crying. I fell back in love with you again," he said angrily.

"You don't understand, Billy," she said softly, her body beginning to rock back and forth.

"The beatings you took, it was all part of it too, the...."

"You do not understand," she interrupted.

"NO! YOU'RE GOD DAMN RIGHT I DO NOT UNDERSTAND. ENLIGHTEN ME!" he screamed as he walked over and grabbed her. Picking her up off the sofa, he just as quickly threw her back down again.

"It was the money," she said in a whisper as she looked him in the eye with no expression on her face.

"MONEY?" he yelled. "It wasn't for love, or hate, or country, a belief. Just money, the God damn money. They were going to kill me and all my life meant to you was dollar signs. My God, how could I have been in love with someone like you? Hell, how could I have fallen back in love with you? Christ, you and that ahole Eastwick make a good combination. Look at it this way Jill, you slept with me for the money, that makes you nothing more than a common whore," he said with disgust as he let his tired body fall onto the sofa.

"Billy, I didn't say I liked it. I had no choice. John and I are wrapped up in this too tight to get out. I've wanted to get out for a long time and so has John, but he can't. He's afraid of St. John and doesn't want to cross him," Jill said as she moved over on the sofa to sit next to Billy.

"No, no way. I don't want you anywhere near me. Get up. Go sit over there," Billy said, pointing to another chair with one hand while pushing her off the sofa with the other. "All right then, you tell me, what the hell is all of this about? What is St. John doing?"

"I don't know, John won't tell me. He always said it was better if I didn't know. The way he said it, I knew he was serious so I never asked," Jill said quietly biting at her finger nails.

"So you just took the money. Not caring or wondering where it came from or how much blood was on it?"

"It was a lot of money," she said dryly.

"How much money?"

"Over $400,000 last year. Looks like it will be more than that this year, may be $500,000."

"Wheeeeeee," Billy whistled. "That is a lot of money. So what was you're part in this whole little deal. I want to know it all."

"Dr. St. John called me," Jill said with no emotion, just speaking the words as she looked out the window at the ocean. "He knew we had been married. John told him about it. Anyway, Will said he wanted me to contact you and set up a meeting about writing a story about my shop. He told me to use my 'feminine wiles' to 'woo' you back to me. I was supposed to keep you busy so that you would stop investigating them. St. John was really worried about what you might find out. John grabbed all his stuff and moved to a hotel. I know you won't believe this but, you can't imagine how great it was to see you again. John really isn't the nicest guy around and we've really had our ups and downs. Making love to him was sexy and dangerous. Making love to you was warm and fulfilling."

"Cut the crap Jill," he interrupted sarcastically. "I'm not buying that line any more. Just tell the story without embellishing on it."

"I am. I just wanted you to know, I had feelings for you. It wasn't as cold as you made it sound..."

"Excuse me," he interrupted holding up his hand. "This was all a set up to eventually kill me dead and you know that, so let's just cut back on the feelings bit AND GET ON WITH THE STORY!"

"When they caught you breaking into the building they were going to kill you. You mentioned something about a company and it really spooked Dr. St. John, so they let you escape. They were sure you'd come back here and lead them to the papers or whatever it was they were looking for."

"They let me escape?" he exclaimed.

"Yea, they were pulling your strings the whole time and you didn't even know it. Dr. St. John predicted exactly what you would do from the first time you met him and you did it, except the part about living in the cornfield. That really threw them for a loop. They thought you'd come straight here and when you didn't, it really scared them. They went nuts. I kind of enjoyed it. Seeing them running around not knowing what was happening. They were terrified that you had gone to the State Police and turned yourself in. But, then you showed up here and it was just a matter of time. Billy, there's nothing you can do. John and the others will be here soon. They know where you are. I called John from the car on my cell phone after you left last night to go wherever it was you went. He was supposed to get you when you came ashore. He knew you were heading back to your trailer."

"You're right," Billy said with a smile. "I'll bet my life on it, so to speak, that they are probably still waiting for a call from you, to let them know the package is here and that it's the right one. You are supposed to call them aren't you?"

"Yes, they will wait for a call, but if it doesn't come soon they'll just come up," Jill said, still speaking in a monotone.

"One last question, how many of them are there? I know of the three doctors and Eastwick and Dave Johnson. Is there anyone else?" he questioned.

"I have no idea. Like I said John kept me out of it. I only did what I was told."

"You would have made a very beautiful Nazi, 'I vas jest following orders.' Hey Jill, it just doesn't cut it, but then I guess I'm going to have to live with the feeling of having made love to you this past week. It really, really, really makes my skin crawl. Gee I wonder why?" Billy said sarcastically as he stood up and walked into the kitchen.

Coming back into the living room, he had the glass with the tranquilizer in it.

"OK, sweetheart, time to take a big drink," he said as he sat down next to her.

"Billy, please," she turned to him.

"Sorry sugar. I need just a little time and this is going to buy it for me. Let's face it, do you really think I would trust you to let me walk out of here and not call them for several hours, while I escaped? I think not," he said sarcastically again as he shook his head. "You really don't have much choice. You can drink this or I'll have to beat you up and knock you out. Frankly, I would prefer the second, but I'm tired and don't think I have that much time. So drink it, really, it's good shit, you'll like it," he said with a smile.

"Billy, I..."

"Jill," he interrupted. "Unlike you. I wouldn't do anything to hurt you. I know you can't understand it because it has to deal with feelings and compassion. Something you're completely devoid of, but I really still have some feelings for you as an individual and former wife and lover of mine. This won't hurt you. It's just a strong sedative. You'll be up and around with no side effects in a few hours. Drink it!"

Closing her eyes, she put the glass to her lips and began drinking as a few tears dropped down out of the corner of her eyes. After drinking half the glass she started to put it back down on the table.

"Uh, Uh, Uh," Billy said gesturing with his hand telling her to pick up the glass and drink the rest of it.

Giving him a cold look Jill put the glass back to her lips and drained the rest of the liquid.

"Satisfied," she said coldly, not looking at him.

"Why, yes I am. Thank you very much." he smiled as he got up and went into the kitchen.

Pulling open the drawer by the sink where she had mixed the drinks, he reached in, searching with his hands and pulled out three more vials of the sedative. Opening them he poured their contents into the sink and washed them away with water. When he went back into the living room he could see Jill, slumped slightly over to one side on the sofa as he took the pistol from his pants pocket and placed it on the coffee table.

"Great shit, isn't it?" he said sarcastically, with a large smile on his face.

Moving her head slightly, she looked up into Billy's eyes and smiled.

"You know, I'm going to miss you, Babe," she said with a smile. "Wow, this is good shit. I feel great, but I can barely move."

"Yea, that was one of the things I thought was a draw back to it too, but, what the hell you just can't get any great animal tranquilizers like the olds days I guess," Billy shrugged as he reached down and picked her up off the sofa. Dragging her to the center of the living room, he laid her down on her right side.

Walking back into the kitchen he picked the tranquilizer vial out of the trash can and the other ones he had emptied off the counter. Grabbing a tea towel as he walked out of the kitchen, he wiped his finger prints off the bottles. Holding the vials one at a time in the towel, he rolled each one around Jill's finger tips and placed them on the floor about a foot away from her hand. Reaching up to the coffee table he picked up the pistol and wiped his finger prints off of that too. Holding the pistol barrel with the towel, he placed the gun in Jill's hand, manipulating it with her fingers, cocking and shooting it several times. He then placed it a few feet from the vials. Standing up he looked down at the scene he had just created.

"I wish I had some blood, Jill. Damn, it's tough for an artist to do great work without the proper tools. Oh well, I guess it will just have to do. Jill let me tell you, it has been a slice and don't take this too personally but I hope I never see you again." he said with a smile as he walked to the kitchen counter, picked up her car keys, then headed for the door. Going out the front door, he closed it, but not all the way, leaving just about an inch of open space. Taking a quick look around the hallway, he turned and slipped down the emergency steps once again. Coming out of the emergency exit on the first floor, he walked over to the courtesy phone by the rear entrance doors and picked it up.

"Yes, may I help you," the cheerful voice of a woman from the front office came through the receiver of the phone.

"Ahhhh, listen, Ahhh. I don't know how to say this, but last night about four in the morning my wife and I went out for a late night walk on the beach. We were walking by a partially opened door. It was room 1108, you know on the eleventh floor. Anyway, I heard a man and woman inside yelling at each other and then I'm sure I heard a pistol firing several times. I used to be in the army and I know what a pistol shot sounds like. It was a small caliber pistol. It definitely was not coming from a movie on TV or anything like that, it sounded too real. I probably should have called earlier but, damn it, I really do not want to get involved, but then I started thinking, well maybe someone could be up there bleeding and dying and I can't live with that either. Listen, I'm sorry, but I think you ought to send someone up to check it out if you can,"

Billy hung up the phone before the young woman had a chance to ask for his name.

Walking out the back of the building, he stopped suddenly. Looking out at the ocean he could see that the sun was just beginning to rise and he lost track of everything as he was caught up in the beauty of it. As he continued walking around the building it made him sad to think that there was not enough time in life to enjoy the beautiful sunrises.

Seeing no one around, he got into Jill's car, pulled out of the parking lot and then across the street to the little strip shopping center that faced the condominium complex. There was a small convenience store at the end of the center and a number of people were coming and going at this early hour of the morning. Driving down to the store, he pulled the car into a space next to another car that gave him a good view of the entrance to the condominium. Several minutes later he saw a police car pull into the parking lot and up to the front doors of the condominium. Before the officer had time to get out of his car, Billy heard a siren and turned to see an ambulance coming up the street, followed by a second police car. They both pulled into the parking lot and up to the front doors. The policemen went in ahead of the emergency medical technicians while they pulled a stretcher out of the rear of the ambulance and followed behind them. Watching them all go into the building, Billy was relieved to see that Dave Johnson was not one of the responding officers. Ten minutes later the emergency medical technicians wheeled out Jill on the stretcher and put her in the back of the ambulance, then took off, sirens screaming into the early morning sunshine.

Pulling south onto the highway, he could see another police car pull up and drive into the Golden Sands. Billy smiled to himself, then began to laugh. Driving down the highway, he made a right turn onto Robin Drive and drove up the road to where his boat was docked. It was just before six in the morning and as he got out of the car and surveyed the area. He could see that no one was out moving around yet. Looking off to his left across the vacant lot and over one street he could see what was left of his trailer. When he swam close to the shore last night, he thought he could see that the door had been knocked off and the windows broken out. In the morning light it looked worse than he had imagined. The shell of the trailer was now a dull black from the smoke and flames. What little possessions he had were now laying in a pile next to the trailer, those that were not burned, broken and smashed. His Jeep had been parked next to the trailer and also was nothing more than a charred frame, its wheels burned and melted. He had no idea if the fire from the trailer burned the Jeep or if Eastwick had done it. Surrounding the whole area was a yellow crime scene ribbon, placed there by the police department, that was twisting and fluttering in the light breezes that were blowing in off the bay.

Turning he could see that a few of the boats usually docked near him were gone and that he was completely alone as he walked down to his boat slip. Climbing into the boat, he took the housing off the engine. Something his neighbors had seen him do hundreds of times. The bow of the boat was facing the dock, moving forward, he picked up a small coil of one quarter inch plastic rope laying in the bottom of the boat. Unraveling about ten feet, he tied it to the bow with a slip knot and let it hang down into the water. Climbing out of the boat and onto the dock, he took off his sweat shirt, then looking around to see if there might be anyone watching, got down on his knees and eased into the water.

The water felt cold as he slipped below the surface and swam down by the retaining wall. Once you go below two feet, the water in the bay loses its clarity and it becomes very difficult to see anything. Knowing that Eastwick was sitting about eight feet below the surface, he began feeling around with his hands trying to locate the body. Coming out of the darkness his face bumped up against Eastwick's head. It scared him, making him scream and pull back. The momentary shock wore off and Billy reached out again, grabbing Eastwick's shirt and pushing up off the bottom, trying to bring the body to the surface. As his head came up out of the water Billy made a grab for the dock and missed. Taking a quick breath of air he disappeared again as the weight of Eastwick's body pulled him back down to the bottom. Reaching out and feeling around Eastwick's waist, he found where he had tied the anchor to his belt and undid the belt. The anchor dropped to the bottom of the bay. Pushing off one more time, he could feel that Eastwick's body was buoyant with the water and managed to keep it afloat once he reached the surface.

Treading water Billy kept kicking his feet until he moved the body around to the bow of the boat. Grabbing the back of Eastwick's shirt with one hand and pulling it up to the boat, he was able to hold onto the boat and body at the same time. Taking the new piece of plastic rope he had tied to the bow, he looped it around Eastwick's body and under his arms, tying it behind his back. Swimming around to the dock, he got up on the dock and climbed back into his boat, fastening the housing back on his motor. Undoing the bow and stern lines, Billy pushed the boat back away from the slip and turned the engine over. Coughing for a second, belching its usual puff of smoke, the engine kicked in and began to chug. Billy put it in gear, heading the boat up the channel very slowly, dragging Eastwick's body under the bottom of the boat.

When he got to the end of the channel, Billy made a very slow, wide turn to his right. He was making sure that Eastwick's body would not come rolling out from under the boat. Motoring north, he went up and under the 90th Street bridge, pulling to within five feet of a barren section of a park around 125th Street. As he had hoped there was no one around at this hour of the morning. He knew he was pressed for time, that in a little while people in jet skis, sail boards and boats would be out exploring all parts of the bay. Making his way to the bow of the boat he pulled at the slip knot. It came undone letting Eastwick's body float freely in the waters of the bay.

Placing the engine in reverse he backed up, careful not to run over Eastwick's remains. The body was floating just barely above the surface. Turning the boat around, he slowly motored away. When he had gone about twenty yards, the engine died. He was left floating helplessly on the bay. Billy quickly removed the housing from the engine. Pulling frantically at the fuel lines, he yanked them off, blowing air through them to clean out any dirt. He could see a jet skier about a hundred yard out in the bay going around in circles and jumping his own wake. Billy worked quickly to hook the fuel lines back together. Grabbing the housing, he placed it back on his engine and fastened it.

He tried to start the engine. It turned over twice without catching and died. Looking over to his right, the jet skier came over closer to him. Trying the engine one more time, it caught and belched its puff of white smoke then began running smoothly. Quickly he pulled away and motored down the bay as the jet skier turned and headed back towards the other side of the bay. Once back in the channel, Billy motored down to his slip, carefully looking to see if anyone was around. He saw a few people walking near their houses and some others doing yard work, but they paid no attention to him as he motored by. Pulling into the slip, he tied the bow and stern lines and was about to get out of the boat when he felt a wave of nausea come over him. Leaning over the side, he emptied the contents of his stomach into the bay and sat back up in the boat feeling weak and tired. Sitting there for a few minutes, he slowly began to regain his strength, but his stomach still felt ill. Reaching under the seat, he pulled the notarized envelope out and standing up on shaky legs, stepped onto the dock. Not wanting to be seen by any neighbors, he walked briskly to Jill's car, climbed in the front seat and closed the door.

"Billy, it's so nice to see you again, we've just got to stop meeting like this!" a voice said jokingly from the back seat.

"Ahh!" Billy shouted jumping at the sound. Dr. St. John leaned forward in the seat with a large smile on his face, pointing a gun at Billy's head.

A car pulled up beside him. Billy turned his head to see Dave Johnson in a patrol car. There was another man in the car with him, but he didn't recognize him.

"Billy, be a good sport, would you please? Slide over to the passengers side. I think Dr. Jackanock wants to drive from here on," St. John said reaching into the front seat and picking up the envelope. "Just think, all that trouble and just for this one little envelope. It doesn't even weigh that much," St. John said bouncing the envelope up and down in his hand as if trying to judge its weight.

Billy slowly slid across the seat as he watched Dr. Jackanock get out of the patrol car, walk around and get into the driver's side of Jill's car. Once in, Jackanock gave a menacing glare at Billy for having caused so much trouble.

"Put your seat belt on Billy, after all, we do want you to be safe," St. John said still smiling. "Gee Billy, you don't seem to have much to say. Cat got your tongue?"

As Billy was buckling his seat belt he looked up to see St. John opening the envelope. Billy thought about jumping out the door, taking his chances on the street, when he felt a sharp pain in his left arm. Dr. Jackanock had stabbed him with a large hypodermic needle. The Doctor's thumb was squeezing down on the plunger forcing the contents of the syringe into Billy's arm. Pulling his arm away the needle bent and was pulled out ripping open Billy's skin leaving a large bleeding gash.

"Son-of-a-bitch," Billy yelled in pain as he swung the back of his hand at Dr. Jackanock, striking him in the jaw but doing no damage. Dr. Jackanock's head moved slightly and he frowned at Billy raising his fist to strike him back.

"Now, now, Jock," St. John said as he was reading the papers in the back seat. "It is to be expected, let's not venture into unwanted violence at this stage of the game. Let's just start the car and head back to the factory. After all, it would be nice if we got there before the employees began arriving, and where the hell is Eastwick anyway? He should have been here taking care of this situation, not us! Since his wife started having that affair with Billy, he's become too unreliable. Billy, you should know, is she really that fantastic, that she can have this affect on men, leading them to distraction and dereliction of duty?"

"At one time, I thought so," Billy said softly, almost in a whisper.

He was beginning to feel weak from the shot in his arm and sat back in the seat resting his head against the head rest. Staring out the window, he watched as a small group of vacationers just a few yards away were preparing to cross the highway. They were loaded down with towels, coolers and lawn chairs, making a very early trip to the beach, eager to get their daily dose of sunburn.

"Wow, Billy, you really have given us a run for our money," St. John said lowering the papers. "But damn it Billy, you were right, you had nothing on us that we could not have explained away. I'm really sorry that we are going to have to kill you for just this, but after all, that is life, isn't it? Jock, be careful, slow down, we don't want to get a ticket, do we Billy Bob? Could create a whole new set of problems. By the way, how are you feeling? That's a new synthetic horse tranquilizer we're using now. Much more potent than that stuff we used the other day. Just picked it up yesterday. It's made by a company in Connecticut, they used to break down perfume formulas and make those fabulous fake perfumes. Sold them at half price in department stores, made millions. They figured they could use their technology from making perfume to get into pharmaceuticals, and what do you know they did it! Stocks soaring sky high, they're going to make millions, I bought a bunch of the stock. I'd advise you to buy some stock in the company too, but Billy, I don't think you're going to be around long enough to see it make any big profits. Oh well, just a thought," St. John said lightly as he sat back in the seat continuing to read.

Billy felt himself beginning to nod off. He wasn't asleep but he wasn't awake either. Feeling his head moving around as the car moved in and out of traffic, he tried to wake himself up but was unable to. The car came to a stop and the doors opened. He had the feeling of floating and a breeze blowing in his face. He managed to barely open his eyes once and thought he could see a cornfield off in the distance. Although he was making no movements on his own, he could feel his body begin to lay down on a bed and it felt like straps were being placed over his arms and chest. He felt another small prick in his arm and as he laid there he could ever so slowly feel himself coming back to life. Slowly his eye lids began to open. His hands were free but not his arms or legs. Opening his eyes, he blinked several times as if awaking from a dream. Looking up, he saw an IV with two bags of liquid draining into a tube that ran into his arm. Lifting his head slightly, he could see that he was strapped into a bed, the same one he had been in several days earlier. He was in the research section of Dr. St. John's Pet Food Company. To his right there were only six Asians left in the beds. Like him, they all had IV's running to their arms, but they were not strapped down like he was. Feeling much stronger now he tried to sit up and break free but couldn't.

"Whoa, Billy, hold on," St. John said from behind him. "Take it easy, you'll only hurt yourself and I don't want that to happen."

St. John walked up by Billy's bed and leaned over, looking into his eyes, then walked over and looked at the IV, adjusting the drip. Almost immediately Billy began to feel a little weaker but his mind was still sharp.

"There, that ought to take a little of the spirit out of you," Dr. St. John said as he sat down on the bed across from Billy.

"What are you going to do with me?" Billy stammered.

"Gee, Billy, I think you know the answer to that one," St. John said folding his arms and crossing his legs. "If you take a look around you will see that all of the other people here are connected to IV's just like you. The only difference being, they are receiving much larger doses of drugs than you are. I am, of course, going to increase your dosage in just a few minutes and you will fall into a coma-like state in just a mere second or two. But before that I wanted to have this little chat first."

"You mean, I'm finally going to find out just what the hell's been going on?" Billy managed to get out, the drug making it difficult to talk.

"Yes you are, Billy," St. John said proudly as he leaned forward and smiled at Billy.

Billy tried to speak but couldn't. He could see St. John get up and adjust the drip into his IV and almost immediately felt better.

"Strong stuff," said Billy.

"Yea, it's really great. Made by that same company in Connecticut I was telling you about earlier, we're paying less than half what we paid for the same item from any other company. Those guys are really great!"

"Quit the good doctor routine, just tell me what you want to tell me and get the hell out of here," Billy said angrily.

"Where to begin. This story is just so great, but I haven't been able to tell it to anyone. After all, if I did, I'd have to get rid of them, like I am unfortunately going to have to get rid of you Billy. Sorry, didn't mean to digress, let me get back to the story. Anyway, it is really great being able to tell this story. Let's face it, Billy you're a smart guy, you will be able to understand it and get the full grasp and appreciation of what we are doing here," St. John said becoming very animated with his hands as he uncrossed his legs and put his hands on his knees.

"Please get to the point, St. John!" Billy blurted out, the drugs making it difficult to speak.

"Now, now, Billy let's not get testy. Well, you know most of the beginning of the story. Let me put the rest of the pieces in place. There I was, out of work, my two partners in prison. Sure I had money to live on, but not the big money I was used to, the money that makes life worth living. Most of the money was hidden in a bank account in the Bahamas, but I was unable to use it. Those damn prosecutors just kept trying to make me give it up. Hell, Billy, I earned it and I was going to be damned if I was going to give it back to them. So, there I was, out of work for a long time. Let's face it there are not a lot of jobs out there for doctors that have been thrown out of the medical profession for fraud. So I was on this, shall we say, extended vacation, until I could get my money. One afternoon I was watching this old movie on TV called *COMA*, staring Michael Douglas, and what's her name, Geniveve Bujo something or other. You know, that cute woman with that French name no one can pronounce, it doesn't really matter to the story anyway."

"Oh my God," Billy said in a terrified voice squirming in his restraints.

"Oh, I see you have seen the movie too. Well, as you know they were keeping people in a suspended state until their body parts were needed, then they would harvest them."

"You sick son-of-a-bitch, you can't do that. It's against the law," Billy yelled out in terror from his bed.

"You know Billy, you are absolutely right, it is. Selling body parts is definitely against the law and if you are caught, there are some very heavy penalties to pay, but let's face it, we kind of worked our way around it." St. John said sounding proud of his accomplishments.

"Let's for the sake of argument, assume you are married and your wife becomes ill and needs a heart or say a liver transplant. You are a very rich man and she is rapidly running out of time, very close to dying. Being an intelligent man, you would check all the alternatives. You would find out that there are approximately 35,000 people right now, today, in the United States, waiting for organs; hearts, lungs, livers, kidneys. Anyway, this year there will be only 5,000 donors. Doesn't take a lot of arithmetic to figure out that there is one hell of a big shortage of body parts out there. Of that 35,000 about 4,500 of them will die without the transplants they need this year, over ten people every day. That's a lot of dead people, but here you are, a wealthy man who loves his wife and will do anything to help her, money is no object to a man who loves his wife and wants her to live. Her tissues are typed and sitting in data banks waiting for a match. One such data bank is HelpMed in New York City. That's right Billy, the company I bought a few years ago. It's really a small little company, just a couple of rooms, a computer and some phones. So there we are, we have your wife's tissue information and there's no match, but wait, we finally manage to come up with a match from another source. One of our representatives contacts you and tells you about HelpMed's branch office in Zurich and that they have a tissue match on a heart. Your problems have been solved. Your wife will live, except for one little thing, we can't legally bring it into this country, and the relatives of the person who own the heart want $750,000 for it. It's you last chance, you know it is illegal, but you want your wife to live, so what do you do? Naturally, you agree. Money is wired to our bank in Zurich and miraculously the hospital is informed by HelpMed in New York that they have found a tissue match and will have the heart shipped out immediately. It is placed on a plane at Kennedy Airport and flown to the waiting hospital. Then cut, cut and stitch, stitch she has a new heart. With luck you and your wife will go on and have a happy life together, living out the rest of your days, however many of them there are, in love. Kind of brings a tear to your, eye doesn't it, Billy?"

"You are a sick son-of-a-bitch," Billy said hopelessly, tears welling up in his eyes.

"There, you see Billy. You were touched by the story also. It's so great being able to donate such things to society," St. John said with a smile.

"So that's what the Asians are for, body parts?" Billy asked half heartedly, knowing the answer.

"That's right and you too, Billy. We made a tissue match on you from some samples we took when we had you in here last time and within the next week your body parts will fly all over the country helping out seriously ill people. It should make you feel good, you'll be living after you die. Think of it as life after death. Isn't it great?"

"Go to hell!" Billy tried to shout but could only get the words out as a loud whisper.

"Billy, bad attitude!" St. John scolded him. "So let me continue. Dr. Jackanock is a pilot and we set it up so that all the parts are shipped at once. He flies the company plane to New York where the body parts are loaded onto their appropriate planes and shipped off in a timely manner to their destinations to be replanted. The real problem was getting the donors. Let's face it, people aren't real happy about donating their body parts before their time. The body must also be alive when the parts are harvested. I love that word, harvested, gives you the feeling of farmers toiling in their fields harvesting wheat or some such stuff."

"Well, when Dr. Ling was in prison, he made friends with some of his fellow country men, he's Chinese, did you know that? He also has a very bad back from that fall he took with you off the loading dock. I'm afraid he'll be wearing a back brace for some months. He is not real happy with you, Billy. Oh well, anyway he made friends with these people and they turned out to be members of a rather prominent Chinese gang in Hong Kong, they have been running people into this country for years. They think we're just grabbing some people for slave labor and prostitution. Wow, if they knew what we really were doing, would they ever want a large piece of the action. Anyway, they are happy to unload groups of people. After all, they have their money from these people, they only agreed to get them into this country and nothing else. Not like some of the others who turn them into slaves to pay off their passage when they get them here. Like I was saying, for a price they were glad to sell us a number of people from time to time. We take my boat out to sea and pick them up from the ship and bring them back here. We can't unload the body parts quickly. Wish we could, but it takes precision timing to make the contacts and set up the delivery. So with each group we get, it takes about four to six weeks to work them through the system. We average from ten to twelve people, sometimes more, sometimes less. After expenses, and I know you'll appreciate this, we net about a million five per person. That's net, not gross, Billy we're talking about a lot of money. A whole lot of money. You know, one thing I've always wondered about. There is such a huge profit margin in this business and it is so easy to get into it. There must be a number of other groups out there, exactly like ours. Just boggles the imagination, doesn't it? It is a shame we cannot get together with them and trade information. That's why we can't take any risks. That's why we had to run you around, just to make sure you didn't have anything on us."

"So what do you do with what's left? Is that your secret recipe you add to the dog food?" Billy asked quietly, his voice getting weak.

"No," St. John answered with a laugh. "That's just some corporate hype. There is no special mixture we add, it's just some vitamins and minerals. Sort of a large liquid vitamin pill. Hell, it might even do the animals some good, who knows or cares? No, when we're finished we just grind the bodies up with the horse and cow parts, at night after everyone is gone, then ship them out the next morning. To be sure there's no problems we only send those to the stores that are really moving our merchandise, mostly in the north and east. That's where we're big. Dog's love our stuff up there. Hey, it is kind of funny when you think about the correlation. Was it the real dog food or the human variety that made the dog food so popular? Now that is an enigma!"

"I don't want to die, I don't want to die," Billy was saying, tears running down his cheeks.

"Gee Billy, I wish I could help, but let's face it. This isn't a book or a movie where the good guys come rushing in at the last minute and rescue you. I don't think there are even any of them out there anymore. Besides, we got a quick match and, well, you've been promised, or I guess it would be more appropriate to say are being promised right this minute to a number of people across the country. Soon as the money comes through, I guess there's not really a better way to say it, but, we operate."

"You sick son of a bitch. You can't do this to me. You can't do this to me!" Billy was yelling as St. John stood up and adjusted the IV solution.

"Just relax Billy. It'll all be over in a few seconds, you will fall asleep," St. John said softly.

"I swear, you bastard, I'll come back from the grave to get you!" Billy was yelling.

As if watching a stage play, Billy's eye lids came falling down like a curtain at the end of a performance. He thought for a second he could just see the last bit of light as they closed.

"I'm sure you will, Billy, I'm sure you will," were the last words he heard as he slipped into a deep sleep.

Chapter 11

Off in the distance, Billy could see a bright light shining. It was a beautiful white light that seemed to be lighting a path for him, beckoning him to come forward.

My god, Billy thought to himself. It's real. I can't believe it, there really is a light out there leading the way. After all these years of denial, a life after death! Son of a... gun."

Without warning the light went out and Billy felt in despair, he could hear himself yelling.

"NO! Please, I'm here, over here. Turn the light back on I want to come home. Helllllp meeeeeee, please! Turn the light back on!" Billy could feel himself begin to cry when he suddenly saw the light shine again just off to his left. He immediately felt a flood of relief come over his body.

"I'm here, I'm here, over here," he yelled again.

Slowly the light got brighter and shapes began to come into focus. He was very groggy but knew he would be safe in heaven. At least he thought it was heaven, wasn't it?

Forms moved around him, moving hurriedly back and forth. Slowly his eyes became more focused and he began to distinguish the forms and shapes as people. He was not in heaven but still in that hospital ward in the dog food factory and coming back to life. Fear swept through his body and he began crying and yelling that he did not want to die. Trying to move, he felt the restraints. He was still strapped down. Then he could feel his right eyelid being pulled open and a bright light, the one he had thought was heavenly, shining into his eyes. There was a person in front of him, but it was not St. John, Ling or Jackanock. The light went off and he heard someone talking to his left.

"He be around soon?" asked the voice.

"Yea, he's coming out of it rather quickly now. He should be alert in another minute or two. Where do you want this one transported to, the hospital in Salisbury?" asked the voice to his right.

"Damn right, he gets a very private room and I'll have the man's ass if there isn't a wide awake alert guard on him 24 hours a day. This is too big to mess up. Anyone slips, it's his ass and you can spread the word along to the others," barked the voice.

"Yes sir, I will."

"And no leaks to the press. I trace any information back to anyone and they are in jail for a long, long time!"

"I'll spread the word, Captain."

The figures began to take shape more quickly now and Billy became aware of a large number of people around him. His vision came back to normal as he was watching one of the Chinese people being wheeled out on a stretcher by what looked like a paramedic. Still feeling afraid, he was quickly taking in just who these people were that were walking around him. He could make out a number of Maryland State Troopers, firemen, rescue workers in uniforms and another small group in suits. The group in suits was over against the wall talking to a very heavy man with close cropped, red curly hair wearing shorts and a T-shirt. Billy shook his head for a second to be sure who he was looking at. It had been a number of years but he was sure it was Oliver Garret.

"Mr. Lee? Mr. Lee? Can you understand what I am saying? Do you hear me properly?" the voice off to his left asked.

Turning his head there was a Maryland State Policeman kneeling down next to his bed.

"Yes," Billy said groggily. "I think I'm all right. Am I going to die?"

"No sir, Mr. Lee. Everything is fine. You are in no danger," the voice said in a soothing and sincere tone. "My name is Captain Jonas, Ira Jonas, of the Maryland State Police. We got here in time to save you. We believe we have arrested all the people responsible for this ghoulish place. Right now, we are more worried about your safety and that you are in no medical danger. We have one of the State Police Emergency Medical helicopters outside and we are going to fly you to the hospital in Salisbury to be checked out. Until we are sure that we have everyone, you will be placed under around-the-clock protection. Now, do you feel up to taking that helicopter ride?" he asked with a smile.

"Get me the hell out of this place!" Billy replied immediately.

"Fine. Let's get him on a stretcher and out to the copter," said Captain Jonas as he stood up.

Billy was following everything with his eyes, watching as they rolled a stretcher next to his bed, picked him up and placed him on it. He felt a prick in his arm and looked to his right, seeing that they had connected him to an IV hanging from a pole on his stretcher.

"No, please, please, don't knock me out again. I don't want to go to sleep. I'm afraid," Billy whimpered.

"No, no, it's all right," said the Emergency Medical Technician. "It's just a glucose drip to keep you from getting dehydrated. Don't worry. No one is going to put you under. You have no serious injuries that would warrant it. I am a little worried about some of the insect bites on your face and that old head and lip wound. They are looking a little bit infected but one of the doctors at the hospital will look into that. As far as I can see you are in pretty good health. BP and pulse are strong, given half a chance you could probably walk out of here."

"No thanks, I tried that once before," Billy said softly as he felt his body being wheeled out of the room.

When they were wheeling him through the warehouse he could see a crowd of people, the plant workers, standing in one corner, surrounded by a group of State Police officers, with side arms drawn.

"They're the plant workers, Mr. Lee," said Captain Jonas as he leaned down to talk to Billy. "At this time we don't think they are involved in anything but we can't take any chances. We'll be interrogating them in a little while, to try and get a handle on just who knows what has been going on around here."

Billy's head was turned and he was staring at the plant workers as he was being wheeled out the rear entrance.

Something caught his eye in the group of people but at that second he could not quite figure out just what it was. Suddenly, he realized what had caught his attention. Standing in the rear of the group was someone with a good sun tan wearing a bright red and yellow Hawaiian shirt. He tried to sit up but the restraints around the stretcher held him down.

"It's St. John, did you get St. John? I think it was St. John. My god, was he one of the one's you arrested? St. John, St. John, I think it was St. John!" Billy continued to scream.

No one could hear what he was yelling, as he was wheeled out the rear of the building. The high pitched whine of the helicopter sitting in the parking lot next to the hole in the fence he had escaped through a few days earlier drowned out all sounds. Immediately he felt strong waves of wind buffeting his face and could barely see through the cloud of debris being kicked up by the rotating blades. Even though he knew no one could hear him, he continued to yell anyway. They had to know. They had to be to catch him. St. John could not be allowed to escape.

Looking up he saw the blank faces of Captain Jonas and the Medical technician as they signaled that they couldn't understand what he was saying. They made gestures with their hands telling him to wait until they were airborne. Laying back frustrated and exhausted, Billy knew there was nothing he could do but wait. He felt his stretcher being lifted into the open door of the helicopter and felt it being mechanically channeled into position and fastened down. The engines began to whine louder, and louder. There was a slight bump as the helicopter pulled from the earth and then began to quickly ascend into the sky. Momentarily Billy forgot what he was trying to tell Captain Jonas as he became overwhelmed by the sight unfolding below him. He could see the cornfield he was in a few days ago getting smaller beneath him. Off to the right was the ocean, looking more beautiful than he had ever seen it. The helicopter lurched to the left. He could see the estuary and the long sandy strip that was Ocean City come into view. Tears welled up in his eyes as he realized that he was really alive and would live to go fishing yet another time in that beautiful bay he loved so much. The whine of the jet engines on the helicopter toned down as the copter settled into cruising speed.

"Captain, did you get St. John?" Billy asked reaching out, grabbing his arm.

"What?" the Captain yelled above the din of the jet turbines.

"DID... YOU... GET... St... JOHN?" Billy yelled slowly so the captain could understand.

"We got everyone in the research section. They were all placed under arrest. I don't have a complete listing of names yet but should have one by the time we get to the hospital. This is all still new and unfolding. We'll be met by some people from the FBI in Salisbury. They are going to join us in the investigation. Looks like these guys may have broken one shit load of federal laws, but it looks like we may get the main jurisdiction because of the murders. Just sit back and take it easy, we'll be there in a minute or two. This baby is really fast."

True to the captain's words, the helicopter reached the hospital just a few minutes later. Billy could see a large contingent of people by the large red "X" on the roof, waiting for them to land. The helicopter engines whined louder as it pulled up and hovered over the hospital in preparation of landing. Billy had a slight sensation of falling and then felt a bump. As he looked to his left he saw the large group of people descending on the helicopter as its doors were opened. He felt the hot outside air come rushing into the helicopter and realized with a smile that it was not damp and did not contain the scent of salt or suntan lotion that he was used too.

Two hours later he was sitting up in his bed drinking a cold Coke from a can as the doctors finished the last of their tests and inspections. They had pronounced him in good health after his ordeal and rubbed some neosporen on his infected insect bites. They advised him to do that for several days and that they would be fine. The large cuts on his lips and forehead were a different story. The one on his head had become infected and would need some attention and drugs. He was also advised that he should have some surgery to repair it along with his upper lip or it would leave some rather nasty looking scars. The doctors also advised him to stay in the hospital for a few days for observation and that the FBI was waiting outside to interview him.

After the doctors had left, the people from the FBI walked into the room and introduced themselves to Billy. There were five of them dressed in almost identical gray suits, white shirts and dark ties that made them indistinguishable from each other. They set up a tape recorder, turned it on and immediately informed Billy of his rights. They explained that they had to do this as the investigation was just beginning and looked to be a very high profile case. As such, they were taking no chances with anything or anyone. Captain Jonas walked into the room and they all began talking amongst themselves about the logistics of getting more information and taking the helicopter back to the crime scene later that day when Billy spoke up.

"Did you get St. John?" Billy asked in a serious tone.

"I have a list of those arrested at the scene in the, ahhhhhhh, research section. Let me see, nooooooooo, no. No St. John listed. Let's start at the beginning and work our way back to today. First..."

"He was there in the warehouse when I left. He's the brains behind the whole thing. You have to get him, he was with the group in the warehouse. Please, call someone and make sure they still have him in custody."

"Mr. Lee, we'll have one of our men check..."

"For Christ's sake," interrupted Billy. "Stop all of this bureaucratic bull shit. Find out if he's been arrested. The names St. John, Dr. Will St. John!"

One of the people from the FBI frowned as he picked up the phone and called the Maryland State Police at the scene in Ocean City. They talked in hushed tones for a few minutes as the other agents stood around like statues waiting to resume their interrogation of Billy.

".. thank you," said the agent. "Well, Sir, apparently there was a Dr. St. John there with the people from the plant who were detained for questioning. When they escorted them all into the office area, he was apparently missing from the group. They are searching for him now and expect to have him in custody in a little while. They think he may have escaped into the cornfield next to the plant."

"Call them back," Billy interrupted again. "There's only one way for him to get away. It's his boat 'Bow Wow', docked in the bay with the rest of the large fishing boats. For Christ's sake send them there first, forget the cornfield. Believe me I've been there!"

The FBI agent picked up the phone again and called back to the State Police alerting them to be sure to check St. John's boat as well as the corn field. The agent gave special emphasis to the words 'corn field.' Billy suspected he had stepped on some toes while telling them how to do their jobs.

For the next two hours Billy laid out piece by piece the whole ordeal of the past week. To Billy's astonishment he neglected to tell them about Jill or her part in the story. When he came to the parts about being in her apartment or with her, he passed them by or said he was delirious and not sure of just where he was or what he was doing. He could not believe that he was not mentioning her at all and was not even aware of why. He used Eastwick's name several times but made no mention of killing him or his connection in the menage-a-trois between Eastwick, Jill and himself. As he was ending his story the phone rang. One of the agents picked it up and spoke in inaudible tones then hung up the phone.

"They made a search of the corn field first. Not finding Dr. St. John, they went to where his boat was and it was gone. They're going to start searching for it by air, but it will be an hour or so before we can get someone airborne," the agent spoke out to no one in particular.

The news was disheartening to Billy and he felt himself becoming very weary and tired.

"Gentlemen, can we put this off until later? I'm feeling very tired and would like to get some rest. Can this wait until tomorrow?" Billy asked wearily.

"That will be fine, Mr. Lee. We will be going down to the plant and would like to look around and check some things out before we come back. It probably won't be until tomorrow afternoon. The doctors have told us that they would like to keep you here for observation. We can provide good security for you in the hospital and would recommend you spend a few days here while we sort things out."

"Sounds great to me. I can use the rest. I also don't happen to have anywhere to go either, so this will be fine."

The FBI agents put the tape recorder aside, removed the tape they had used during the interview and left the room. Once they were gone, Billy breathed a sigh of relief and put his head back on the pillow and instantly fell into a deep sleep.

The sun coming in through the hospital window woke Billy. Laying there looking out the window at the clouds, he realized that he was starving. Reaching for the buzzer next to his pillow, he squeezed it twice. A minute later a nurse came into his room.

"Yes, Mr. Lee, is everything all right?" she asked with a concerned look on her face.

"I'm sorry to bother you but I'm starving. Is it possible to get some food, please?" Billy begged.

"Yes sir, the doctor left some instructions. I'll see something is sent up right away," she said as she walked out the door.

"And a very, very large cup of black coffee," he yelled after her, hoping she had heard him.

Ten minutes later the nurse returned with a tray, pulled the lap table across his bed and placed it in front of him. Carefully she removed the plastic wrap from the Jell-O, toast and glass of yellow liquid that was definitely not juice and not at all inviting.

"Ahhh, coffee. Is it possible, please, to get some coffee, please?" Billy asked in a kind and mannerly tone.

"I'm sorry Mr. Lee, but the doctors feel you need some light nourishment first, to build your strength back up. You can probably have some coffee in a day or two," the nurse said as she turned and headed for the door.

"Wait. Cigarettes. Can I at least have a cigarette?" he yelled after her.

The door had not closed behind her when it opened again and she walked back in with a sour expression on her face.

"Mr. Lee, you are forbidden from smoking. There is no smoking allowed in any public buildings in the State of Maryland and I am sure you know that. So, I am warning you now that the police may control this room, but I control this floor, do you understand?" she said curtly.

"Oh yea, sure, no problem," he said with a small smile on his face as he held the palms of his hands up in defense.

As the door closed behind her, he breathed a sigh of relief as he tilted his head with an astonished look on his face. Picking up the piece of toast, he took a small bite, then pulled it back out of his mouth with his fingers and threw it on his plate.

"Damn, that tastes the way this hospital smells," he mumbled out loud.

Picking up the glass of yellow liquid, he took a small drink and gagged on the taste.

"Jesus Christ, it tastes like lemon Kool Aid with antiseptic in it. Damn this really sucks!" he again mumbled to himself as he sat up and moved to the edge of the bed. Holding onto the table just in case he was weaker than he felt, he stood up. Realizing that he was in fine shape and completely mobile, he walked to the door and opened it. Standing out side his door were two of the largest State Troopers he had ever seen. One was African American and the other white. They turned, looked at him with a smile and nodded their heads.

"Good morning, Sir," said the African American officer.

"Hi, guys," Billy said with a smile as he surveyed the corridor outside. "Listen, I am kind of new at this protection thing. Am I being held in here or is it possible for me to come out and walk the hall?"

"No, Sir," smiled the African American officer. "You are not restricted to your room, but if at all possible we would prefer that you stay there."

"Look, I understand, but you would not believe what they just tried to give me for breakfast," Billy whined.

"Ahhh, yes, Sir, I would, they provided us with some breakfast also," the officer said pointing to two trays sitting on a chair a few feet away. The plastic wrap was pulled half off of both trays and it looked like a small bite had been taken from each tray then abandoned.

"Guys, look I want to make your jobs as easy as possible," Billy said looking up and down the hallway to see if anyone was listening. "But I need a cup of coffee and I need it NOW! If one of you guys could get me a cup of coffee and a pack of Marlboros, I'd be in heaven and never mention where they came from. I'd stay in this room and never bother you again, at least until lunch. Otherwise, I'll have to start exploring this whole hospital for a coffee vending machine."

"You'll stay put and not try to go out, do whatever we say we need you to do to protect you?"

"Cross my heart," Billy said making an 'x' with his finger across his chest.

"Mike, you look like you have to take a pee," the African American officer said to the white officer with a smirk on his face.

"Yea, it's been building all morning. You guys want anything other than black?" Mike questioned.

Watching Mike walk down the hallway, Billy was not sure of what to do next. The African American officer reached into his shirt pocket and pulled out a pack of cigarettes, Camel filtered, and handed them to Billy.

"My name's George," said the officer. "It is against the law to smoke in a public building in the State of Maryland..."

"Yea, that's all anyone seems to be able to say around here," Billy spoke over George.

"However, I know from experience that if you open the window wide and wait a minute or two you can smoke in there without anyone knowing. Besides, I'm not allowed to just walk in anyway, so enjoy," George said with a smile. "What the Governor has done to smoking in this State's a crime. I ever get the chance to bust his ass, he's mine."

"You bet," nodded Billy as he looked down the hall and saw the other officer coming up, easily balancing three coffees in his huge hands.

"Thanks guys, I promise I'll do whatever you want, but we need to talk about lunch later," Billy said with a smile as he disappeared into his room with the coffee and cigarettes.

Opening the window by his bed, he could smell the warm soft air as it flowed in the window, carrying with it the slight smell of chickens. The Purdue Chicken Company owned most of Salisbury and employed the majority of the county in one way or another. A few minutes later the air began to filter out the window and as it did, Billy lit a cigarette, took a drag and followed it by a large gulp of coffee.

"Breakfast of champions," he said looking out the window and over the town, happy that he was alive to enjoy the morning. Beginning to feel tired he crawled back in bed and started thinking about Jill, replaying everything that had happened and trying to figure out why he had left her out of his talk with the FBI.

Two hours and two more cigarettes later Captain Jonas came walking into the room. Looking tired and worn, he sat down in the chair next to Billy's bed. Billy reached for the remote control and clicked off the game show he was watching on the TV.

"We just finished interrogating Dr. Ling an hour ago. He's being held along with the others in the lock up in Snow Hill," Jonas said with a bewildered look on his face. "My god, after twenty-five years in law enforcement, I thought I had seen everything, but nothing prepares you for something like this. The scope of it is unbelievable. He spilled everything, names, dates, companies in New York and Zurich, where the records are, even the money, everything! It's just too unbelievable to think that something like that could really have happened, let alone around here. Scares the shit out of you. I swear I think we're doomed as a species."

"Yea, I know what you mean, scares the hell out of me too. I was told most of my parts were heading for other bodies. Still makes me shake when I think about it," Billy said in a soft voice, almost a whisper.

"Well, anyway, Ling agreed to turn State's evidence. I'm not sure why, even with a reduced sentence there's no way he won't spend the rest of his life in jail. He's corroborated everything you told us yesterday. With both of your testimonies that'll be enough to just about tie everything up. We got everyone but St. John and the FBI's hot on his trail now. There was one other person you had mentioned, Eastwick. He's dead, we think his wife killed him, but we're having some problems with that investigation. She's not being too cooperative, but we'll sort it out soon. Currently she's under observation since her suicide attempt a couple of days ago. With the evidence we're compiling it's beginning to look like she may be indicted for murder."

"There's something I've been wondering about. How did you come to rescue me? No one knew where I was," Billy questioned.

"Oliver Garret, he's outside. Been chomping at the bit since yesterday to get in to talk to you. I told him, after everything he'd done, that it would be all right to see you if you agreed. You want to talk to him? I'll let him explain it all to you."

"Yea, I would, if you don't mind."

"No, I'm done here, the District Attorney's handling this thing now that we have Ling's confession. I'd imagine they'll be talking with you in great detail in the coming months. This is really going to be a big case for this area. It's going to make a lot of careers. Be careful Billy, past experience in this sort of thing, even the good guys may try to climb over you for a shot at the top. District Attorney wants to keep you under guard until they catch St. John. Probably be a wise thing to do. Well, take care, I'll send Mr. Garret in," Captain Jonas said as he stood up and shook Billy's hand.

Jonas was only out the door a second before Garret walked in, a very large smile on his face. He was easily six feet tall and weighed about 225 lbs. and was sweating profusely. Billy was unsure if it was from the heat or nervousness.

"Oliver, I think I owe you my life and a very large thank you," Billy said extending his hand.

Oliver shook Billy's hand vigorously and pulled a chair up close to the bed. Taking a quick look around to see if anyone was within listening distance, Oliver sat his large frame down and leaned forward towards Billy.

"This is big," Oliver said quietly with a large smile on his face. "BIG! I mean really B-I-G, BIG."

"I'm feeling fine Oliver and how are you?" asked Billy sarcastically.

"Cut the bull shit Lee, you don't know what has been going on out there. The press is having a field day with this. You would not believe how many of them are out there, right now. Dan Rather's coming down for a local on the Evening News Tonight. Dan Rather, Billy! It's that big. Bits and pieces of the story have slipped out and it's electrified the country, hell the world. It's bigger than O.J. Simpson. It's really big, Billy. Really BIG," he finished in a whisper.

"That's nice Oliver. Listen. What happened? That guy Jonas said it was you that saved me. What happened?"

"Christ, Lee, that's small stuff. Listen, I quit my job at the Washington Post yesterday. This thing's..."

"Oliver, damn it, tell me what happened first!" Billy said angrily.

"Oh, all right," Oliver said begrudgingly. "I thought you had blown me off the story. I'm reading some local State wire copy and I saw where your trailer and car were torched. On a hunch something was going on, I drove down here. I checked things out and, naturally, no one knew anything about anything, except that you were missing. I had to get back to the Post for a story I was finishing. For the hell of it, I made an early stop at your trailer before heading back to Washington. I drove in just as you were getting in this Caddy and a cop pulls up beside you. I followed you to that dog food company and knew something was wrong. Cops don't arrest you and take you to dog food plants, so I called the State Police. At first they didn't want to do anything but check around, so in my own friendly way I started leaning on them and they got a search warrant and next thing you know, BAM we're in the headlines. Billy, this is really BIG!" Oliver said excitedly.

"Yea, you keep saying that, but I don't know what the hell you're talking about."

"This thing's playing like some big fucking movie. Swear to God. The District Attorney is trying to sit on this whole thing and keep it quiet so they don't get a tainted jury and blow the trial, like O.J.'s. He's a small town boy made D.A., but hell, between him and the guy I heard they're picking for the judge, who knows they may be able to do it. But Billy, you and I have the WHOLE story. THE... WHOLE... STORY..., YOU AND I. I'm not giving it out to anyone, especially those pricks on TV. Hell, they thought I would be dying to tell my story on *Night Line* last night, you know a chance to be on TV! Hell, were they ever surprised when I told them to fuck off. I have an agent, he's been talking to some book publishers already. Billy, you and I can write this book together and split the profits. We need each other for each other's part in the story. It'll be a lot like Woodward and Bernstein. Hollywood's interested too, they think it's got block buster written all over it," Oliver stopped talking and sat back in the chair giving Billy a smile as he nodded his head in approval.

"Oliver, what the hell are you trying to say?"

"Billy, my agent's already got the bidding for the book rights up to five million and the whole story isn't even out yet. They don't know how much more there is to it yet, but they do know they want to get our story because no one but you and I, a couple of sharp writers, knows what really happened and can explain it. My agent thinks we can get at least ten million for the book and at least that much for the movie rights plus a piece of the gate. Billy, that would be ten million a piece, less say, twenty percent or so to blood sucking attorneys and agents. By the time this gets to press, you'd be looking at at least eight million dollars. Not bad, huh dude?"

Billy narrowed his eyes and looked around the room. Oliver tried to speak again and Billy held up his hand to quiet him.

"An hour ago I was homeless, no job, not a dollar to my name and now I may be a millionaire. Damn, this will take some getting used too," he said with a bewildered look on his face.

"Billy, you and I will write this story together from both of our perspectives. Just take a second and think, does it or does it not look BIG?" Oliver asked making a large gesture with his hands.

Billy sat there thinking for a few seconds, reviewing the ordeal he had been through and then a smile came to his face.

"My God, Oliver, you're right. This is big. I've never really had a chance to sit down and take an objective look at this as a story yet. Oh my God, oh my God, Oliver, this IS BIG, really BIG!" Billy smiled at Oliver as he clapped and rubbed his hands together.

Chapter 12
Tuesday, July 27

It was just after 1:00 p.m. and Billy was sitting in the cool shade of the balcony enjoying the sea breeze blowing gently into his face. Gazing out at the Atlantic Ocean he was carefully contemplating the last few days and trying to prepare himself for the days to come. After spending three days in protective custody in the hospital, they had found St. John's boat "Bow Wow" moored at a local dock in New York city. Receiving word of sightings of him in and around Zurich, the FBI surmised that he had left the United States and were searching for him in Europe. Feeling that Billy was no longer in danger, the State Police removed their protective custody and Billy was released from the hospital along with a bill for $8,000 for three days stay which was promptly paid by Billy and Oliver's new publisher Salient Press.

They had all come to terms on a book deal. Salient Press was guaranteeing them $8 million dollars for their book plus a percentage of the profits. The papers were to be signed at a fancy press conference in New York next Monday, August fourth. The movie rights were also just about concluded and it looked like they were going to go for $10 million plus two points gross profit. The only hold out on the deal was Oliver, he was hoping by delaying agreement he could get them to kick in an extra million.

All told, Billy was about to become a very wealthy man next Monday when he signed those papers. When the book publisher heard that Billy had no place to go after he left the hospital, they promptly leased him a condominium on the ninth floor of the Golden Sands. Naturally it was going to be set off against sums to be paid to Billy, but he didn't care. Once out of the hospital, he had little time or desire to go apartment shopping. Deluged by the press, he was happy for an anonymous place to hide, even if it was there.

Looking up, Billy felt that it was more than ironic that he was two floors below and one condo over from where Jill had lived. Since her arrest, no charges had been filed against her but a grand jury was about to be convened to look into her case. Bail had been set at $900,000 considering her connection to Eastwick and the fact that she was in no way cooperating with the police investigation. Newspaper reports had stated that she had refused to say one word during several interrogations.

Glancing at his watch, Billy saw that it was two o'clock. Standing up, he took a last look out to sea, picked up a pair of very large sunglasses and left the condominium. Pushing the elevator button he looked over towards the emergency stairs he had learned to navigate so well and for the first time today smiled. The elevator doors opened with a ding. He stepped onto the elevator loaded with people in swim suits heading for the beach. On the trip down to the lobby he could hear the whispers coming from behind him.

"I'm telling you that's that guy Billy Lee, bet my ass on it," said one.

"Yea, I heard someone say he was living here, I can't believe it, this is really cool," someone whispered.

"What, what did you say? Billy Lee? Who, him? Jeez, I thought he'd be bigger than that. Helen, that's that guy Billy Lee," another person whispered.

Feeling very embarrassed, Billy could hardly wait for the elevator to get to the first floor. It had been the same every time he had ventured out of his apartment and he had contemplated taking the emergency stairs, but the memories of them made it to difficult. Once off the elevator he walked quickly to separate himself from the crowd. When he got to the front doors of the complex he was about to go out when he saw a TV crew set up waiting for him. Turning around he walked back through the lobby to a side entrance and into the parking lot. Watching the TV crew carefully, he walked across the parking lot and got into his rented Chevy Cavalier. Sinking low in the seat, he picked up a ball cap from the back seat and placed it on his head as he drove by the TV crew and left onto Coastal Highway. When he reached 6501 Coastal Highway he turned right into the Ocean City municipal complex and up to the city jail.

Once in the jail a small commotion started. Several officers he knew came up to congratulate him and try to talk about the case. Saying he was under a court order to say nothing he was able to dodge the questions, but other officers, people and a few reporters hanging around looking for a story began coming up to see him, the media star from TV. The commotion got even louder when he walked up to the desk and said that he wanted to see Jill Eastwick. One of his friends on the force, Sergeant Phil Elliot, seeing things were beginning to get out of control, took Billy by the arm and escorted him out of the foyer and into a private room.

"Thanks, Phil, I really appreciate it. You would not believe what my life has been like in the past week," Billy said quietly.

"I don't know Billy, sounds pretty profitable to me. I think I could put up with it for that kind of money. You ever feeling philanthropic, don't forget your old buddy. I'd be more than happy to relieve you of some of that awful money that's ruining your life," Phil was saying as both men started laughing.

"All right, all right, as usual you're right. When this dies down a little, let's go out for some beer like we used to. Hell, I'll even buy for a change."

"I don't know, you buying the beer. Shit, Billy, that might just be a little more than I can handle."

"Phil, I want to see Jill Eastwick, in private. Can you arrange it for me?" Billy asked quickly, sounding apologetic.

"Jesus, Billy, when you come out in public, you really know how to create a scene. Yea, I can fix it up, but between the press and the District Attorney Wight, you're really going to make my life hell for a few days," Phil said as he rubbed his forehead.

"ALL RIGHT! The next four times we go out drinking. I'll pay!"

"Five and it's a deal," Phil smiled.

"Deal," Billy smiled back as he shook Phil's hand.

"Look, I can set it up for in here instead of the visitor's room. I can get away with it in the interest of public safety, considering the scene your presence started out there. She will have to wear chains and an officer will have to be present in the room. He'll sit on the other side of the room so you can talk quietly without being overheard, but in no way, manner or form are you allowed at any time to touch each other. Understood? Also she has to want to talk to you. I can't drag her out here if she doesn't want to talk and I can tell you she has not said one word since she was brought in here."

"Agreed," Billy gestured with his hands as he walked over to the corner of the room, dragging two plastic chairs with him.

His heart was beating rapidly and even though the air conditioned room was cool, he could feel that he was sweating. The palms of his hands wet and cold, his mouth dry. A few minutes later the door opened and Jill came walking in, her hands cuffed behind her to a chain around her waist. She was wearing a disposable blue jump suit and looked worn and tired. Saying nothing, she walked up to the chair and sat down a few inches away from Billy. She had a vacant look on her face and even though she was without makeup, she still looked very pretty. Her once perfectly coifed blond hair was now hanging limply down and he could see a number of lines around and under her eyes that he had never noticed before.

"I need to talk to you," Billy said softly as he looked over at the guard on the other side of the room watching them. "I want to know the truth, was it just for the money?"

"What's the difference, Billy. What does it really matter?" she asked quietly and unemotionally as she stared at the floor.

"I guess that's the point. I doesn't matter anymore, that's why I would like to know the real truth."

"There sure hasn't been a lot of that around here lately, that's for sure. Let's look at the truth, the truth is, like you used to say, 'I'm fucked,' that's the truth. You are a smart man Billy Lee, you did a beautiful job of framing me, much like St. John did to you. If I say I didn't kill John then they'll probably go after me for my part in this thing with St. John and you. If I say I did kill him, then they'll get me for that and not for St. John. So if I just say nothing, all they can do is run around in circles until they decide which murder to pin on me. So, I'm fucked. I have no choice but to just sit here and say nothing. You really did it great, Billy," she said as a small smile came to her face.

"So then you can feel free to tell me the truth. I have to know, was it just the money?" he asked again softly.

"Billy, I could sit here and tell you anything and you'd probably believe me, so what's the point? Just let it go and get on with your life," she said coldly.

"Jill, you've got nothing to lose, so let's have the truth," Billy said throwing his hands up in the air for emphasis.

"I don't think you can handle it!"

"Jesus, Jill, get to the point!"

"All right," she said taking in a large gasp of air, then exhaling. "You remember that story I told you about John and me?"

"Which one? Let's face it, there were a number of them," Billy said sarcastically.

"When we were eating at Fagers Island. About what life was like living with him. The beatings and rapes that passed for sex."

"Yea, sure, go on."

"Well, that was the truth. That bastard made my life a living hell. There was nowhere I could go and no one I could turn too. Like I told you I was too embarrassed to come back to you. The store, *Jill's Place*, is not mine, it's his. He needed a way to launder the money so he could explain where the condo, cars and big spending were coming from. I never saw much of it. What little I did see I had to use for the hair, clothes, nails, etc. It was important that I looked good in public. It wasn't by choice, it was an order. It justified his ego. I was one of his possessions to be shown around. I often dreamed of killing him and even planned on doing it, but never had the courage to carry it out. Eventually I would have, it was just a matter of time. It would have been the only way out. That's sort of my penance, I guess. I would have killed him and ended up here, so he is dead and I am here. Sort of poetic justice and you know what? It's even worth it to be away from him. I'm actually somewhat happy, just a little concerned for my future, though," she shrugged her shoulders and looked up at Billy.

"So why did you do it? You and me?"

"I didn't want to. I refused to. St. John, that fucking psycho, put the pressure on John and he put it on me. I refused and he beat me up. John was a cop. Hell, he knew exactly how to beat you up bad so's you wouldn't show any marks. I must say, of all the beatings he gave me, unless he wanted to, he never left as much as a finger print. Man was a genius at it. Real talent! I couldn't help myself, after the second beating I knew I had no choice, so I agreed. I was originally just going to go through the motions, see if I could scare you away from me. But when I saw you, the old memories and emotions came back. Emotions and feelings I hadn't had in years. You'll probably laugh, but I realized that I was still in love with you. I knew what they were going to do to you and knew I couldn't stop it. I was a pawn in their little chess game and after all those years to suddenly feel loving emotions come back, I went for it. I couldn't help myself. I know it wasn't fair to you, but I didn't care. One last time I wanted those feelings of love and tenderness. Even though they were going to be tragic, I still wanted them, just one more time in my life. I'm sorry, Billy, but it was all worth it. I know it was at your expense, but it was all worth it to me for just a few days of love and passion. I know you can't understand that, but that's my problem, not yours. Look, I'm feeling a little tired. I'd like to get back to my cell now... Billy, I love you and because I love you I'm going to do you a favor. Don't ever come back. You come back, I'll refuse to see you no matter where I am. Let it go, Billy. Forget it and me. You're better off," she said tears falling from her eyes.

Billy felt a lump in his throat and could feel his eyes filling with tears. Jill stood up and walked away as he sat there staring at the pattern on the green floor tile, watching as his tear drops formed a small puddle on it. She said nothing as she walked over to the guard and was escorted back to her cell.

Standing up, Billy put his sunglasses on to hide his crying. Walking out the door and into the hallway, he was greeted by a large group of photographers and TV cameras. Once surrounded, the people began thrusting microphones in his face asking what he and Jill had discussed. Trying to push his way through the crowd he felt a hand grab his arm and was about to pull violently away when he saw that it was his friend Phil. Turning, Billy followed him out of the hallway and into a small room. Bending over and breathing a sigh of relief he looked up and saw the District Attorney, William Wight, sitting on a chair, nervously smoking a cigarette.

William Wight was only thirty years old but looked older than Billy. He had very short, fashionably greasy black hair and was dressed in an expensive suit. Even though he had been born and raised in Ocean City, he talked with a Southern drawl that no one else who grew up in this area ever possessed. Billy had known Wight's parents and disliked them for being stuffed shirts. Every time he had ever met Wight over the years he had always felt the same thing about him too. The man was a born politician who loved the lime light and now with a big case, had visions of being Governor or a Senator in the next elections.

"Thanks, Phil," said Billy.

"Yea, thanks, Phil, now get the hell out of here," Wight said rudely as he motioned with his arm for the Sergeant to leave.

"Mr. Lee, I must ask this. WHAT IN THE HELL IS GOING ON? Why are you here? What did you discuss with her and why did you not talk to me first before coming here? You may have just created some very serious legal problems on the prosecution of her case. Do you realize that Mr. Lee?" Wight asked the question as if he were scolding a small boy for misbehaving.

"More than you know," returned Billy with an exasperated look on his face.

"Now, what does that mean, Mr. Lee? I think we need to talk and talk now."

"Yea, I think we do. Remember when you were taking my deposition last week? I told you about some blank spots I couldn't recall. Well... I have been having these nightmares the past couple of days. Only they seemed too real. They stopped being nightmares yesterday when I realized that the things in my dreams had actually happened," Billy stopped and took a deep breath and turned around. Waiting for a few seconds to make it dramatic enough he turned and faced Wight.

"I remember killing John Eastwick."

Billy watched as the life slowly drained out of Wight's face. He could see Wight coming to the realization that it was going to be one less high profile case that would keep his name and face in the news and out of voter's minds..

"Good Lord," was all Wight could say.

Standing there for a minute, Wight walked around in a small circle then kicked at a plastic chair by one of the tables. The chair sailed across the room and made a large thud as it struck the steel door then bounced like a toy across the floor. Almost immediately the police officer on guard outside came running.

"Get the Hell out of here!" Wight yelled in his best southern accent as the officer immediately turned and ran back out the door. "Wait, get the hell back in here," he yelled again.

"Yes, Sir?" the officer said as he stuck his head in the door.

"Get me a tape recorder and bring it in here quickly, ya'll understand? Say nothing to anyone. Go, boy, GO!" Wight ordered.

Looking thoroughly exasperated, Wight sat back down on the chair. A minute later the officer came back in with a tape recorder, set it up and left the room.

"Go on, Mr. Lee, proceed. Let's hear it all," he said as he cradling his face in his hands, his eyes closed.

"As best as I can recollect, it's all still coming back. I'm not sure I have it all yet but I know I have a great deal of it. I think. Well, it's kind of hard to tell. I guess I know a lot of what happened. I remember vividly some things and others are still a little fuzzy. You see..." Billy was mumbling.

"Mr. Lee, could you please get to the point and tell me what in the Hell you do know?" Wight asked sarcastically as he interrupted Billy.

"Well, Sir, I had escaped and it was just before I was recaptured by St. John. That last time, the one where Oliver Garret saw me, that led to my rescue. I remember being down by my boat. I was going to try and get away in that. It was after they had burned my car and I had no way of getting around. I was going to head up to Delaware and hide out. It was dark, about three or four in the morning. I was casting off when Eastwick caught me. He sat there pointing a pistol at me. I remember asking him about Jill and how she figured in this whole thing. I don't remember why I asked it, but I did. I wondered why he had used her to lure me away from the investigation by asking for my help at one point in writing a story about her business. You following all this, Mr. Wight?" Billy asked sincerely.

"Yes, Mr. Lee. I believe so. Please proceed," he said slowly.

"Well, like I was saying, she had contacted me just after I had seen the Chinese people on St. John's boat. She called me and asked me to write a story about her shop, *Jill's Place*, I went out to see her and we met and had dinner. Being my ex-wife, I wasn't real happy about seeing her again. It was very awkward, the first time we had talked in years. I was really uncomfortable and so was she, but anyway we went to dinner. It was real strained and we didn't exactly hit it off and that was all. So, anyway, John and I were talking and I asked him how she fit into this whole thing. He told me she was just a stupid bitch and that he had never told her anything about St.

John and what he was doing. All of a sudden, without saying anything, he walks up and starts hitting me in the face with this little pistol. I grabbed a hold of him and we fell on the dock. The pistol popped out of his hand and I picked it up as we rolled into the bay. I remember putting the pistol right about there," Billy walked up and stuck his finger in Wight's stomach, just where he had shot Eastwick. "I just kept pulling the trigger. I don't know how many times I shot him, no less than two or more than six, that's all the bullets the pistol held. So after he's dead, I panic. I'm still out of my mind from that knock on my head I took when I escaped and not really thinking very well. I saw Jill's car parked a few hundred feet away, so I reached in Eastwick's pocket and took her car keys. I'm not sure but I think I was afraid I'd be charged with killing a police officer, so after I climbed out of the water I cut a piece of rope off a line in my boat and tied it up under his arms. You probably found the rope around his body, I left it there. If you go to my boat you can check it against the piece I cut it from. I wanted to hide his body so I got in the boat and towed his body up to around 125th street. I let it loose in that general area and he just drifted away. So I have his keys. I go back to get his car and am recaptured by St. John. That's it."

"So why did you come here to see Mrs. Eastwick?"

"To tell her the truth. That it was me that killed her husband. I didn't want her to hear it from others. I loved her once. I felt I owed her that."

"How did the pistol get from you back to her apartment?"

"St. John, I guess. You know he was good at that sort of thing, setting people up. When you catch him you'll have to ask him about it," Billy added facetiously.

The room became very silent except for the whir of the tape recorder. A few minutes later, Wight reached up and switched off the machine and the room was silent.

"Thank you for your deposition, Mr. Lee," Wight said in a sullen, quiet voice as he rubbed the temples on the sides of his head with his fingers. "I'll have one of our investigators look into your story."

"You need me for anything else, Mr. Wight?" Bill asked in a cheerful voice.

"No, Mr. Lee, you may go. Thank you," Wight said very slowly.

"Well then, I guess I'll just go out and run the press gauntlet. You know where to find me if you need anything. Have a nice day, Mr. Wight," Billy said as he ducked out the door.

"You too, Mr. Lee. You too," Wight said very quietly.

Out in the hall, the TV reporters and photographers descended on him once again. This time he was prepared for them and much like a half back on the football field. bending over, he plowed through the crowd, answering no questions. The throng of people chased him into the parking lot and he managed to jump into his car and take off just seconds ahead of the crowd.

It was about five o'clock when he got back to the Golden Sands. The TV crew was gone, probably back with the others at the jail. There were no other people hanging around. Pulling into a parking space, he went in the front doors and to the elevator. The last groups of sunburned and wet people were returning from their day on the beach. Billy could feel the stares as he waited for the elevator. When the doors finally closed behind him, he heard the voices whispering again from behind him. They were saying the usual things. When the elevator reached the eighth floor he stepped off and turned around with a smile facing the group on the elevator.

"Catch the eleven o'clock news if you really want to see something," he said with a broad smile as the elevator doors closed.

Chapter 13

Sitting on the couch drinking a beer. Billy waited for the Ten O'clock news on Channel 5 from Washington. He stared out the window at the moon hanging over the ocean.

"More big news out of Ocean City tonight. We'll have tape and a live feed on the Ten O'clock news next!" the reporter said over the credits from the show that was just ending.

Turning his attention to the TV, Billy sat there with a smile on his face, this time looking forward to the news.

"Our top story of the night," the newsman said in an extremely serious manner. "One of the doctors being held in what's come to be called the Transplant Case was found hanging in his cell tonight. Dr. Jolaris Jackanock was found just a short while ago, hanging in his cell. Reports are sketchy at this time but we do know that he was pronounced dead at the scene. We have a live report from Mike Johnson at the County Jail in Snow Hill, Maryland. Mike, what can you tell us about what has happened?"

"Not much, Morris. We do know that Dr. Jackanock was found dead, hanging in his cell at approximately nine o'clock this evening. Attempts were made to resuscitate him but they were futile. As you can imagine, things are a little crazy around here right now as the police begin checking into how he was able to hang himself. There's a press conference planned for ten thirty and we hope to have more information then. Back to you, Morris."

"Thank you Mike. We will come back to you at nine thirty to follow up on this important and still unfolding story. In still other news on this case, the man who broke this whole story, Billy Lee, visited the Ocean City jail today to see his ex-wife, Jill Eastwick. Eastwick is being held in connection with the murder of her husband whose body was found floating in the bay behind Ocean City a week ago. As you can see by the tape, Mr. Lee's coming out in public created quite a scene. After the surprise meeting with Mrs. Eastwick, who is rumored to have given no information to the authorities on this case, Mr. Lee had a conference after his meeting with the District Attorney, William Wight, at the jail. Fred Smith is standing by live at the Ocean City Jail tonight. Fred, can you shed some light on what is happening there tonight? I know with everything that's been happening in Snow Hill, rumors must be flying everywhere."

"Right you are, Morris. To say that the crowds of people at the jail and District Attorney Wight were stunned today when William 'Billy' Lee showed up unannounced would be a gross understatement. I was here when he came in and the crowd was electrified. No one had expected it. As you can see from the tape rolling there when he left, hundreds of reporters and photographers were converging on him trying to find out just what he was doing here. My sources have told me that Mrs. Eastwick, since being arrested, has said absolutely nothing to the authorities. They say that she just sits there refusing to give even her name or affirm that she is in fact Jill Eastwick, which they know that she is. My sources also tell me that Mr. Lee had a very heated meeting with Mr. Wight, the District Attorney, after his meeting with Mrs. Eastwick and that her case is in jeopardy. Mr. Wight has scheduled a news conference for eleven-thirty tomorrow morning when we expect to find out more about what is happening. Once again, Morris, this whole Transplant Case has taken yet another very bizarre turn, much as it has many times this past week. The eyes of the nation and the world are focused here wondering just what the next turn in this case will be. Back to you, Morris."

"Thank you, Fred for your report, we will be back to you at the end of the hour just in case any new events..."

Billy flipped the switch on the remote control and the TV went off leaving the living room nearly dark save the light from the moon that was shining in the windows. Billy sat thinking about the newscast when the phone rang. After it rang a second time he switched on the light and looked at the caller ID. It was Oliver Garret.

"Hello," Billy said softly into the phone.

"Billy, Billy I love you. God damn, but I love you. I want to have all of your children. I will bear them for you, just tell me how many you want and they're yours. I'll even throw in my first born when I find a woman to marry me after I get rich," Oliver said very excitedly.

"How are you, Oliver?"

"How am I? You know how I am. I just saw the ten o'clock news. Billy, Billy you've got to tell me the truth. Is there a love angle to this?"

"Keep it under your hat, but yea, there was and if things work my way there might still be. I think we'll find out more tomorrow by noon. The D.A. is making an announcement. It must be important. He's going to make it just before the news at noon so he'll get the best press coverage."

"Oh my God, a love story! Not only do we have this great story but it's also a love story? Please, please tell me you're not lying," Oliver begged.

"Nope, it's a love story but we don't know the ending yet. We should, hopefully, in a few days."

"Oh my God, a love story. A LOVE STORY TOO! Billy, this is BIG! The public will really eat this up if there's a love story in it too. Oh GOD, this is BIG, Billy. You should have told me this before we made the deal with the publisher. Hell, with a love story in it we could have gotten another million out of them easy and the movie... My God, the movie people. Christ, when they find out there's a love story in this they might double the money. Gotta go, bye," Oliver said quickly as he slammed down the phone.

"Bye, Oliver," Billy said after Oliver had hung up the phone.

He could almost hear Oliver, twisting a producer's arm for more money. Laying back on the couch he laughed as he watched the moon shining in the window then fell into a deep sleep.

Waking up around ten the next morning, Billy got up from the couch. Stretching his back, he walked to the window. It was going to be an overcast day but there were still a handful of people on the beach waiting and hoping for the sun to shine. Walking to the kitchen, he put some water in a pot and boiled it for coffee. Ten minutes later he was sitting on a stool at the kitchen counter, smoking a cigarette and finishing his first cup of coffee. Opening the drawer under the counter, he took out the phone book and turned to the blue, city pages, then dialed the phone.

"Good morning, Ocean City Jail, may I help you?" the voice answered.

"Could I speak to Sergeant Elliot please," Billy said.

"Yes, Sir. Just a minute I'll transfer you."

"Sergeant Elliot," Phil's voice came curtly across the phone.

"Phil, it's Billy Lee."

"Oh Christ, not again. Jeez, Billy, we're still trying to recover from yesterday. You really shook things up around here bud," Phil said in a joking tone.

"Well, you know. I like to spread a little light wherever I go," Billy said.

"A little light, hell we were almost blinded by that light. I was here to after eleven last night. Reporters were all over the place. Hey, did you see me? I was on the eleven o'clock news on Channel Eleven in Baltimore and Channel Four in Washington."

"Naah, sorry, I missed those. I caught the ten and went to bed. Listen, can I pump you for a little information?"

"Depends, Billy, we are friends but this is a public job and it has to handled honestly. If I can help I will. What do you want to know?"

"Wight's got a news conference scheduled for eleven-thirty. I think he's going to drop all charges and release Jill. Can you tell me if it's true?"

"You son-of-a-gun, you really did do it yesterday didn't you?"

"What?"

"There've been rumors flying around here all morning that you admitted killing Eastwick and cleared his wife. Damn, that explains the news conference then. No, I haven't heard anything officially, but I can tell you the scenario. If he says he will drop charges and release her, it will take about two hours for us to process her out. He would give us the papers authorizing her release before he speaks, so he can say he has ordered her release. That what you need to know?"

"That's it, Phil, but you're not off the hook yet, there's more."

"Christ, Billy, lay it on me!" Phil said nervously.

"I'm going to really owe you for this one. I want you to talk to Jill if you find out she's being released. See if she will allow me to pick her up out front. Media coverage and all and call me here at, ahhh 555-1616 and let me know when and if I can pick her up."

"Christ, Billy, do you know what kind of a mob scene that will make?"

"Yes I do, Phil, that's what I want. Will you do it for me?"

"If that's the way it's going down, I will. If not, I won't bother to call back, you'll find out what happens in the press conference."

"Thanks, Phil."

"No problem, Billy," he said hanging up the phone.

For the next hour Billy paced back and forth through the living room, hoping, even praying, that things would turn out like he had planned. At eleven o'clock he turned the TV on to Channel 5, waiting for the news at noon and the possibility of any news flashes. When the clock said eleven-thirty he knew that the news conference was in motion and was beginning to feel desperate. Phil should have called by now. Sitting down on the sofa in the living room he sat staring at the phone on the coffee table.

"RING, damn it!" Billy yelled. As he finished saying it the phone rang and he made a mad grab for the receiver.

"Billy, it's Jill, what the hell's going on? This guy who say's he's your friend comes to my cell and tells me I'm being released, they're dropping charges and it was because of you. Billy, what's happening?" she was talking in the phone in urgent and questioning tones, her voice very strained on the verge of breaking.

"I told the District Attorney yesterday that it was me that killed John and how John had told me before I killed him that you never knew anything at all about St. John and the dog food company."

"... why Billy?" she asked very softly after a long pause.

"... because I still love you. I want to come pick you up. Can I?" Billy held his breath and crossed his fingers.

"... are you sure Billy, after everything we've been through?" she said cautiously.

"I'm sure, the question is, do you want me to come to get you?"

"Yes I do, Billy. Very much so. I never in my wildest dreams believed it might turn out like this. I'll be waiting for you and yes, like I told you yesterday, I love you too... Wait the sergeant want's to talk to you." Billy heard her breaking down and crying as she finished the last statement.

"Billy, Phil, listen, this place is a mob scene now. By the time she's released it will be worse. Why don't you let us bring her to you? It might be better that way," Phil said sounding concerned.

"Not a chance, Phil. I want the world to see she's innocent and can walk away with her head held high."

"Well, I can tell by the tone of your voice I'm not going to be able to change your mind. Look, let's at least try and coordinate this circus. We'll clear a way for you in and out at three o'clock. Be here right on time, I'll handle processing her out. It's getting a little weird around here."

"How's Jill? Can I talk to her again?"

"She's fine. A little broken up over this whole thing but fine. I'd let you talk to her but we have to get moving to get everything ready by three. I probably won't get to see you then. Listen, good luck!"

"Thanks, Phil, I owe you. See you then."

Hanging up the phone, Billy rubbed his eyes to get rid of some of the emotion he was feeling. Next he called the man who handled security for the Golden Sands. He was less than happy to hear that Jill was coming back, knowing that it would be a strain on the few people who worked there as security guards. The guard brightened up when Billy told him that he had the authority to hire all the private guards he deemed necessary for at least the next week and that Billy would pay for it all. Billy told him he was also appointing him as his official spokesman for the next week. The thought of dealing with the press, being on nationwide TV, telling the reporters to get the hell out of the Golden Sands made the guard ecstatic.

Billy knew he couldn't pick her up in his rented Chevy Cavalier, he called a limousine service. Even though it was on short notice, they were able to get a pickup scheduled for an hour from then. They were happy to accommodate him, especially after they heard where they were going and who it was for. The advertising value from this would be tremendous.

At two-thirty Billy put on his only pair of jeans and a T-shirt, he still had not been able to replace his clothes from the fire, and took the elevator down to the lobby. At this time of the afternoon everyone was already at the beach so he was by himself on the ride down. Walking out into the lobby he could see a limousine out front and walked to it. The driver recognized him from the news reports on TV as he walked out the doors of the complex.

"Good afternoon, Mr. Lee. My name's Robert, I'll be your chauffeur for the day." Billy stepped quickly into the car and the door was closed.

"Robert, you know what's going on?" Bill asked after Robert had gotten into the car.

"Yes sir, Mr. Lee. It was me you talked to on the phone earlier. To the jail, through a crowd and then back here, correct?"

"Correct. Look, here's a hundred bucks for a tip. I really appreciate your doing this on short notice and I hope we can get in and out clean. Don't get out to get the door when we get there. I'll handle it. You just get ready to take off, it might be a little crazy."

"No sir, it's going to be a lot crazy. I went by there on my way up here. You won't believe the scene. This is really going to be something, thanks for the business. No matter what happens, this is going to be a blast!" Robert said with a large grin as he looked in the rear view mirror at Billy.

The chauffeur stepped on the gas. The car lurched forward rolling Billy onto the back seat. He tried to get up as they flew out of the parking lot but when the limo made a hard left onto the Coastal Highway it made him roll over against the door hitting his head. Laying half on the seat and the other half on the floor, Billy looked up at Robert. He could see a demonic smile on his face that immediately became infectious, causing Billy to begin laughing wildly.

Billy was not prepared for the scene that was awaiting him at the city jail. Traffic was backed up as people were slowing down to see what was happening. Hundreds of media trucks were parked in and around the jail. Microwave dishes, cranes and large antennas were coming out of all sorts of trucks and trailers. As they pulled up to the scene Billy could see Robert start flashing his lights on and off. The police officers recognized it as a signal. As if on que, they opened up a path for the limousine to drive to the entrance of the building. Once there a contingent of police officers held back the crowd, creating a path for Billy. Jumping out of the car he was greeted by loud cheers coming from all around him. Embarrassed by the scene he walked quickly to the front doors. Opening them he walked in and was surprised to find the place practically vacant. Looking to his left he saw Jill come running out of one of the rooms and she almost knocked him over as she threw her arms around him.

"Take me home, Billy," was all she said as Billy looked into her eyes and saw tears running down her cheeks.

"Let's go!"

Taking her hand he started walking to the front door. He saw Phil standing there waiting to open it for them and Billy smiled and said thanks as they walked quickly through and out into the crowd. The police could barely hold back the crowds of reporters as they were yelling questions at them while other onlookers cheered. Practically running they jumped into the limousine. Pulling the door shut behind them, Robert sped off through the crowd, barely missing a few TV reporters.

"All right, Robert!" Billy yelled as the limousine pulled back onto the highway and headed home. "Jill, I've got a place for us, I hope you don't mind. It's at the Golden Sands, the ninth floor."

"Billy, you know I'll go anywhere with you, even there, but how can you afford that let alone this limousine?" she asked nuzzling up close to him as he put his arm around her.

"Haven't you heard?" Billy asked.

"Heard what? They put me in solitary when I refused to talk and cut me off from everything. I'm still not sure what's going on. I wasn't sure if you were alive or dead until yesterday. I haven't had any news for a week. Are we out of trouble?" she asked fearfully.

"Oh yea, we're OK, but I think you have some surprises coming," Billy said with a smile.

Chapter 14
Wednesday, September 22

Around this time of the year Ocean City begins to look like a ghost town, except for the weekends when the crowds pick up a little. By now the last of the late vacationers who wanted solitude have gone. There would still be a few more people vacationing up through the last warm days in October but not many. The seasonal help is all back in school and there's a severe shortage of cooks, waiters, waitresses and shopkeepers. The news coming from the Transplant Case began to subside and with it so did the number of newscasters hanging around Ocean City. The last big story was about the surviving Chinese Aliens who were granted green cards and allowed to stay in the United States. Occasionally someone from the Washington or Baltimore stations would come down, but only for an update about how there was no new news and then they would return home.

The past two month's had been very profitable for Billy. He signed the book deal with Oliver in New York at a press conference full of cameras and questions, most of which Billy and Oliver deferred to the book that was expected to be released in early February, long before the trials were scheduled to begin. After expenses and taxes, he and Oliver each netted about four and half million free and clear. When Hollywood found out that it was not only a suspense thriller but a love story with a happy ending they were able to make a deal for the film rights for twenty million plus one point each for Oliver and Billy of the gross profit. That deal was signed in Hollywood with even bigger fan fair than the book deal. Billy netted about eight million out of that deal. Hollywood had fallen in love with the yet unwritten story and were already working on nationwide casting extravaganzas that hyped the movie larger than those for *Gone With The Wind*. All told he had about twelve million tax free dollars in various banks and investments.

When Billy and Jill returned from the jail they spent most of that night and following day talking, finding out how much in love they really were with each other and if they would be able to make it work after everything they had been through. Then they spent the next several weeks making rather loud and passionate love. After that part of their relationship cooled down, they began to move into the next stage, becoming best friends as well as lovers. They found a nice five bedroom house in Ocean Pines on the bay with a large dock for $600,000 and were going to settlement on it next week. Jill had been trying to get Billy out to look for furniture for weeks, but he was working on the book now and did not have the time. Given the circumstances she graciously deferred to the book.

"Won't it be nice, Billy, when we can get out of this little apartment and into the new house?" Jill asked as she took off her bathrobe and laid down on the couch naked.

"Uh, huh," muttered Billy as he continued pounding away at his laptop computer, editing the story.

It was a warm day in the mid seventies. Not hot enough for air conditioning, the balcony doors were wide open and the sheer curtains were flopping around in the gentle breezes traveling up the beach.

"Maybe you should take a little break and get something to nibble on. You've been working at that all morning now. You could use a little time off."

"No, I shouldn't, I want to get this one section just a little smoother before I email it to Oliver," Billy said glancing around to see her laying seductively on the sofa. "Of course, on the other hand, I could possibly use a little recharging of my batteries."

Standing up, he walked over and reached for her hand to pull her up.

"Uh, UH. Here!" she smiled.

Taking off his clothes Billy got down on the couch with her and they made passionate love for the next fifteen minutes, then laid in each other's arms for the rest of the afternoon, talking about the new house. At four, Jill called out for some pizza and they got dressed. Once back at his work, Billy lost all track of time as he carefully and skillfully re-edited his copy. The front door rang and Jill went to get it. Looking through the peep hole she saw the pizza box and opened the door.

"Pizza ready, Jill? Jill?" Billy said as he turned around.

A man with silver hair had his hand around her throat, pinning her to the wall.

"Stop it!" yelled Billy as he flew across the room.

When he was two steps away, the man turned his head and pointed a gun at Billy stopping him dead in his tracks.

"Billy, so nice to see you again," St. John said with a warm smile on his face.

"Christ, St. John, you son-of-a-bitch, I thought I'd seen the last of you," snarled Billy.

"Oh, come on now Billy, you know you and I have this thing for each other. Why else would we keep meeting like this?" he laughed.

"You fucking bastard!" Billy replied.

"Billy. Billy. Let's try and keep it cordial! OK guys, over on the sofa," St. John said taking his hand from around Jill's neck and motioning them to the couch with his gun.

Jill ran into Billy's arms and they walked over and sat down on the couch together.

"What do you want with us, why don't you leave us alone?" Jill asked angrily.

"Oh Jill, such a bad attitude. I had to come back to this country for a few days and make some arrangements, so I thought I'd drop by and see my old friends. I used to read a lot about you two in the papers. Sounded like you guys were the *Dating Game* duo of the news. Course, I haven't heard much lately. How you guys doin' anyway?"

"What do you care, what do you want?" Billy asked curtly.

"Oh, I had to come back and make some arrangements for Dave Johnson and Dr. Ling. Seems they're going to be checking out of this life next week. I'm sorry, but you won't be around to see it. Hate to hit and run," St. John said as he pointed the gun at Billy.

"NO!" yelled Jill lunging off the chair at St. John.

Chapter 15
Tuesday, March 28

There had been a light rain earlier in the morning but it had stopped an hour ago. The sun was coming out but the air was very cool for late September. Although Billy was walking bare footed, he had to wear a light jacket. The rain had caused the sand to become crusty in spots and Billy's feet broke through to the dry sand underneath and it sifted up through his toes. Opening the glass vase, he spilled its contents slowly as he walked down the beach.

"This is the best way," Billy said softly as he continued to pour the contents as he walked along. "This is what you came here for, the beach, and this is where you belong, not in some land locked hole under a tree. No, this is best," he shook his head.

After walking three blocks the last of her ashes were poured from the urn. Walking up off the beach and onto the boardwalk, Billy turned to look back over the beach and wiped a tear from his eye.

"All right, cut and print it. That wraps up that shot. Thank you, Mr. Bridges that was wonderful," said the director.

Jeff Bridges turned and walked back across the boardwalk to his trailer. He saw Billy leaning up against it and smiled as he walked up and shook his hand.

"Hi, Billy. Nice to see you again. What did you think about that scene? I play it right?"

"Brought tears to my eyes. Only difference was when I did it I was bawling like a baby, could hardly walk. I was staggering like a drunkard, but this is Hollywood on the Atlantic, isn't it?" Billy said wistfully.

"I know, but this way, trust me, it will have more impact on the audience. It's going to be one hell of a blockbuster. I was watching the dailies last night. This is really going to be one hell of a hit. Hell, wish I had been able to hold out for some more points. That crazy son-of-a-bitch Oliver around?"

"Yea, he's back at the hotel, trying to hustle some girls who want to get on the set. What scene you shooting next?"

"The one where you killed St. John. Listen, what kind of a look did you have on your face? What were you feeling when he fell off that balcony? The book said you were looking in his eyes and could see he was afraid, knowing he was about to die. Did you have a fierce look, was it angry, what?"

"No," Billy said as he looked around making sure no one was close enough to hear what he was about to say. "This is just between you and me. I'll deny ever eve saying it. Understand!"

Jeff nodded his head as he stared intently at Billy.

"I had my hands tight around his throat," Billy said unemotionally. "Looking up I could see that Jill was dead. Somehow I knew it would be too easy just to strangle him. In the book I wrote that he knocked me off and we stood up wrestling with each other near the balcony and he went over. Truth is, he was exhausted from the fight, I dragged him over to the balcony, picked him up and rolled him over the edge. I could see that cold look of fear and panic in his eyes as he was screaming for me not to let him go. What was I feeling at that moment? Strange. I don't think I was really feeling anything at all. I was just numb. But I'll never forget that look in his eyes when I let him go, just watching him fall, screaming into the darkness.

The End

Look for

The Mason and Dixon Line

the next book

by Tom Croft

scheduled for release

at Christmas time.

About the Author

A Native of Hagerstown, Maryland, Mr. Croft graduated from Hagerstown Community College, then attended the University of Maryland. He was employed for seven years as a business analyst for Dun & Bradstreet. At the age of thirty he decided to leave the business community to attend the Maryland College of Art and Design in Silver Spring, Maryland. After leaving art school he working for various agencies in the Washington, D.C. area. Two years later he opened his own advertising agency which he successfully operated for fifteen years.